Doctor's Orders

'I've always had a thing about lady doctors,' said Duncan.

'Have you?' said Helen, with a wry smile on her face. 'So you like to see women in positions of authority?'

'They fascinate me,' he confessed.

'And would you like to be dominated, Duncan?' As his expression told her all she needed to know, Helen realised she was playing with fire. He was her patient, and he was supposed to be recovering.

Doctor's Orders
Deanna Ashford

BLACK LACE

Black Lace books contain sexual fantasies.
In real life, always practise safe sex.

This edition published in 2003 by
Black Lace
Thames Wharf Studios
Rainville Road
London W6 9HA

Reprinted 2004

Originally published 2000

Printed and bound by Mackays of Chatham PLC

ISBN 0 352 33453 3

Chapter One

Dr Helen Dawson was the friendliest and most even-tempered senior registrar at St Matthew's Hospital – a crumbling NHS edifice situated in a run down area of London, close to the Docklands development. It was most unusual to see her in a bad mood, and the two nurses, gossiping outside the entrance to Laburnum ward, looked up in amazement as Dr Dawson strode past them, her full lips set in a tight angry line.

Helen Dawson was far too involved in her own problems to even notice the surprised glances from the various members of staff she passed as she marched determinedly up the stairs to the second floor. One of Helen's decisions regarding a patient's treatment had been overruled by Professor Max Fenton, the senior consultant in charge of her department. It wasn't the first time Max Fenton had done this to her, and she intended to get this matter sorted out once and for all.

Max Fenton's office was in the west wing, located in the Byron Suite, the private part of the hospital. Soon the scuffed linoleum floors and peeling cream paint disappeared, to be replaced by thick grey carpet, pink wallpaper and soft lighting. Helen usually noticed the difference, frustrated by the constant lack of adequate funding in the NHS, but today she wasn't conscious of the change in her surroundings as she strode past the office of Professor Fenton's secretary, Ella Carter.

'You can't go in, Dr Dawson,' Ella said agitatedly. 'He left orders not to be disturbed.'

'Damn his orders,' Helen muttered under her breath as she ignored Ella and strode into her boss's office.

Max was seated behind his large mahogany desk, sifting through a pile of papers. The morning sunlight streamed through the window just behind him, and his steel grey hair looked almost white in the bright light. Max had only recently returned from a medical conference in Southern California and the deep tan he'd acquired made his eyes appear even more startlingly blue.

'Dr Dawson?' Max Fenton said coldly. 'Just what do you think you are doing, barging in here like this?'

'I'm sorry to disturb you,' Helen replied, trying to contain her fury. She knew that Max wouldn't appreciate an unseemly outburst. Sometimes, Helen thought, Max was just too damn controlled. 'I have to speak to you right now.'

'What's so important that it can't wait a few hours?' Max enquired, removing his steel-rimmed spectacles. 'I told Ella that I wasn't to be disturbed under any circumstances. I've a lot of work to do and I'm due at the TV studios by one at the latest.'

As well as carrying out all his medical duties, Max Fenton was a regular presenter on a high-profile medical programme that dealt with all aspects of women's health. His good looks and charm, coupled with his medical expertise, had gained him a legion of female fans. Because of this his private practice had increased to almost unmanageable proportions. Nevertheless, Helen didn't begrudge Max his success; he still remained true to his origins, often working long hours to see as many NHS patients as possible.

'You overruled my decision and refused treatment to Laura Marchant,' Helen challenged.

'I did,' Max Fenton confirmed. 'I happen to think that

2

cosmetic surgery won't solve Laura Marchant's problems. She'd be better off if we referred her to the psychiatric department. We can only treat the most needy on the NHS and you know how limited we are by this year's budget. If she is really desperate to have the surgery she can find the money to pay for private treatment.'

'That's a pretty hard-nosed attitude,' Helen retorted. 'Frankly, I don't agree with your diagnosis. She's my patient and Laura doesn't need a psychiatrist, she just needs the surgery. Her financial circumstances would never allow her to find enough to go private. I want you to reconsider, Max.' Laura had aroused a sympathy in Helen that totally outweighed logical medical considerations.

'Helen, you're a brilliant doctor, but you've still a lot to learn. You should never allow emotion to take precedence over your medical judgement,' Max said, leaning back in his chair and subjecting her to a penetrating stare.

Helen's skin prickled under his gaze. Max was just too attractive for her peace of mind and she fancied him like crazy, but she wouldn't let that get to her. She was determined not to let him sidetrack her in any way. She would keep her mind focused on the matter in hand. 'In our line of work I think that sometimes we have to do just that,' she countered defiantly.

'You're too self-opinionated at times.' Max looked her up and down with a slow sensual precision that, despite all Helen's outward control, made her heart beat faster.

Someone had once told her that in order to retain command of a situation like this, one should try to imagine the other person clad only in his underwear. However, the thought of Max dressed only in a brief white pair of Calvin Klein's served to have the opposite effect and unsettled her even more. He was tall and slim with the muscular physique of a swimmer or long distance runner. Visions of his long limbs, tanned a deep golden brown, with only a sliver of white cotton covering his bulging crotch, crowded into her mind. Helen

3

swallowed, her mouth going suddenly dry as she was overcome by a multitude of obscene thoughts.

She tried to concentrate on her patient's problem. But it became even more difficult to focus her attentions when Max smiled at her and said in a soft, mesmerising tone, 'I think we should continue this discussion undisturbed, don't you, Helen?'

Max walked over to the door, and turned the key in the lock, while Helen watched him in silence, feeling aroused, yet also apprehensive. Max generated a multitude of conflicting emotions inside her whenever they were together. She was attracted to powerful men. They acted like an aphrodisiac on her senses, and she found a perverse pleasure in being controlled by them. Max had somehow sensed that when she had come to work for him, and he often took advantage of that fact.

Today was clearly no exception, she thought, as he moved to stand in front of her. The thin white cotton of his shirt clung to the firm contours of his chest and slim waist. She glanced downwards, seeing the proud shape of his cock half-concealed by the soft pleats of his grey trousers. She suppressed a shiver of desire, wanting to fling herself into his arms and beg him to fuck her. Max was the dominant partner in all aspects of their private and professional relationships, but for once she was determined to fight the hold he had over her, and insist on having her own way. 'My decision to treat Laura Marchant should stand. You gave me full control over the clinic, didn't you, Max? What gives you the right to countermand my decisions when it suits you?'

'You're so arousing when you're feisty, Helen.' Max chuckled. 'Perhaps I should countermand your decisions more often.'

He leaned towards her and his warm masculine odour, a heady mixture of pheromones and expensive cologne, filled her nostrils. Helen's nipples grew taut against the thin cotton of her dress, and the heat between her thighs increased, her panties dampening, the moist gusset stretching tightly against her swollen pussy lips.

4

'This is serious, Max,' she said curtly, anger and arousal sending a rush of colour to her pale cheeks.

'Even if I did agree to operate on Laura Marchant the results we could achieve would be minimal. She's not going to turn into a raving beauty overnight,' he said, with a trace of cynicism. 'Reading your reports, I'm certain that her problems run far deeper than just her physical appearance. In the circumstances, don't you think our limited resources would be more efficiently employed elsewhere?'

'I don't think we should always consider cost,' Helen argued. 'If we did that, most medical advances would never be made.'

'In some instances you may be right, Helen. However, on the subject of Laura Marchant, I've yet to be convinced.' Max glanced at his watch. 'I'll give you ten minutes. Go ahead, find a way to persuade me to change my mind.' He sat back against his desk, looking at her expectantly, his gaze focusing pointedly on the upper swell of her breasts, which were revealed by the low scoop neckline of her brief cotton dress.

The room was deathly quiet, a cocoon of luxury protecting them from the noise of the busy hospital. For a moment Helen faltered – Max was playing games – and she knew exactly what he expected her to do next. Fighting her need for him, she shook her head. 'No, Max, not this time . . .' she murmured.

'I'm not making you do anything you don't want to do, Helen, you know that,' he purred. 'Go ahead, offer me any number of credible reasons why we should operate on Laura Marchant.' He paused. 'However, to quote an old adage, don't actions always speak louder than words?'

Helen looked at his hands resting on the desk. They were slim, with long graceful fingers. Beautiful hands that were capable of carrying out the most intricate miracles of surgery, yet also able to take her to the very peak of pleasure. She couldn't deny that she wanted him touching her right now. Her knees felt weak as she let her imagination run riot. 'You're a bastard, Max.'

'You wouldn't have me any other way.' Ice-blue eyes challenged hers.

'Damn you,' she muttered, not giving herself time to think of the consequences as she shrugged off her white coat. She pulled impatiently at the buttons running down the front of her short cotton dress. Her fingers, usually so agile and precise in their movements, fumbled awkwardly with the tiny fastenings. The front of her dress parted to reveal full breasts, slightly over-generous for her slim frame, then her narrow waist and the faintly rounded curve of her belly. Underneath Helen wore only a pair of brief, white lace panties that barely covered the tangle of pale blonde curls at her groin. 'Is that convincing enough?' she challenged.

Max remained silent, his cool gaze seeming to caress every inch of her exposed flesh, and she shivered, feeling goosepimples form on her skin. Helen hated herself, hated the pleasure she found in such submissive behaviour, but at this moment in time all she wanted was Max. Her body ached with longing as Max stepped forwards and gently cupped her left breast in his hand.

'Very,' he murmured, pinching her nipple. Helen gave a soft moan as he pulled at both her teats until they grew into fat pink cones. 'What would your male patients think,' Max added in a throaty tone, 'if they knew how little you were wearing under that white coat.' Hooking his fingers under the lacy sides of her panties, he pulled Helen close. 'Perhaps you should be assigned to the male impotence clinic?'

'That's not a very professional comment,' Helen countered, all too conscious of the blatant boldness of Max's erection which pressed enticingly into her stomach.

'I dropped all pretence of professionalism the moment you chose to invade my office, Dr Dawson,' Max said. 'Now all I want to do is fuck you until you beg for mercy.'

He spun Helen round, forcing her back against the

6

desk, caging her with his arms. The rolled wooden edge of the desk dug into her thighs, just below the curves of her buttocks. Max picked up a small silver paper knife and sawed through the lacy strip that held her panties together. As the lace fell away to reveal the full beauty of the pale-gold curls guarding her sex, Max gave a ragged groan. Jerking Helen close, he held her, grinding his engorged penis sensuously against her stomach.

'Why do I always end up giving in to you,' Helen said breathlessly as Max bit hungrily at her full breasts, flicking his tongue over the hard points of her nipples. A delicious coil of lust uncurled in the pit of her belly, and her quim grew even wetter as Max pushed his tongue into her mouth, voraciously exploring the moist interior.

'Because you enjoy it.' Max caressed her back, his fingers tracing the line of her spine and the gentle curve of her buttocks. He stroked the sensitive skin of her inner thigh, just brushing her pubic curls and she trembled in anticipation, desperate for him to invade her sex. As Max's teasing fingers slid between her pussy lips, thrusting deep inside her, Helen gave a soft, pleasure-filled sigh.

Taking hold of her wrist, Max pressed her palm against his groin. Helen could feel the hardness of his prick, straining eagerly at the confining fabric of his trousers.

'Fuck me,' she begged, pulling down the zipper tab. 'Fuck me now, Max,' she added pleadingly as his stiff, naked cock reared from the opening.

'Greedy bitch,' he grunted as he pushed her down on to the desk, impatiently shoving the piles of books and papers on to the floor. The polished wood felt cold and slippery against her buttocks as Max pulled her thighs wider apart and thrust his fingers further into her, his knuckles roughly grazing her sensitive G-spot, arousing her senses to a fever pitch. Leaning forwards he cruelly squeezed her left nipple until Helen squirmed with excited, painful pleasure.

Max looked down at her quim. Moisture glinted on the pale curls of her pubic hair which delicately framed the rosy slit of her sex. 'So pretty,' he grunted, replacing his fingers with the hot hardness of his prick. He thrust into her with one smooth stroke that seemed to penetrate the very depths of her vitals as the root of his shaft rammed against the sensitive tip of her clitoris. Immediately, Helen wanted to lift her legs, twine them around his narrow hips, but as always Max retained control. Digging his fingers into the soft skin of her thighs, he held her body motionless as he continued to pound into her.

Helen surrendered to Max's passion as his thrusts became faster, deeper, forcing her upwards, towards the brink. His thick root nudged repeatedly against her clit until the intense sensations overwhelmed her. Helen felt her interior muscles tense around him, spasming out of control as she came in a sudden rush of ecstasy.

After, she lay there, wide-eyed and silent, the strength drained from her body, while Max, breathing heavily, his brow dotted with perspiration, pulled away from her and wiped the scent of her from his cock with a handful of tissues. He pushed his semi-erect organ back inside his trousers and looked down at her. She still lay limply, spread-eagled across his desk, her tangled blonde hair fanning out across the dark polished mahogany.

'You've convinced me,' Max said, smoothing his ruffled grey hair. 'If you wish it, Laura Marchant can have her operation.'

'Sometimes I almost hate you,' she said breathlessly, refusing his extended hand as she sat up.

'I know you don't mean that.' Max smiled teasingly as he watched her climb from his desk, totally naked, her hair falling in tangled strands around her shoulders. 'If only your patients could see you now. Their prim Dr Dawson, a sexy seductress.'

'I look a mess,' she said, her voice trembling as Max bent to retrieve her dress.

'Unfortunately, your panties are beyond repair.' Max picked up the ragged scraps of lace, stuffed them in a manila envelope and threw it in the waste paper bin.

'You're costing me a fortune in underwear,' Helen complained half-jokingly.

'Then allow me to buy you some new undies. I know a delightful little shop in Mayfair that has the most erotic garments I've ever seen. Consider it, if you like, an early Christmas present.'

'In June?' She gave a soft, uneasy laugh. 'You know that I don't feel comfortable letting you pay, Max.' It was bad enough that she let him hold sway over practically every other aspect of her existence.

'How can you be so stubborn about some things, and so acquiescent on other occasions,' Max murmured. 'You're a contradiction, Helen.'

'That's what you like about me, Max,' she remarked, struggling to do up the buttons of her dress.

'Helen.' Max pushed her hands aside and fastened the buttons as though she were a helpless child. 'You're too bloody independent,' he said, tenderly kissing her. 'You're also intelligent and very beautiful. You could be successful in anything you tried to do. Why, when I've offered you the occasional spot on the programme to help supplement your income, do you always find some reason to refuse?'

'I don't think I could handle all the attention that goes with the notoriety.' Often during their dates they'd had their private moments interrupted by overzealous fans. Max had a natural ability to take such moments in his stride, but Helen hated the regular unwanted intrusions on their privacy.

'It's not so bad.' Max removed a few stray pins from her hair and ran his fingers through her tangled locks. 'I suggest you use my bathroom and do something about your hair before Ella sees you, Helen. You know how much of a gossip my secretary is.'

'Ella often confides in me. She's certain that you're having a secret affair with someone in the hospital,' Helen replied with a smile. 'She just hasn't cottoned on that it's me,' she added as she pulled on her white coat and picked up a felt-tip pen which had fallen from the pocket and rolled half under a chair.

Max piled the scattered books and papers back on to his desk, then straightened and looked at his watch. 'I'll have to leave soon,' he said.

'Can you make dinner tonight?' she asked.

'Sure. We'll eat at my place. I'll order in,' Max replied, then added in a more serious tone. 'We have a lot to discuss.'

She tensed. 'Have you heard? Has the final decision on the hospital's future been made?'

'Yes,' Max replied. 'I got a call this morning, just before you barged into my office.'

'Judging by your expression, the news isn't good?'

'You're right,' he confirmed.

'Damn,' Helen exclaimed in angry frustration. 'Then St Matthew's will definitely close?'

'It's not the end of the world, Helen.' Max shrugged his shoulders. 'We'll talk about the future tonight.'

'Sure,' she agreed, trying to contain her disappointment. The staff had worked hard lately in a last ditch attempt to save the hospital from closure. 'As you say, Max, we can talk tonight.'

Inamoratia – an elegant, very expensive restaurant close to the Tower of London, was crowded as usual. There were a number of major celebrities among the regular clientele, and the owners prided themselves on the fact that their diners could enjoy themselves in peace. The restaurant had a strict rule; fans, or admirers of any kind, who troubled the personalities, were always asked swiftly and politely to leave.

It had been three days since Helen had discovered that St Matthew's was closing, and a lot had happened in that short length of time. She and Max had some final matters to discuss and in the restaurant she knew that they would be able to enjoy each other's company undisturbed.

Helen had chosen to wear a scrap of designer black

10

satin that she knew had cost Max an obscene amount of money. The short, bias-cut dress had a low neckline and was held up by thin shoestring straps. It had been Max's birthday present to her. The dress was cut so low at the back it was impossible to wear a bra, but Helen was lucky; despite the fact that her breasts were large and full, they were still as firm and uptilted as they had been in her teens. Also, at Max's behest, she'd left off her panties.

When she walked into the restaurant, Helen felt bold and blatantly sexual. The soft satin caressed her erect nipples, brushing sensuously against her belly and sex as she moved. The skimpy garment was short – a good eight inches above her knees – and it flared out at the hem. She felt even more excited and apprehensive knowing that one indiscreet movement would bare the blonde curls of her pubis to public gaze.

Max was already seated at their usual table, and Helen moved to join him, oblivious of the admiring glances from a number of the other male diners. Helen was twenty-nine years old, and not only was she extremely clever, she was also beautiful: tall and elegant, with delicate features, grey-blue eyes and hair the colour of spun gold.

'I've already ordered,' Max said, as she sat down beside him at the small round table.

'I'm not very hungry,' she replied, picking up her glass of red wine.

'Still upset about the hospital closing, and me moving to the States?'

Max had told her all his plans the evening she had discovered the hospital was closing. He, along with a small group of financial backers, was planning to open up a string of plastic surgery clinics all across America.

'Everything's happened so quickly,' she said. She still couldn't help resenting the fact that he'd not confided in her as fully as he could. As far as she had known the US business venture was still only in the early planning stages. Now she'd discovered it was almost complete.

11

'I understand how you feel.' Max smiled reassuringly as he put his hand on her knee under the cover of the tablecloth. He slid it slowly upwards past the lacy tops of her hold-up stockings. His blue eyes darkened with desire as, from then on, he encountered nothing but bare flesh. 'You did as I asked,' he whispered huskily.

'Does that turn you on?' she smiled seductively, feeling empowered by the expression on Max's face, 'Knowing that I'm naked under this dress.'

'More than you know,' he growled, ceasing his exploration and letting his hand rest on the upper part of her bare thigh. 'I'm going to miss you like crazy.'

'Me too.' She would miss the great sex if nothing else, although Max could be a selfish bastard and was sometimes more concerned with his own pleasure than hers.

'You could join me sooner if you wouldn't insist on being so independent.'

'I won't let you keep me, Max, even for a few months. I'll come as soon as I can get a green card, and authority to practise medicine in the States.'

In the meantime, Max had offered Helen a senior registrar's job at the Princess Beatrice Clinic – an exclusive private hospital that was owned by him and his American financial partners. Helen would have preferred to follow her NHS patients who were transferring to the King's Cross Hospital, but the plastic surgery clinic there was already fully staffed. In the normal course of events Helen would never have accepted a job at a private hospital, but they had offered almost double her current salary. At present her outgoings substantially exceeded her incomings, a fact that had more or less forced her to agree to the very generous short-term contract.

'How will I ever manage without this?' he purred, his hand moving higher again, his fingers pulling teasingly at her blonde pubic curls.

'Perhaps you'll find someone else?' she said lightly, opening her slim thighs, wanting his searching fingers to slide between her pussy lips. There was something highly titillating about knowing that Max intended to frig her in front of all these people.

'No one else pleases me like you do, Helen.' Max leaned closer and whispered in her ear, 'This hot little pussy is all mine, never forget that.'

Helen gave a soft sigh, her eyes glazing over, the sounds of the other diners receding, as Max's tantalising fingers began their slow sensual exploration. However, her pleasure was interrupted by the unexpected sound of a male voice.

'Max – I never thought I'd see you here!' The deep voice, with its strong mid-Atlantic undertones, made the hairs on the back of Helen's neck prickle.

'Duncan!' Max smiled warmly at the man. 'What brings you back to England?' he asked, ceasing the subtle movements of his fingers, but letting his left hand remain where it was, lightly cupping her sex. He seemed casual in his greeting, making no attempt to stand, or shake hands, as he normally would when coming across an old acquaintance.

Helen couldn't fail to recognise the famous movie star, Duncan Paul. During her teenage years, Helen had been mad about Duncan, having a crush to end all crushes on him. He hadn't been quite so well known then; it was at the beginning of his career, when he had been starring in an action-adventure TV series. Tall and muscular, with black hair and dark brown eyes, Duncan was even more devastatingly handsome in the flesh.

'Mind if I join you for a moment?' Duncan did not wait for a reply. He pulled up an extra chair and sat down at their table. 'I'm filming here during the coming months. I'm executive producer on this one, so I'm heavily into pre-production work.' Duncan's deep voice caressed Helen's senses. Goosepimples formed on her skin and her stomach tightened, just as Max's fingers closed possessively over her naked pubis.

There was barely room for an extra person at the small table, and Duncan's presence proved quite overwhelming for an already highly aroused Helen. Duncan was undeniably sexy, and the close proximity of the two men, coupled with the feel of Max's hand on her crotch, made her feel incredibly horny. Her breasts swelled and her nipples stiffened even more, until the aching peaks lewdly distended the thin satin of her dress.

'Helen.' Max glanced over at her. Fully aware, by the way her juices were steadily dampening the palm of his hand, that she was now even more highly aroused. 'This is my cousin, Duncan Paul. Duncan, may I introduce Dr Helen Dawson.'

Helen smiled, surprised that Max had never bothered to tell her he was related to such a famous movie star.

'You've been keeping this one very quiet, Max.' Duncan looked admiringly at Helen as he lifted her hand to his lips. 'It's a pleasure to meet you, fair lady.'

Lust crawled slowly over her skin, and she shivered slightly. 'I'm an admirer of your work, Duncan,' Helen managed to say in a husky voice, although it was difficult to sound composed. Max's fingers were sliding inside her now, teasing and tantalising her senses, while she was so close to Duncan she could smell the musky maleness emanating from his body.

Helen's senses were so inflamed, so on edge, she felt as if she were floating and about to climax at any moment. Taking hold of her wine glass, she gripped the stem tightly, fighting to retain control of herself. It wasn't easy. Max's searching fingers ventured deeper, until she thought she would scream aloud with pleasure. Agitatedly she glanced over at Max, who had a calm unconcerned expression on his face, which belied what he was doing to her under the cover of the tablecloth.

'Helen's a great fan it seems,' Max said. 'Judging by the effect you're having on her, Duncan. I've never seen her so overwhelmed.' As he spoke he pressed his thumb down hard on her clit, and it took all the self control Helen had to remain still and stop herself from gasping aloud. Her thighs shook slightly, and beads of sweat formed on her brow, as Max doubled the assault on her senses.

'It's great to meet someone who likes my work. Max never tells his friends that we're related,' Duncan said to Helen. 'Too embarrassed I reckon. He thinks most of the movies I make are rubbish.'

'Not all of them,' Max amended. 'Just the ones where you save the world single-handed,' he added jokingly.

As Helen's orgasm exploded, the stem of her glass snapped under the pressure of her grasping fingers, spilling blood-red wine over the white tablecloth. 'Oh, God!' she gasped.

Grabbing a napkin, Duncan blotted up the wine and looked worriedly at Helen. 'You didn't cut yourself, did you?'

'No. I feel so silly, it just snapped,' Helen said, pulling down her dress and standing up in one agitated movement. 'Excuse me, I have to go to the ladies,' she added shakily. Picking up her bag, she moved swiftly away from the table.

'Duncan really turned you on, didn't he?' Max said, managing to sound remarkably cool and untroubled.

Duncan had gone back to join the people he was dining with, before Helen returned from the ladies'. Max had never resented his cousin's movie star looks and fame before, but he did now. Judging by her response, Helen really fancied Duncan, and that knowledge annoyed him and made him feel extraordinarily jealous.

During dinner Max had managed to deftly brush aside Helen's curious questions about Duncan. Instead they had talked about her new job, and Max's impending move to the States. They were now about to leave, and Max could contain his curiosity no longer. He had to find out exactly what Helen thought about his world famous cousin.

'I have to admit he is gorgeous looking. I had rather a crush on him when I was a teenager,' Helen owned up, laughing in an embarrassed kind of way. 'I never expected to meet the guy, certainly not here of all places. Then to discover you and Duncan Paul were related . . .'

'Perhaps you're not quite over your youthful crush,' Max remarked as they entered the lift. They were followed by an elderly couple. The woman was wearing a genuine mink coat. As the lift started to move she stared thoughtfully at Max, who pointedly ignored her and leaned closer to Helen.

'Do you know that every time I lifted my fork to my mouth during dinner I could smell your come on my hands,' he whispered in Helen's ear. 'It made me feel so bloody horny. I wanted to bury my face in your quim and suck you dry.'

'If you had, I'd probably have destroyed the rest of the glass and crockery on the table. The head waiter was upset enough about one glass,' she whispered back, colouring slightly. She cast a wary glance in the direction of the elderly couple, before adding,' I want you right now, Max.'

Max gave a husky chuckle. 'I'd be only too happy to oblige, but those two old fogies would probably have a heart attack. I'm in no mood to give CPR,' he replied, just as they reached the basement car park.

Max and Helen followed the elderly couple into the small concrete passage, eager to reach the privacy of Max's Mercedes. However, the old woman turned and smiled hesitantly at Max, her overweight bulk half-blocking their way. 'Aren't you that wonderful TV doctor? The one who does the programme on women's health?'

'I am indeed.' Max pulled Helen closer to him and slid an impatient hand under the back of her dress to cup her bare buttocks. He fondled her soft tempting flesh, so hungry for her now it was unbelievable. Max was in no mood for an extended encounter with an adoring fan tonight.

'I do love your programme,' the woman continued in a tremulous voice. 'The last two have been so informative. You are wonderful and I –'

'I'm so glad,' Max interrupted, his fragile patience running out. 'Horny' didn't even describe the way he was feeling. 'I can understand your interest in the segments on plastic surgery, but at your age I fail to understand how you could find female fertility problems so fascinating,' he continued curtly. 'If you'll excuse us.'

Max pulled Helen past the couple, out into the underground car park. The lights were dimmer here, the cavernous depths filled with the odour of musky dampness and spent exhaust fumes.

'That was unnecessarily cruel,' Helen pointed out. 'You could have been more diplomatic. You probably upset the old dear.'

'Who cares!' Max snapped, feeling tense yet aroused. The heady mixture of lust tinged with jealousy was steadily gaining strength. 'I just said what I thought for once.'

'That's so unlike you, Max. You never lose your cool when confronted by adoring fans.'

'Perhaps I should more often,' he growled, pulling her impatiently towards the spot where he'd parked his car.

'Slow down – you're hurting my arm,' Helen complained.

'Too bad.'

'I'm not sure I like this new side of you, Max.'

His mouth set in a grim line and Max ignored her. Helen's response to Duncan's arrival was the one thing now consuming his thoughts. Max was suddenly feeling insecure, an uncomfortable emotion for a man usually so certain of his own sexual attraction.

'Fuck you.' Helen stumbled slightly on her high heels as Max dragged her between his black Mercedes and the white Rolls Royce parked next to it. 'What the hell is wrong with you?'

'Nothing!' He would soon make her forget Duncan, show this randy little bitch who was her master. Max had never experienced such overwhelming jealousy. Helen was his, his alone, and he intended to prove that to her in no uncertain terms.

'Why are you being so unreasonable?' Helen sounded

17

angry as he pushed her against the bonnet of the Mercedes. 'You're drunk, aren't you?'

'On a couple of bottles of burgundy?' he growled. 'On
the contrary, Helen, I'm frighteningly sober,' he continued. 'I just didn't like your behaviour this evening. I
suppose you think it normal to act like a bitch in heat
when another guy sits next to you!'

Blood pounded through Max's veins, his cock growing
harder until it pressed urgently against the zip of his
trousers.

'You're jealous.' She feigned surprise. 'That's
irrational. I was aroused because you were finger-
fucking me in the middle of a crowded restaurant.'

'Do you think I'm stupid? You were barely damp
when I touched you. Duncan appeared and your quim
was dripping wet. The difference was unbelievable,' he
growled, letting his fury erupt.

'I want you, not him.'

Max knew Helen was lying, but it didn't matter.
Grabbing hold of the straps of her dress, he yanked them
down her arms, feeling the fragile satin tear at the seams.
His lust magnified as the black bodice slid downwards,
exposing her bare breasts, the full globes glowing palely
in the dim light.

'Helen,' he groaned, bending his head, pulling one
pert nipple into his mouth and sucking on it like a
hungry child.

Helen whimpered softly, the sound echoing eerily
around them, and Max knew that he still held full sway
over her senses. He felt the tenseness leave her limbs as
she lifted her hands, threading her fingers through his
hair, clutching his face even closer to her bosom. Max
sucked harder, squeezing and kneading her breasts,
grazing her nipple with his teeth until she gave a sobbing
gasp of surrender.

'Fuck me,' she begged. 'Right here, right now!' Her
eager hands pulled at his trousers, jerking down the zip,
freeing his aching prick.

Max covered her lips with his, kissing her passionately, his tongue plunging deep inside her mouth, while Helen ran teasing fingers up and down the shaft of his penis. It jerked excitedly, and Max's desire magnified, his cock feeling as if it was ready to explode.

'Seeing you so out of control like this turns me on.' Helen dipped her hand into the opening of his trousers, her fingers cupping the soft sac of his balls.

'Then I'll lose control more often,' he growled, his hands reaching for her pussy.

His searching fingers invaded her hot damp slit, while she continued to stroke and tease his throbbing testicles. By now he was so aroused that he was forced to grit his teeth, barely able to keep control of his senses. He swung Helen around, pushing her against the bonnet of the car, and lifted up her skirt. She made no attempt to resist as she leaned obediently forwards, belly pressed to the cool, gleaming metal.

Helen was naked apart from her hold-up stockings, the black satin dress lying a crumpled band around her waist. She reminded Max of the whores he'd frequented in Amsterdam. From one in particular he'd learned the delicate art of dominating a woman.

Her body looked even paler, her skin luminous in contrast to the polished black metal. Max fastened his gaze on her bottom, which had never looked more appealing. Shoving a foot between her legs he forced them wide apart, and pulled open the cheeks of her buttocks. Her rosy arsehole was so tempting, hungry to be filled by his hard dick. Helen had shied away from anal penetration, so Max had never made any attempt to persuade her to try it. Now, he would have given anything to slide his dick into that sweet, tight virginal opening, but he knew this was neither the time nor the place. Soon, he thought, as he dug his fingers into her buttocks and positioned his cock-head against the moist channel of her sex. As he entered her with one swift thrust, she gave a sharp scream of ecstasy.

'You're mine, all mine, baby,' he whispered in her ear. Placing an arm either side of her, he splayed his fingers across the car bonnet. He ground his belly against her buttocks, then drew back and thrust deeper into the all-embracing flesh. As he began to move his hips in the age-old rhythm, he was barely conscious of the car bouncing slightly on its wheels, rocking in time to his powerful thrusts.

In the distance Max heard the sound of an engine, followed by the slamming of car doors and voices. The new arrivals would move towards the lift, perhaps pass this bay and glance casually into the dark depth, just in time to see him fucking Helen in the smelly warmth of this car park. He found the idea of being watched stimulating, and the blood began to pound savagely through his veins.

As their wild dance of lust continued, Max's movements became stronger, more violent, and the car rocked even harder. Just as the sweet pleasure began to overwhelm him, the raucous sound of his car alarm filled his ears and the headlights began to flash. The intrusive noise seemed to increase in intensity as Max reached his powerful, gut-wrenching climax.

'Shit,' he muttered, slumping spent and exhausted against Helen for a moment, while fumbling in his pocket for the key fob. As he pressed the button, the car doors clicked open, at last silencing the alarm. 'The bloody security guard will be here at any moment,' he added, sanity and reason returning in a sudden rush.

As he jerked open the door of the Mercedes, Helen recovered herself enough to adjust her crumpled dress with trembling hands, and climb into the passenger seat. She sat there not moving, not saying a word, as Max jumped into the driver's seat and started up the engine. In the rear view mirror Max saw the parking attendant walking swiftly towards them. He backed out of the bay and turned. Car tyres screaming, they drove off.

Chapter Two

'Well, what do you think?' Max asked.

'Very impressive,' Helen replied.

Max had insisted on driving her down to the Princess Beatrice Clinic. Now he was taking her on a guided tour of the exclusive private hospital. The huge Georgian mansion was set in extensive grounds, and had been seamlessly extended to provide the most up-to-date and well-equipped hospital Helen had ever seen. The operating theatres, intensive care facilities and laboratories were superb, as was everything else. There was even a swimming pool and gym.

'We have the very latest and best medical equipment there is,' Max boasted. 'The staff pride themselves on being able to cater for every conceivable need of our patients.'

'Quite a contrast to St Matthew's,' Helen observed. Now that she had seen all this, Helen wasn't surprised that the Princess Beatrice was the most expensive private hospital in England. She would be better paid here than she'd ever been, yet in essence she was taking a step backwards in her career.

As a senior registrar in this relatively small hospital, she would be responsible for the general wellbeing of all patients, both surgical and medical cases. It would be a big change. Helen had left general medicine behind her when she'd decided to become a surgeon. For almost two years she had been working for Max, furthering her chosen career path by concentrating wholly on plastic surgery.

'This is our new maternity unit.' Max led her towards a pair of double doors at the end of the corridor. 'It has only just been completed, so we've no in-patients at present.'

'I suppose it would be stupid to ask if you can accommodate all the very latest birthing techniques.' Helen followed Max inside the unit. She knew that only a few, fortunate women could afford to have their babies delivered here, but she was still looking forward to perhaps helping at the occasional birth. She could still vividly recall her stint in maternity. There was something profoundly humbling about helping a new life enter the world.

'We try to keep the operating theatres in maternity as much like home as possible.' Max guided Helen into a large room which had floral patterned wallpaper on the walls and frilly curtains at the windows. The large amount of necessary medical equipment ranged along one wall was half-hidden by screens.

'It can't be easy to keep this sterile,' Helen commented, moving to examine a unit at the side of the bed – one of the very latest foetal monitoring machines.

'The mental well-being of our patients is just as important to us as everything else. Most patients feel more at ease in these sort of surroundings. Here we can deal with just about every complication. Unlike most private clinics, we've no need to resort to transferring patients to an NHS hospital when things get difficult.' Max pulled back the padded counterpane. 'Looks like a normal bed, doesn't it? It is a tad hard but quite comfortable, and we can use it for caesareans if the need arises.' He touched a button, and soundlessly the top half of the bed was raised into a sitting position.

'There are stirrups underneath. A little old-fashioned for such an advanced unit,' Helen said with a wry smile.

'Maybe so,' Max agreed. 'But there are times when they come in handy. We have a number of very wealthy patients from cultures far different from ours – where it is still considered necessary for the birth of an heir to be witnessed by those in positions of authority. With the woman flat on her back, her legs raised high and wide, it makes it easier for the witnesses to see the birth clearly.'

'Rather barbaric.' Helen shuddered as she sat tentatively down on the bed, wondering what it would feel like to give birth in front of a crowd of people, all most likely male. 'And very demeaning.'

'Do we have the right to question such customs?' Max slipped off Helen's shoes and lifted her feet on to the bed. 'How does it feel?'

'Surprisingly comfortable,' she admitted. Max bent down and swung the shiny stainless steel stirrups into place. 'What are you doing?' she asked as he took hold of her ankle and placed her leg in the padded cup of the stirrup.

'Just letting you get a feel of the place.' He smiled, put her other leg in the opposite stirrup, and fastened the Velcro straps in place around her ankles.

Helen had never much liked the stirrups, they had always reminded her of barbaric torture equipment. However, sometimes they proved necessary; for instance, during forceps deliveries or when the need for stitches arose. 'They feel a little strange. I've never put myself in the position of the patients before.'

'Every doctor should, however briefly,' Max said seriously.

'Even male doctors?'

'I suppose so, but it's not quite the same.' He walked past the foot of the bed and pulled aside a floral screen. Helen was surprised to find herself facing a huge mirror, the size of a large window, set in the wall. Not the sort of thing one usually found in a delivery room or operat-

23

ing theatre. 'Personally, Helen, I think you look rather sexy.'

'That's a weird comment.' She had to agree with Max. There was a certain sensual vulnerability about the woman she saw reflected in the mirror. Her legs, fastened to the metal stirrups, were held high and wide in a bizarre position. Between her open thighs, Helen could see the pale gusset of her cream satin panties, straining tightly over the pouch of her sex. 'I suppose there is something rather alluring about the indignity,' she admitted with a shrug of her shoulders.

Max laughed. 'I know what you're thinking, Helen, and the answer is no. Seeing my patients like this doesn't turn me on. They are sexless to me, just part of my job, while you, my sweet –' he lovingly stroked her leg, then eased the metal stirrups even wider apart until she felt the strain on the muscles of her inner thighs, the position making the satin gusset tighten even more, hugging the contours of her pussy lips '– you are very arousing.'

'You can let me go now.' She was unable to tear her gaze from the vulnerable woman in the mirror. Part of her wanted to stay like this, beg Max to touch her, bring her to a climax. But she was all too aware that someone could easily walk in here at any moment. What would the staff think if their new senior registrar and one of the owners was found playing sensual games with the medical equipment.

'Not quite yet.' His voice had taken on a husky, demanding note. 'Seeing you like this gives me pleasure.'

'But anyone could walk in on us.' Helen leaned forwards, trying to reach the straps holding her ankles. As she did so, Max touched the control and the back of the bed lowered into a semi-supine position. Using both hands he pressed her back against the mattress. 'No, Max,' she said worriedly.

'There's something I want to do before I release you.' He held her down with the weight of his body while he

24

grabbed hold of her left wrist and fastened it to the side of the bed with a Velcro strap.

'Whatever it is, I don't like it.' She struggled, an icy shiver running down her spine as she saw the wild expression in his blue eyes. They had played a number of games involving bondage recently but always in the privacy of his apartment. 'It's neither the time, nor the place.'

'On the contrary, I think it's perfect,' he grunted, continuing to pin her down as he grabbed her other flailing arm, securely fastening it to the side of the bed.

'Please, Max.' Helen felt agitated yet aroused. She was just able to see her reflection in the mirror, and she looked even more erotically vulnerable as she pulled uselessly against the straps that bound her. 'No silly games, not now.'

'This isn't a game,' Max said in all seriousness. 'There is something I want to make very clear to you before I leave for the States.' He rolled her cotton skirt upwards, bundling it around her slim waist. Then he unbuttoned her thin cotton top, pulling it open to bare her breasts. 'You're mine and you stay that way all the time I'm gone.'

'Why should you believe otherwise . . .' she faltered, as she recalled his anger over Duncan. 'I care for you Max, you know I do.'

'Maybe that's not enough.' Tenderly he stroked the creamy skin of her bosom, pressing and rubbing the firm flesh, until Helen gave a faint gasp of pleasure. Firmly he pinched each nipple, squeezing hard until they turned a dark rosy red. 'I know a place in New York; the silversmith there specialises in sexual jewellery. I think I'll get him to make you a pair of ornate clamps to decorate those pretty teats.'

'Don't they hurt?' Helen winced at the thought of tiny clamps cutting into the sensitive flesh of her nipples, cruelly restricting the blood flow.

'I'm told the constant pressure is highly arousing.' Max whipped the sterile cloth off the trolley close to the bed. Helen saw the carefully laid out rows of surgical instruments. They were all highly familiar to her, yet they looked different now, taking on a subtly erotic, almost ominous element.

'What are you going to do?' she asked anxiously.

'Nothing you've not secretly wanted my sweet.'

Max selected a small pair of blunt-ended surgical scissors. He ran the flat edge of the closed blades slowly up her inner left thigh, pausing when he reached the springy blonde curls spilling out of the sides of the panty gusset. Helen unconsciously held her breath as he ran the blade slowly across the tightly stretched satin.

'I'm about to ruin even more of your underwear, I'm afraid. Don't worry I've ordered a dozen new pairs from that little place in Mayfair. Every time you wear them you'll be reminded of me.'

New panties were the last thing on Helen's mind as Max snipped delicately at the cream satin gusset. The fabric sprang apart, and he flipped the cut fabric away from her sex. Keeping the scissors closed, he caressed her quim with the flat cold blade. The metal felt hard, frightening even, as he carefully slid the closed blades between her pussy lips. The cold steel touched her clit and she gave an unconscious moan, not wanting the lifeless feel of hard metal, craving the warmth and softness of Max's fingers and lips.

Gently, and with great precision, Max move the scissors in a smooth caressing motion along the channel of her sex. Despite her fears and apprehension, her senses were aroused and her juices began to flow in abundance.

'I want you, Max,' she murmured, her gaze fastening on the tempting bulge at his crotch, desperate now to feel his hard cock plunging inside her. 'Please, I can't wait,' she added breathlessly.

'You always were a randy little bitch,' Max grunted, smiling coldly as he dropped the scissors in a kidney bowl with a loud clatter. 'I think you need to be taught a lesson,' he continued picking up a slim, flat-ended probe.

'No, Max!' Helen's eyes widened nervously as he slapped it against his hand.

Leaning forwards, Max hit Helen sharply on her inner thigh, just below the juncture with her pelvis. He had playfully punished her before, but never as cruelly as this. Her skin smarted, colouring slightly. Max hit her again and again, laying the blows in a regular pattern that criss-crossed her inner thighs until the discomfort increased considerably and her skin started to redden and burn. 'Stop it,' she gasped. 'That's enough, Max.'

Max paused and looked thoughtfully down at the pouting pouch of her open sex. Helen couldn't tear her gaze from him as he absentmindedly rubbed his palm across his bulging crotch. His cock seemed to increase in size as he slid down the zip of his jeans and eased the swollen organ out of the opening.

Helen stared hungrily at his huge prick, watching him ring the shaft with his fingers and wank it smoothly until it stiffened even more and a tiny bead of moisture escaped from the tip. Her inner thighs burned, amplifying the aching need in her sex. She would have given anything now to have him, but she still jumped nervously as Max pressed the bed control and the lower end fell away, leaving only her lower spine supported. Helen's buttocks and sex were left even more exposed and open, with her legs still spread high and wide. It made her feel even more vulnerable and excited as Max stepped between her open thighs.

Gently, he peeled open her swollen pussy lips and ran the tips of his fingers along her warm, moist slit. Helen moaned in desperation, then flinched in surprise as he placed a stinging blow across her open sex with the slim metal probe. The fiery heat seared her quim and she barely had time to draw breath before Max hit her again, this time across the tip of her bud. The agony was terrible, yet subtly arousing.

As he hit her again, following the line of her pussy lips, Helen moaned helplessly. Each stinging blow brought a fresh burst of moisture inside her and lights danced before her eyes. Helen begged him to stop, thrashing her limbs, pulling agitatedly against her bonds but Max ignored her pleadings. There was no way she could escape his punishing assault on her senses. She was forced to bite her lip to stop herself from screaming aloud as the pain and pleasure mingled into an exquisite ecstasy that knew no boundaries. As she surrendered her senses to the burning bliss, Max leaned forwards and pulled her abused clitoris into his mouth. He sucked on it hard and her pleasure erupted into a sudden, quite earth-shattering, climax.

Helen, trembling in the aftermath of her orgasm, caught sight of her reflection in the mirror. She could see the red angry slash of her sex standing vividly out against her pale pubic curls. She found the sight of her own inflamed secret parts wildly arousing.

Max eased the stirrups wider, putting even more strain on her leg muscles, until they ached with the unaccustomed pressure and her pussy lips gaped crudely open, revealing the delicious pink moistness of her quim. Casually he rubbed his cock shaft as he stared thoughtfully down at her exposed sex. A bead of moisture seeped from the plumlike head, and Helen could literally smell his lust for her. Desperate for him to take her, she agitatedly licked her lips, confused by his hesitancy. She wondered what thoughts were whirling around inside his head. As usual, she had no idea what Max was planning to do next.

'Do it now. Or let me go,' she pleaded.

'Do what, sweetheart?' Max asked with a wry grin.

'Fuck me,' she replied.

'There's time enough for that, but first I want to show you a new device that a gynaecologist friend of mine has started prescribing for his patients. He says they work far better than the pelvic cones he usually uses to help strengthen the internal muscles.' Max held the objects up for her inspection. Three polished metal balls, fastened together by finely meshed, flexible silver chains. They looked more like sex toys than medical equipment. 'He swears the patients tell him that they often reach a climax just by wearing them for a short length of time.'

Helen swallowed nervously as she imagined them filling the channel of her sex. 'Do they really work better?'

'Apparently the results have been remarkable.' The balls looked heavy and as Max moved his hand they rolled together with a soft clink. 'Why not try them yourself?'

Helen shivered as he leaned forwards, spreading lubricating jelly around her vagina and down the valley of her sex. He eased the first ball inside her, followed by the second and third in quick succession. Helen gave a soft moan as she felt the unaccustomed weight lodged high inside her body. The cold hardness of them, coupled with their weight, added to her arousal. She tensed her pelvic muscles, surprised by the strong ripple of erotic delight that filled her sex.

'They feel strange.' She tensed again, savouring the alien feel of the objects.

'But so good,' Max purred, stroking and caressing her open quim, further stimulating her heightened senses. His lubricated fingers drifted downwards, teasing the tight circle of muscle guarding her anus. Helen took an unsteady breath as he continued to gently caress the rosy ring until it began to relax.

'Yes,' she gasped, surprised at how good it felt as he slid a fingertip inside the virginal opening. She was filled with the sudden urge to bear down against the invading digit. Helen fought the need, her thighs trembling, and the heavy balls in her vagina rolled together, sending a surge of blissful pleasure through her entire sex.

'You like that, don't you?' Max crooned, pulling apart her arse cheeks, and gently rubbing the head of his penis against the previously unexplored opening.

Helen tensed, feeling fearful yet also excited. She had fantasised about this moment, wanting to try the unknown but something had always held her back. Now Max was about to fulfil one of her darkest and most unspoken desires. She tensed unconsciously as he paused to slip on a condom, then tenderly eased his huge cock-head inside the tight ring of muscle. The unfamiliar sensations were strange, breathlessly uncomfortable, yet also supremely arousing. As his hot hardness slid deeper into her forbidden depths, she groaned with painful pleasure, her nerve endings stimulated to fever pitch by the double assault on her senses.

Helen experienced such tightness, such bliss, that she felt her body could take no more of this erotic abuse. However, it did, automatically adjusting to the strangely delectable sensations as Max began to move his hips, thrusting deeper. The pleasure was white hot, sharp and so perfect she became conscious of nothing else. She was overwhelmed by its strength as she surrendered to the ever deepening tide of lustful bliss.

Sandra Pope opened her thighs even wider, her fingers busily stroking her sex, pinching and rolling her clitoris between finger and thumb. She was further inflamed by the sight of the erotic antics in the adjoining room as she felt the electric currents of pleasure flood her, leading her steadily upwards towards her climax.

Curiosity had prompted Sandra to slip in here, hoping to catch a glimpse of the new senior registrar, but she had never expected to be rewarded by the steamy scene she witnessed from behind the two-way mirror: the titillating vision of the gorgeous Max Fenton arse-fucking the latest hospital recruit.

Sandra wished it was her tied down on that bed, forced to submit to Max's every brutal whim. She wanted his dick to be powering into the crack of her buttocks. She could imagine how good it would feel – huge, hot and incredibly demanding. Lost in her wild fantasies, she frantically rubbed herself even harder, all the time keeping her eyes firmly fixed on Helen and Max. She gave a soft groan as the sensations peaked, her body shuddering as her orgasm came in a sudden rush of pleasure.

Leaning back in her chair, she took a deep unsteady breath, allowing herself time to recover. Idly, she envisaged the moment when she and Helen Dawson would meet again. They had been fellow boarders at a private school in Sussex. In their teens they had been close friends for a time. Sandra would never have expected the prim fifteen year old, who'd always claimed to dislike boys, to turn into this uninhibited, sexy woman. Most of the youths they had met at the time thought Helen frigid. She had never let any of them kiss her, let alone persuade her to open her tightly closed thighs.

Time was a great leveller, Sandra thought, as she pulled down the skirt of the smart blue dress. Helen had changed a lot in the intervening years, and she might well prove to be a very useful addition to the hospital staff.

Sandra moved to the wash-basin, scrubbed her hands, then readjusted her white frilly cap. All the nursing staff at the Princess Beatrice wore old-fashioned uniforms; dresses, starched aprons, frilly caps, and black seamed stockings.

Sandra was senior nursing officer, or matron, as she liked to be known. She relished the power and kudos that came with the position. It would be nice to feel on the same par as Helen for once. At school Sandra had always thought herself academically inferior to her friend. Helen had always been the pretty, clever one; the girl voted most likely to succeed.

Quietly she left the observation room. When the architect had first suggested this hidden observation room, Sandra had thought it rather a waste of space and money. Now, she decided, she could put this place to good use. It would be fun to lure other members of staff into the maternity unit and spy on their sexual antics.

Walking briskly along the wide corridors, Sandra made her way to the nurse's station on the second floor of the West Wing. Most of the really expensive private suites were situated here. One in particular was currently occupied by the famous movie director, Christopher

31

Skinner. Sandra made a point of visiting him regularly, at least twice a day. There were certain things she did for him that nobody else could. Mr Skinner had mild diabetes, but it was easily controlled by pills and the proper diet. However, the strains of his job – the snatched meals, location work and long hours – meant he often felt under the weather after he had finished a movie. Then he came to the Princess Beatrice, ostensibly to rest and ensure his condition was stabilised, but mainly to avail himself of the services of his friend, Sandra Pope.

'I left the trolley inside, ready,' Nurse Cowan said as Sandra approached.

'Thanks.' Sandra stepped inside Mr Skinner's room, closing the door behind her, knowing that she would not be disturbed. The last nurse who had intruded on her sessions with Christopher had been forced, by her, to resign the following day. Sandra now carefully vetted all nursing staff due to be assigned to the West Wing, ensuring they were all of like mind to her. Otherwise it would be impossible for the hospital to live up to the reputation of catering for every whim of its wealthy patients.

Christopher Skinner was lying on his bed, his eyes closed, as though asleep. He was a middle-aged, slightly portly man; not unattractive to a woman who knew just how rich and influential he was in the movie business. Over the last couple of years, since he'd been coming here, Sandra had grown fond of him. She sometimes wondered if their association might eventually grow into something more positive and enduring. Christopher knew he could rely on her discretion – she never spoke of her patients differing needs to anyone outside the hospital.

'I hear you've been a naughty boy, Christopher,' Sandra said curtly.

The patient opened his eyes and nodded. 'Yes, matron, I have,' he admitted, grinning like a naughty schoolboy.

'You know that you have to be punished if you don't

behave?' Sandra continued in the cold officious tone Christopher loved.

'Yes,' he agreed, with an excited shiver.

Sandra pulled on a pair of thin surgical gloves with a decisive snap, then jerked back the bedcovers. 'Very naughty, it seems,' she added, staring at the very visible bulge in his pyjama bottoms. She pulled open his flies to reveal his already enlarged penis, which stiffened even more as she stared down at it, her lip curling in disgust. 'Have you been masturbating again,' she challenged.

Christopher flushed, his breathing quickening as Sandra ran her rubber-gloved fingers down the side of his cock shaft. 'I only touched it for a moment,' he admitted nervously.

'You know that I told you to do no such thing.' Sandra gave the organ a gentle slap.

'I couldn't help it,' he gabbled staring up at her. 'I try to do what you tell me, matron. Really I do.'

'Not hard enough it seems,' Sandra said sternly. 'Punishment is the only way you'll learn, isn't it Christopher?' She slapped his penis again, this time much harder and it twitched excitedly and stiffened even more.

'Yes, matron,' he agreed with a cautious smile.

'Pull down those pyjamas and turn over,' she ordered curtly.

Obediently Christopher pulled down his pyjama bottoms and turned over, exposing his hairy butt to her gaze. Sandra ran her fingers over the round cheeks, squeezing the flesh between her rubber-gloved fingers and Christopher gave a soft moan of excited anticipation, knowing exactly what was coming next.

'Keep still.' She slapped his buttocks hard with the flat of her hand. Christopher pushed his belly down against the tightly stretched white sheets and gave a soft grunt. 'And keep quiet, no noise at all,' Sandra added, slapping him again.

She began to inflict his punishment, spanking him soundly, every hard slap making a satisfying crack as her rubber-gloved palm made contact with his quivering buttocks. After a few moments of this abuse, his skin began to turn a fiery red, her hand-prints standing out boldly against his pale flesh. Christopher gave a soft whimper, and unconsciously began rubbing his fat dick against the mattress beneath him.

'Don't move again,' Sandra hissed through gritted teeth, hitting him so hard this time that it made her wrist ache. 'Otherwise I might change my mind and decide not to come and see you again later tonight.'

He froze, clutching at the sides of the bed, fighting to stay still and do as he was told.

Sandra continued the brutal spanking until Christopher's entire buttocks were stained a deep ruby red, and he could no longer repress his agitated movements or his unconscious moans of pleasure. She smiled, savouring the sensual warmth growing deep in the pit of her belly. She was aroused just by the sight of him squirming helplessly on the bed.

Sandra had never appreciated her true calling until she came to work at the Princess Beatrice. It had been quite by accident that she had first discovered Christopher's unusual sexual needs. When she had offered to satisfy them, she had discovered how much she enjoyed dominating a man, inflicting abuse and punishment on her willing charge. As further opportunities had presented themselves, she had learned how to explore every sensual need to its fullest extent. Sandra, however, wasn't a totally committed dominatrix. Her sexual needs were a contradiction even to her, and recently her friend and hospital colleague, Justin, had shown her how exciting it was to be on the receiving end of such erotic domination.

In the last two years, since she had become matron, she had concentrated on attracting the right kind of patients to this part of the select establishment. The private suites in the West Wing were now dedicated to becoming a place where the rich and famous could relax and recover from the strains of life, well away from prying eyes – where they could explore every sybaritic pleasure in a discreet, secure environment.

'Now, what do you say, Christopher?' she prompted.

'I'm sorry,' came the muffled reply.

'Good boy.'

She picked up a tube of cream and began to spread a cooling antiseptic ointment over his fiery buttocks. When she had soothed his abused flesh, she concentrated on spreading the cream between his arse cheeks, and around the entrance to his anus. At first he remained silent, but couldn't repress a gasp of excitement as she eased the tip of one cream-covered finger inside the tight ring. She ventured deeper, until she could apply pressure to a most sensitive spot. Employing her medical knowledge, she carefully massaged the area, knowing that if she continued for too long she would bring him to an abrupt climax.

Christopher gasped with delight, lifting his hips. 'Don't you dare come,' Sandra hissed deliberately reducing the pressure. 'If you do, I won't let you use the plug.'

He gripped the mattress tightly, pressing his face into the pillow. 'I'm trying to do as you say, matron, but it's difficult,' he replied in a shaky voice, as she slowly withdrew her finger.

Sandra selected a white plastic anal plug from the ready-prepared trolley. It was the largest of the set Christopher always brought with him. Slowly, and with great precision, she slid the smooth object deep inside his rectum, twisting it gently to increase the sensation of fullness. Grunting with pleasure, Christopher lifted his buttocks up to meet the longed-for intrusion until it was firmly embedded inside him. She lodged the rim of the plug snugly between his arse cheeks. 'Clench tightly,' she said tersely. 'Keep it in position as you turn over.'

Christopher's face was flushed, his muscles tense with fevered anticipation as he rolled over. 'Let me come now,' he pleaded, glancing down at his distended dick, which looked so red and hard it appeared ready to explode.

Sandra was sorely tempted to continue their game to its ultimate conclusion. She wanted to come herself, right now, as she was feeling incredibly horny. Determinedly she held back on seeking her own pleasure. That would come later, when she returned to see Christopher tonight. First he had to wait and contain his need for a number of hours – that was a specific part of the punishments he expected and enjoyed.

There was something extra arousing in forcing someone famous and important, like Christopher, to comply to all her sexual demands. She had the power to reduce him to a quivering wreck if she chose, willing to do anything to obtain his release. She derived great pleasure from the services she offered, and had never sought anything other than simple gratitude from her patients. However, some of them insisted on giving her substantial monetary gifts. She now had a sizeable sum in her off-shore bank account. If she wanted she could retire in a couple of years, but Sandra wasn't sure she could ever bear to leave this place willingly.

Lost in thought for a brief moment, she didn't notice that one of Christopher's hands had strayed down to his aching prick. 'No,' she snapped, just as he took hold of the rigid shaft. 'If you do that again, I won't come back tonight.'

Christopher frowned. 'I'm – I'm sorry,' he said hesitantly.

'Behave yourself now and I'll let you do everything you want later,' she replied, secretly not wanting to miss out on the pleasures of their evening session.

'You'll wear the rubber corset under your uniform?' he asked.

'Maybe,' she agreed charily. 'You'll just have to wait and see.'

Sandra picked up a pair of black rubber pants, dusted them inside with talcum powder, then slid them over Christopher's feet, working them slowly up his thighs and over his hips. The tight rubber moulded to his stocky body, compressing his excess flesh. Apart from the waistband and leg holes, there was one other opening in the garment. A small round hole designed to allow Christopher's cock to protrude through it. The rubber fitted extra snugly around the base of his shaft, ensuring his erection was kept firmly in place and would not diminish as long as he wore the pants.

'It feels good,' he admitted with a shy smile, and she knew how much he was relishing the combined sensations: the tightly constraining rubber, the compression around the base of his penis and the smooth hardness of the plastic plug filling his arsehole.

Sandra almost envied his exquisite feelings as she stared thoughtfully at his stubby penis. Red and swollen, it stood rigidly out from the corset of black rubber. 'If I find you've rubbed yourself off before I return . . .' she warned, tapping his cock-head which quivered excitedly, rampant and hungry for release.

'I won't, matron,' Christopher promised, his expression showing how eagerly he envisaged the tortuous hours ahead. 'Not until you return to me tonight.'

'You're a good boy.' She took hold of his left hand, placing it on her leg, beneath her starched skirt. Tentatively he ran his hand upwards, past her stocking tops, to the juncture of her thighs, eager to explore the valley of her sex.

She knew that the discovery of underwear, which she wore rarely, would disappoint Christopher. 'Panties,' he groaned. 'They're damp,' he added, fingering the moist gusset. 'Have you come already?'

'No – it's all down to what I saw earlier,' she said teasingly, wanting to arouse his curiosity, as she recalled the enticing sight she'd witnessed between Helen and Max.

'Tell me?' he begged sliding a finger under the fabric to stroke her moist quim.

'Perhaps later tonight,' she said forcing herself to pull away from him. 'I have work to do, Christopher. Now pull up the sheet, and cover yourself, you dirty boy. I'll return after dinner to check if you've been good and kept all your promises to me.'

* * *

37

'Do you like the apartment?' Max asked as they left her new abode and walked across the old stable-yard back to the hospital. He had helped Helen unpack and settle into the staff flat which had been allocated to her. It was one of half a dozen situated in the stable block, a short distance from the main building.

'Very comfortable,' she agreed. 'Especially the bed.'

'Pity we didn't have more time,' he said huskily.

Max had insisted that Helen keep the balls inside her while they made their way to her new apartment. They were heavy, and she'd been forced to concentrate hard to keep them in place. Feeling them roll around inside her as she walked had been wonderfully stimulating, and by the time they reached the privacy of her bedroom, she was desperate for Max. Not surprisingly, they'd had sex again, spending nearly an hour trying out her new four-poster bed.

'I'm going to miss you, Max,' she admitted, very conscious of the rather pleasant discomfort between the cheeks of her buttocks.

'As you should.' He slid his arm around her waist and pulled her close. 'Initially I should only be in New York about six weeks.'

'Six weeks is a long time.'

'It'll pass quickly enough. You'll be busy adjusting to your new position,' he said, pausing outside the office of the senior nursing officer.

Helen wasn't looking forward to this meeting. She had never liked the officious senior nursing officer at her old hospital. This one was bound to be as starchy and middle-aged as all the others she had known. However, she would do her best to get along with the woman, just to make life easier adjusting to this new hospital routine.

'Relax,' Max whispered as he escorted her into the brightly decorated outer office. 'Sandra,' he continued with a warm smile as he greeted the dark-haired woman dressed in a distinctly old-fashioned uniform. 'I brought Helen Dawson, the new senior registrar, to meet you.'

'I recognised the name when Max mentioned it, but

somehow I never really expected it to be you, Helen. I heard a rumour that you'd moved to Australia,' Sandra said, smiling in an impersonal but quite welcoming way.

'You should never believe all that you hear,' Helen replied, struggling to hide her surprise. She had never discovered what happened to Sandra after she left their school at the age of sixteen. Helen had certainly never expected the pleasure seeking, flirtatious teenager she'd known to become a nurse. She must have done really well in her career to become matron at such an early age.

'You know each other?' Max asked in surprise.

'Very well,' Sandra replied, smiling knowingly at Helen.

Helen felt a faint flush rush to her cheeks, as a number of repressed memories surfaced.

'We were quite good friends at school,' she explained to Max.

'What a coincidence. It'll be nice for you to have an old friend here, won't it?' Max said, presuming wrongly that she was pleased to see Sandra again.

'I'll do my best to make her feel right at home,' Sandra told him.

'That would be great,' Max said. 'Now, if you'll excuse me ladies, I really do have to get back to London.'

'Sure,' Helen smiled at Max, casually as if they were just friends. They had decided to keep their relationship secret here as well, so they had already said their more passionate goodbyes in the privacy of her new apartment.

'I'll phone you from New York,' Max said to Helen, then turned back to Sandra. 'I've shown Dr Dawson around, but I'm sure you will help her get acquainted with the hospital routine.'

Sandra nodded, smiling agreeably at Max. 'It would be my pleasure. In fact I've already ordered tea to be brought to my office. We can talk about the hospital, then have a cosy private chat. We've a lot to talk about, haven't we? Especially that holiday we spent together in

Cornwall so many years ago. It was fun wasn't it, Helen?'

'Lovely,' Helen agreed nervously, preferring not to recall what had happened during the nights she and Sandra had shared a double bed.

Chapter Three

*T*he two women made their way into Sandra's office and sat down on the couch by the French window. There was a glorious view of the hospital grounds, but Helen was more interested in surreptitiously examining Sandra while she was busy pouring the tea.

Physically Sandra had changed little in the intervening years. She was still a good few inches shorter that Helen, but far more voluptuous. Sandra's breasts appeared to be much bigger than Helen remembered. Her hair was as dark and curly as ever, and her brown eyes still held a wicked sparkle. Men probably found her very attractive. In their teens, it was Sandra who all the boys had fancied. Helen had been very shy and they had all seemed a little put off by her cool, blonde beauty.

'Milk and sugar?' Sandra asked.

'No sugar, and just a splash of milk, please.' Helen felt rather unsettled by Sandra's reappearance in her life. She would much rather forget most of what had happened when they'd been friends.

'You always took at least two sugars in your tea if I remember rightly,' Sandra commented, handing Helen a cup of tea. 'You're still very slim, so you can't possibly be worried about your figure.'

'I'm not concerned about putting on weight. It's just that my tastes have changed as I've got older.'

'Have they?' Sandra leaned back against the floral cushions and stared thoughtfully at Helen.

'Very much so,' Helen replied, made even more uneasy by the odd way Sandra was now looking at her. 'Don't they always as we grow and mature?'

'Not always. Funnily enough I got the distinct impression that you and Max Fenton were an item,' Sandra mused. 'In the circumstances I was surprised. I always rather thought that you'd turn out to be a lesbian.'

'A lesbian,' Helen repeated. 'Of course not.' She blushed awkwardly. 'I don't know what gave you that idea.'

'What could have?' Sandra smiled teasingly. 'Perhaps your behaviour when we shared a room. You were the one who led me on after all.'

'I don't remember it like that. It was just girlish curiosity, nothing more,' Helen said defensively, as even stronger memories of that time flooded her mind.

It had all started out quite innocently. When they were teenagers they had gone on holiday with Sandra's parents and stayed in a creepy old Cornish farmhouse. On the first night, fearful of ghosts and frightening apparitions, Helen and Sandra scurried nervously into their double bed. The mattress was old and lumpy with a deep dent in the centre, so they had little choice but to cuddle up close. Helen found the feel of Sandra's warm curvy body incredibly comforting.

During their ensuing conversation, she admitted to her friend that she didn't know how to French kiss and Sandra offered to teach her. Their lips tentatively touched, then Sandra's tongue squirmed its way into her mouth. Helen had been overcome by this first sexual encounter, as they had continued to kiss, their tongues sensuously exploring each other's mouth. Turned on by the intimate contact, Helen had run her hands nervously over Sandra's body, secretly wishing she was unclothed.

One of them, Helen couldn't remember who, suggested they remove their nightgowns. After that their caresses had become bolder, more uninhibited. They stroked and squeezed each other's breasts, then slid their hands downwards to seek out their partner's most secret feminine parts.

The stroking, and rubbing of hands between open thighs, had proved highly exciting, stimulating them to proceed further. Clumsy caresses gradually became more proficient, and they soon discovered exactly what to do to bring a feminine body to the peak of pleasure. Their mutual delight, the orgasms they shared, acted like a drug on their senses. They spent the remaining days of their holiday looking forward to the intimate privacy of the nights.

When they returned to school, the liaison continued, and would probably have gone on much longer if a teacher hadn't discovered them naked in bed together late one night. They had been threatened with expulsion. It had only been prevented when they both promised not to see each other again. They were assigned to different dormitories, kept apart in lessons, and soon their friendship faded along with their youthful passions.

'I seem to remember that it was far more than just girlish curiosity,' Sandra said softly. 'At the time I really fancied you, Helen. You knew exactly how to turn me on. The sex we had was far better than the fumblings of the inexperienced boys I knew,' she added with a teasing laugh.

'Well, it's all in the past now, and best forgotten,' Helen said curtly.

'The past can often come back to haunt us,' Sandra pointed out, seeming amused by Helen's discomfort. Finishing her tea, she put her cup down on the low table in front of her. 'How long have you and Max been together then? I always thought him incredibly sexy. Is he good in the sack?'

'I prefer not to discuss my relationship with Max

Fenton.' Helen couldn't understand how Sandra could have so easily figured out that she and Max were involved, as neither of them had made it at all obvious. As far as Helen knew, no one at St Matthew's had ever realised they were going out together.

'I should guess that he's a pretty inventive lover.' Sandra smiled in a knowing, rather unsettling way. 'Enjoys fucking in unusual places, does he?'

Helen blushed even more. Sandra couldn't possibly be privy to what had happened between her and Max earlier today, could she? 'My private life is none of your concern, Sandra. Let's keep our relationship here on a purely professional level,' Helen replied, struggling to retain her composure. 'Officially Max and I are good friends, nothing more.'

'Whatever you say.' Sandra smiled sweetly. 'In the circumstances I understand why you would want to keep your liaison with Max quiet. He is a major shareholder, and the most senior member on the governing board of the Princess Beatrice. Most people consider him the big boss around here. You know how staff gossip – '

'Are you implying that they'll think I got this job because of my relationship with Max?' Helen slammed down her cup on the table.

'Goodness, no. I'm certain that Max isn't the sort of guy who would give you a job just because he's fucking you. You're well qualified for the position, Helen. A little too well qualified if you ask me.'

'I have very good reasons for coming here,' Helen replied.

'Of course you do. It's a great pity you lost your old job when they decided to close St Matthew's. The hospital had a good reputation. It was the salary that attracted you here, wasn't it? They pay very well, and initially most of the staff come here precisely because of that fact. Now of course they all stay because they love it so much. We are a very close-knit community.' She put a hand on Helen's knee. 'Very close.'

'Really,' Helen stuttered as she felt Sandra's fingers

44

gently caressing her leg. She wanted to pull away, but somehow she couldn't. Sandra was the only woman Helen had ever found attractive, and she could feel the sensual pull even now, after all these years. It was something she couldn't rationally explain and it troubled her.

'We were such good friends when we were young, and we shared virtually everything,' Sandra said in a soft hypnotic voice as she slid her hand up Helen's leg. 'We could take this opportunity to renew our close friendship, couldn't we, Helen?'

'I don't think that's a good idea,' Helen stuttered, suddenly beginning to feel weak and a little shaky.

Helen glanced downwards nervously, mesmerised by the slow upward movement of Sandra's hand. Soon it was resting intimately on her upper thigh, and Sandra's fingers were straying dangerously close to Helen's crotch. The warmth of Sandra's palm seemed to sear Helen's skin, even through the thin cotton of her skirt.

'Why isn't it a good idea?' Sandra asked, leaning closer until Helen could smell the tantalising odour of her musky perfume, mixed with the faintly familiar womanly scent that time had almost erased from her memory.

Sandra's crisp, old-fashioned uniform fitted snugly, the pinched-in waist adding further emphasis to her full breasts. They were tightly encased by a bra, and Helen wondered what they would look like free and unfettered. Big as melons, they would be soft and infinitely pleasing – a total contrast to Helen's firm, uptilted bosom. She could still remember Sandra's large, rusty-brown aureoles, and her nipples had always been permanently erect; huge reddish-brown teats, just right for nibbling and sucking.

This was insane, Helen told herself, trying to push such erotic thoughts out of her mind. There was no way she was going to rekindle the relationship. It had been a youthful mistake, driven by curiosity, during a time of rampantly burgeoning sexuality. She wasn't a lesbian and never would be. Apart from her brief liaison with

Sandra, all her relationships had been totally heterosexual. Her attraction to Sandra was over and done with years ago. She liked men fucking her, not women.

'The past is over and done with,' Helen said in a hesitant voice as she felt Sandra's fingers slide between her thighs, moving closer to her aching pussy. She fought the sudden urge to lean back, pull up her skirt and open her legs, welcome the pleasure Sandra could give her.

'Whatever you say. But I still turn you on, don't I?' Sandra purred.

Her soft breasts pressed temptingly against Helen's arm. Helen shivered, feeling her heart rate increase, as the tips of Sandra's fingers moved teasingly across her sex. The gentle touch was so good. The feel of Sandra's fingers even through the layers of skirt and panties was still incredibly exciting. Helen bit her lip, wanting to beg Sandra to push harder, to put more pressure on her throbbing quim.

'You don't turn me on,' Helen lied, having no desire for Sandra to know how aroused she felt, how much the intimate contact was affecting her senses.

Helen couldn't allow relationships to complicate her life here at the Princess Beatrice. There was no way she could become involved with Sandra Pope, of all people. Even pausing to consider it was madness.

'You always were a lousy liar.' Sandra's laugh was softly mocking as Helen pulled away from her and slid to the end of the sofa.

'As I said before,' Helen responded, her voice shaking slightly, 'I intend to keep all my relationships here on a purely professional level.'

'You can try,' Sandra replied coolly. 'Keep yourself to yourself as much as you like, but it won't be easy.' She glanced out of the window. 'As you can see this place is pretty isolated, and we're miles from the nearest town. If you don't make friends you're bound to be lonely.'

'I can get out and about, explore the countryside.' Helen, still conscious of the throbbing heat between her thighs, took an unsteady breath. 'Or buy a car if I find I need one. I've never bothered before; it would have been an unnecessary extravagance in London. Here it's a different matter.'

Sandra stared thoughtfully at Helen through narrowed eyes. 'You should at least get to know your fellow workers. The person you'll be mostly dealing with is the other senior registrar, Ben Taylor. He's planning to pop round to your apartment about eight this evening. He'll take you to the staff bar, show you the recreational facilities, introduce you to some of the hospital personnel. That's if you don't object, of course.'

'Not at all,' Helen said coolly. 'I look forward to meeting him.'

'Ben can fill you in on hospital routine, what nights you'll be on call and suchlike. You'll like him, he's a charming guy.'

'I'm sure he is,' Helen replied. Sandra didn't appear at all upset by her rebuttal, but Helen still felt a tad uneasy in her presence. 'Well, thanks for the tea, Sandra.'

'It was a pleasure,' Sandra replied. 'I'll see you tomorrow sometime, when I do my rounds.'

'Yes,' Helen agreed, standing up, and managing to disguise the fact that her legs still felt a trace unsteady. 'Tomorrow, then.'

'Tomorrow,' Sandra echoed, as Helen left the room.

Zara Dawn's hospital room was awash with flowers. Large bouquets from her manager, publicist, the producer of her most recent movie, and most importantly from all her fans. However, at this moment in time such lavish signs of affection meant little to Zara because she was in one of her nervous, apprehensive moods.

Like many glamorous movie stars, Zara was extraordinarily insecure about both her talents and her looks. In her youth she'd been far more positive, confident that she could conquer the world with her beauty. Sadly, once the odd faint wrinkle, the merest suggestion of sagging skin, had begun to mar her looks, Zara's insecurities had magnified beyond proportion. Every tiny sign of ageing, every blemish, looked so much worse when inflated on a large movie screen.

Over the past few years, in order to counter her insecurities and bolster her image, Zara had found herself seeking out younger and younger men. It looked good in public, and felt even better in private to have a young handsome guy always beside her.

The last in this line of young men was the wannabe rock star, Warren Hart. Warren's first record, made in a converted garage at his parent's house, had been fairly successful, reaching number five in the charts. His second, made in a de luxe studio and backed by a major record label, had been a total flop. Nevertheless, Warren was convinced that one day he would be bigger than the Stones or Oasis. Bigger even than Presley, if he found the right songs.

Zara and Warren had met at a show-biz party nearly six months ago. Zara had been attracted by Warren's raw, unpolished sexual charisma and his hard, lean body. He wasn't conventionally good looking, with his bad skin, strong features, long dark hair and small goatee beard. But his compelling dark eyes, and his oddly satanic quality had drawn Zara towards him like a moth to a flame.

At first, like all the other guys, Warren had been flattered by Zara's interest in him, but Warren was selfish with an over-inflated ego, and to her amazement she soon found herself pandering to his whims. But the sex was so great that Zara put up with his selfishness and sometimes brutally cruel behaviour. Zara, with her many years of experience with a multitude of different men, was a skilful and inventive lover. Warren, on the other hand, was rough and often coarse, with an uncut sensuality which led him to experiment in just about every conceivable sexual perversion. Their lovemaking was the most exciting she'd ever known.

Zara was certain that Warren was far too self-interested to care deeply for her, despite the fact he often said that he loved her. She tried to ignore the fact that he stayed with her mainly because she was rich, influential, and could help him get to know all the right people – eventually help bring him the fame he craved.

Today, Warren had been due to record a brief spot for a TV programme, and had promised to visit her afterwards. He was very late, Zara realised, anxiously glancing at the clock and seeing it was almost 5 p.m. She ran her fingers through her artfully styled, shoulder-length, honey-coloured hair, which was much darker than the platinum blonde she'd favoured in her youth.

Lately she'd been feeling even more insecure. Warren was only twenty-six, while she didn't even acknowledge her age. Knowing that he was coming to visit her for the first time since her operation had made Zara extra careful with her make-up. She'd easily managed to cover the marks left by the liposuction on her previous suspicion of a double chin. To her relief her jaw-line looked cleaner and sharper now, giving her a more youthful appearance. There were a few faint bruises still visible from her upper eye lift but they weren't half as bad as she'd expected. One thing she hadn't bothered about were the purplish yellow marks on her stomach and thighs, all due to the liposuction carried out in that area. The marks would have faded completed by the time she returned home and Warren saw her in the nude once again.

Fear of the future, fear of losing her renowned beauty, had prompted Zara to splash out a large amount of money on the plastic surgery. In public, she had always insisted she would never resort to such extremes to retain her looks, so her publicist had announced she'd come to the Princes Beatrice to be treated for a recurrent chest infection. Once she was recovered, she and Warren planned to fly to the Bahamas for three weeks' holiday, after which she was due to start work on a TV miniseries.

Suddenly the door of her room swung open. 'Well!' Warren exclaimed, kicking the door shut behind him with a loud slam. 'How goes it, babe?'

49

'Fine,' she said brightly. 'I'm feeling very well.'

'You don't look bad at all,' he conceded almost disinterestedly. 'Much better than I expected. I'm totally fucked.'

He leaned forwards to kiss her cheek, and Zara almost recoiled from the smell of stale cigarettes and booze. 'How did the interview go, Warren?'

'Bloody awful,' he growled. 'The bitch didn't ask me one of the fucking questions I'd agreed to. She just kept on blabbering on about how badly my last single had done in the charts. Tried to humiliate me. Even mentioned I was living with you. Inferred I was some kind of frigging gigolo, stupid cow.'

Zara sighed. Warren was his own worst enemy at times. 'Perhaps it would have gone off better if you hadn't drunk so much beforehand,' she suggested.

'I didn't drink a bloody thing this morning.' Warren flopped down on the chair beside the bed. 'Just had a couple last night with a few friends.'

'Where?' she enquired casually.

'Your place, where else?'

He grinned revealing yellow uneven teeth. Zara, who was used to his excesses, thought Warren looked worse than usual today. His face was pale and spotty. There were heavy dark circles under his eyes and his hair was greasy and lank. Even his clothes looked crumpled and none too clean. Zara couldn't prove it, but as well as overdosing on booze, she suspected he was also using. He would never admit it to her as Zara was an outspoken anti-drugs campaigner. She had been ever since a close friend of hers had died of an overdose ten years ago.

'Don't worry, we haven't fucked up your precious pale furnishings,' Warren growled. 'You made such a bloody fuss last time, I made sure they all behaved themselves.' He grinned at her in a youthful cheeky kind of way, which made her heart race. It was only occasionally now that she got glimpses of the cocky young man she'd fallen for all those months ago. 'Look, do you like it?'

He pulled back his lank greasy hair to expose his left earlobe. Just beneath his usual gold sleeper was a huge, sparkling, canary diamond stud.

'Is that mine?' she asked in concern.

It looked like one of the diamond earrings she'd been given by a former lover, an obscenely rich Arab Prince. The earrings were worth a fortune, and one of her most precious possessions. All Zara's jewellery was carefully catalogued and stored. She looked upon it as insurance which would help ensure her financial security in her old age.

'Of course it's yours.' Warren's grin widened. 'Looks great doesn't it? Made the hole myself with a needle – bit messy, but worth it. I haven't figured out where to put the other one yet. My nose, or my dick, what do you think?'

Zara couldn't believe what she was hearing. No one was allowed to lay hands on her secret hoard, it was hers alone. 'They were in the safe along with the other pieces,' she said angrily. 'How the hell did you get hold of them?'

'How d'you think?' he sneered. 'I opened the safe – used the combination. I didn't blow the bloody door off.'

'I never gave you the combination.'

'Didn't have to,' he said proudly. 'You're so damn scared of forgetting things that you write everything down. I watched you stick a piece of paper containing the combination to the underside of one of your dressing table drawers.'

'And you spied on me, then stole it,' she accused.

'Shouldn't have been so fucking careless. Anyone with any sense would know to look there.' He fingered the diamond possessively, while staring at her through narrowed eyes. 'There's no need to look so put out.'

'Put out!' she repeated. 'That's an understatement,' she added in disgust. 'You stole my jewellery.'

'Just took what I earned.' His expression hardened.

51

'Earned?'

'Yeah, with this.' Warren rubbed his hand against his crotch until his cock hardened, bulging visible against his skin-tight jeans.

'You bastard,' she hissed. Even though she was angry she still wanted him. She stared at the very visible rod of male flesh. Warren might be slightly built and none too tall, but in contrast his dick was magnificently large. 'Did you expect to be paid?'

'For fucking you, why not? I made sure you always enjoyed it.'

'You enjoyed it too,' she challenged.

'So you thought,' he countered. 'Maybe I'm just a bloody good actor. I'm only twenty-six, while you're middle aged, but also rich and very famous. Work it out for yourself,' he added cruelly.

'You told me when we first met that you were a great fan, that you'd always fancied me.'

'When I was thirteen I did, but that's a long time ago. The years are catching up on you big time, Zara. Why else would you be having plastic surgery?'

'How dare you say I'm old,' she screamed. 'Get out of my sight you bastard.'

'Don't order me about, bitch.' Jumping to his feet, Warren jerked back the bedclothes and plunged his hand inside the bodice of her nightgown. 'You know that I just need to touch you and you'll do anything I say.'

He squeezed and kneaded her breast so roughly that she gave a whimper of discomfort. 'No, Warren, don't.'

'No, Warren, don't,' he repeated in a high-pitched parody of her voice. 'You want me – admit it,' he added, pinching her nipple, rolling and pulling at the sensitive peak, while flipping up the skirt of her nightgown with his other hand. She was bared to the waist, her badly bruised stomach and thighs on full show. 'Not such a pretty picture down here,' he sneered, thrusting a hand between her thighs. 'But I bet your little cunt is as hungry as ever.'

'You bastard,' she muttered, as he roughly caressed her pussy, yet she found herself opening her legs wider.

'Soaking wet.' He thrust three bunched fingers deep inside her vagina.

His brutality turned her on, and she didn't have the strength to fight the assault on her already heightened senses. 'I don't want you,' she gasped unconvincingly, as tears of humiliation stung her eyes.

Warren thrust his fingers in and out of her soaking sex, and Zara gave an unconsciously loud, submissive moan. Warren laughed triumphantly. 'You can't get enough, can you, Zara? Now you've had your surgery you could go for someone even younger. Why not hang round the local school, pick up some fresh meat – some fourteen or fifteen-year-old kid.'

She wanted to tell him to go to hell, but the words wouldn't come out of her mouth. It was days since she'd had sex and despite her disgust for him, she found Warren's crude invasion arousing. She whimpered, wanting him to continue finger-fucking her as his thrust became harder and deeper. Zara couldn't fight the inescapable pleasure building inside her aching quim, moving her closer and closer to a climax.

'So desperate for it – so easily controlled,' Warren taunted.

Zara lifted her hips to meets his thrusts, no longer caring at this moment in time what he said. Warren gave a harsh chuckle as he ripped the fragile bodice of her nightgown, and leaned forwards to pull one full breast into his mouth. He sucked on it hungrily, grazing her enlarged nipple with his teeth. Then he pressed his thumb down hard on her clitoris, and the combination of sensations was sweet perfection itself. Her desire and hatred combined into an overwhelming emotion that drove her up and over the edge, into a pulsing climax.

Zara was left shaking with spent passion, suddenly feeling used and deflated as she stared up at Warren. 'Stupid bitch,' he growled, laughing triumphantly. 'Now I've proved who's in control.'

'Damn you.' Lifting a trembling hand, she hit him hard across the face.

'Bitch,' he yelled furiously, slapping her so hard in retaliation that her ears sang and her head buzzed.

Grabbing Zara by the shoulders, he shook her, then thrust her roughly back against her pillows. 'I've a mind to open that bloody safe and take every piece of your precious jewellery. I'll sell it or hide it somewhere you'll never find it.'

'Do that and I'll have you arrested. You'll be in jail before you even know it,' she screamed, watching fearfully as his raised his hand again, while the other went to the zip of his jeans.

Staff nurse Colin Deakin was standing in the corridor issuing instructions to two young nurses, who'd just come on duty, when they heard the commotion coming from Zara Dawn's room.

'Leave this to me,' he told the nurses, recalling that he'd not liked the look of Miss Dawn's visitor when the man had strolled passed the nurses' station a short time ago. 'You attend to the other patients.'

Not bothering to knock, Colin barged into Zara's room. He was just in time to see Warren, hand raised to hit her again, while the other unzipped his flies. Colin's reactions were quick, honed by the years he'd spent in the army. 'Don't you dare,' he barked loudly, crossing the room in a flash and pulling Warren away from Zara's bed.

'Take your fucking hands off me,' Warren growled as he spun round to face Colin. 'I'll punch your lights out, arsehole.'

'Don't even try it if you value your life. It'll be the last move you ever make,' Colin warned, staring scornfully at Warren's scrawny body.

Warren muttered something incomprehensible under his breath, raising his clenched fists, desperately trying to look menacing. He failed miserably and it was clear he was scared of Colin, threatened by his impressive

54

height and muscular build. Despite the fact that Colin had only served in the army as a medic, he'd still been behind enemy lines on a number of occasions, forced to fight for his life. He looked every inch the former soldier.

'Well?'

'Cool it,' Warren muttered. 'Calm down, man – this was a private argument.'

'Not when my patient's well-being is at stake. You, out!' Colin pointed to the door.

'You can't order me around,' Warren sneered, nervously clenching and unclenching his fists. Glancing down, he self-consciously rezipped his gaping flies.

'Try and stop me.'

'The bitch isn't worth any of this.' Warren cast a brief, scathing glance in Zara's direction, before moving towards the door with undue haste. 'You can both go to fucking hell,' he yelled boldly, slamming the door shut behind him.

Colin moved solicitously over to Zara. It was the first time he'd been on duty since Zara Dawn had arrived at the hospital. He was way too old at thirty-four to indulge in crushes on movie stars, but he'd admired her for years. He'd been looking forward to meeting her, though not in a situation like this.

'It's OK now, Miss Dawn, he's gone,' Colin said reassuringly. 'Did he hurt you?' he asked, seeing a mark, which looked suspiciously like a hand-print, marring the smooth paleness of her cheek.

'My pride more than anything else,' Zara sobbed, fighting to regain her composure.

Tears rolled down her face, streaking her mascara as she reached for the box of tissues on the bedside table. Colin couldn't believe the colour of her large tear-filled eyes; they were an even deeper violet than they appeared on screen. 'Would you like me to issue instructions not to let him visit you again?' he suggested. 'You need peace and quiet to recover from surgery.'

'And there's never any peace when Warren's around.'

Zara picked up a small mirror and tried to concentrate on removing streaks of mascara from beneath her eyes.

As she moved, she didn't notice that the sheet she'd so hastily pulled up had slid down again. Where her nightgown had been ripped away, Colin got a clear view of her magnificent bosom. The nipple of her left breast looked red and sore. Damn the bastard, he thought, but his expression betrayed nothing. Despite his familiarity with women's bodies, and his medical training, he couldn't help feeling aroused by the sight. Zara was even more beautiful in the flesh than he'd ever imagined.

'I'll tell reception not to let him in again.'

'I doubt he'll be back anyway,' Zara replied. 'When Warren gets angry and upset, he disappears for days. Most likely he'll pick up a couple of tarts, book into a cheap hotel and go on a drinking binge.'

'Sounds a real nice guy,' Colin remarked in disgust.

'I'm a fool, aren't I?' Zara regained some composure, but her hand still trembled as she replaced the mirror on her bedside table.

'We all do foolish things at times,' said Colin. He wanted to ask Zara what she saw in a creep like Warren. She was famous, beautiful, and according to the tabloids had a number of rich and influential admirers. 'Would you like me to give you something to help calm you down? You're pretty shook up.'

She shook her head. 'I don't like taking drugs. I'll just have to get over it myself.'

'There are other things,' he pointed out.

'Like what?'

'Herbal remedies, essential oils. I've just been away, doing a course on aromatherapy massage. That can be extraordinarily soothing in times of stress.'

'So that's why I've not seen you before.' She stared admiringly at his strong tanned arms and muscular physique, which were well displayed in his form fitting white uniform. 'Warren didn't scare you, did he?'

'I'm ex-army. Compared to a herd of angry Iraqis your

friend Warren is a pussy-cat.' Colin smiled wryly. 'Let's get you tidied up. Where do you keep your spare nightgowns?'

'Oh!' She looked down at her torn bodice, which did little to conceal her breasts. 'No matter.' She tried to sound unconcerned. 'I've shown far more in movies.'

'It's not quite the same, is it?' Colin replied with understanding.

'You're very astute.' She pointed to the low dressing table. 'They're in the top drawer. Any one will do.'

Colin pulled open the drawer and removed the first nightgown he saw – a fragile white lace garment that had probably cost more than a month of his wages. 'This is pretty.'

'A shade virginal,' she said cynically. 'I'm far from that.'

'It's perfect.' Colin laid the garment on the chair beside her bed. 'Almost as beautiful as its owner.'

'You flatter me,' she said, lifting the sheet to cover her. 'Now about this aromatherapy. Do you really think it would help?'

Colin selected and mixed the essential oils, adding them to the oil base he would use for the massage. The combination would calm Zara down and help her to forget the unpleasant incident with Warren. Colin could only guess what had happened between them, but his surmising was extraordinarily close to the truth.

When he entered the hospital room again, he found Zara already prepared for her massage. She lay on her stomach on the bed, a large white towel beneath her, another discreetly covering her body.

'You'll soon start to feel better, more relaxed,' Colin assured her as he turned the towel back to her waist, then rubbed his hands together to warm them a little.

Zara's skin was a pale ivory and blemish free, while her body was just perfect; curvy, not stick-thin like most of the actresses Colin had come across since working there. She looked more like a thirty year old than a woman fast approaching fifty.

Colin tried not to think of her in a sexual way, but he found it far from easy, as he poured the sweet smelling oil on her back and started to massage her with long, smooth strokes.

'That feels nice.' Zara pillowed her head on her folded arms.

'Relax, think of nothing,' Colin said, so very conscious that he was touching a woman he'd adored for years. A hungry ache of longing formed deep in the pit of his belly, and no matter how hard he tried, it couldn't be totally ignored. Her full breasts were compressed by her weight, and they spilled enticingly out of the sides of her body. As Colin slid his hands up the sides of her back his fingers brushed the soft curves. He wanted to roll her over, cup them in his hands, cover then with gentle kisses. His heartbeat quickened at the thought as life blood flooded his groin. His cock hardened – God, how he wanted this woman.

Slowly he eased down the towel, only to discover that beneath it she was totally naked. This was the first time he'd massaged a patient. During all his practice sessions the ladies had discreetly kept on their panties. Zara's bottom was pert and tight, with no sign of softness or dimpling – a testament to the time she spent working out in the gym. Colin dug his fingers in her gluteus muscles, kneading and squeezing. The movements pulled apart the cheeks of her buttocks and he caught a glimpse of her rosy brown anus. Aroused by the delicious sight, her tried hard to concentrate on the massage, sliding his hands lower to stroke her legs.

Zara gave a soft appreciative sigh, relaxing even more, and her legs rolled open just a little. Colin's fingers, slick with oil, unintentionally slid between her thighs, just brushing her dark blonde pubic curls. He felt her shiver, and was so very tempted to proceed further; to mesh his fingers in the silky pelt, dip them inside the lips of her sex and seek out the throbbing heat of her quim. A sheen of perspiration formed on his brow, as he fought against his desires. Trying to ignore the dark inviting shadows between her thighs, he ran his hands downwards to stroke her calves.

'You were right, this feels good,' she said softly as he massaged each foot in turn.

'I'm pleased it makes you feel better,' he replied, his voice husky with need. 'You can turn over now,' he added, pulling the towel up to cover her again, wondering how he was ever going to contain himself as he massaged her front.

Zara rolled over, then looked up at him, an unreadable expression on her face. 'Let's not bother with this,' she said, casting her towel aside. She glanced at his name tag. 'You really are a very good looking guy, Colin,' she added, her violet eyes softening.

Was this an unspoken invitation to intimacy, Colin asked himself as he stared at her naked body: lush full breasts with rosy tipped nipples and a slightly rounded belly, marred at present by the bruises of surgery, but enticing all the same. He swallowed hard as his gaze fastened on the triangle of dark gold curls at her groin. The sudden rush of lust he experienced was almost overwhelming. His cock stiffened into a rigid rod. Now highly visible as it pressed against his tight-fitting white cotton trousers. Yet he dare not glance down, dare not look Zara in the face, or express how horny he was feeling.

'You're too kind, Miss Dawn.' He turned away, concentrating on pouring more oil into his palm.

'Do I embarrass you?' She folded her hands behind her head, bringing the lush breast into even greater prominence.

Colin struggled against the rising tide of lust, the sudden need to rip off his clothes and fling himself on top of her. 'This is my job. Naked bodies don't disturb me,' he replied, trying to sound professional, and in full control.

He began to massage her front, sliding his hands up

each arm, then concentrating on her midriff, all the while sternly reminding himself he was a professional and this was part of his job. There was talk in the hospital, much of it about the goings on between staff and patients in the West Wing. Colin had never worked there, and he kept himself apart from the gossip, the tales of sexual proclivity. Now he began to wonder if the fanciful tales were maybe true. For the first time he was allowing himself to be seduced by the sexual attractions of one of his own patients.

Almost of their own accord, he found his fingers creeping upwards, until they were just brushing the undersides of her magnificent breasts. Zara uttered no words of protest, on the contrary she gave a soft moan of encouragement. Colin's hands slid higher, cupping her bosom. Becoming bolder, he stroked and kneaded her breasts, until they were slick and shiny with the aromatic oil. His hands trembled as he circled her rosy brown nipples, squeezing the firm peaks, rubbing and pulling at then until they darkened and hardened.

'You have magic in your fingers, Colin.' A half-smile hovered at her lips, as she took hold of his wrist, leading his hand downwards to rest on her quivering belly. 'Lower,' she softly commanded.

Colin needed no more encouragement. He caressed her stomach, and meshed his oil-covered fingers in her silky pubic curls. Restlessly Zara moved her hips and opened her thighs. Light-headed with excitement, Colin slid his fingers into the dark cleft of her sex. The flesh felt warm and deliciously moist as he eagerly explored her pussy, pausing to play with her swollen clitoris until she moaned with pleasure.

'Are you sure?' he asked, his voice thick with passion.

'Yes,' she groaned. 'Frig me.'

Colin thrust three bunched fingers into her hot wet depths, burying them as deep as he could. She groaned again, lifting her hips upwards as he began to thrust his fingers in and out of her.

'Does that feel good?' He was filled with the need to

remove his fingers, replacing them with his hungry cock, bury it deep inside her hot, tight cave of pleasure. Instead he clenched his teeth, held back on his own desires and moved his fingers harder and faster.

'Oh, yes.' She bucked against the movements of his hand, as he finger-fucked her in a smooth erotic rhythm, crying out with pleasure as he pressed his thumb down on her clit again.

Colin's breath came in short urgent gasps. He tried to rub his cock against the side of the bed, wanting to somehow relieve the pressure gathering inside his groin, all the while doing his best to imagine that his dick was buried deep inside her sex. She climaxed, her flesh contracting around his fingers in deliciously tight waves. Colin was hard-pressed to hold back his groan of agony, consumed by the need to quench his own physical frustration.

As her orgasm died away, Zara collapsed limply against the pillows, her beautiful face flushed in the aftermath of her spent passion. Colin meanwhile lifted his come-covered fingers to his face, and inhaled her musky, sexy odour, longing to spend hours making slow sensual love to her and spend long erotic nights in her bed. Yet he was conscious that he could never aspire to such precious delights. He could never expect more than the brief intimacy of this moment from this famous and beautiful woman.

'Thank you, Colin,' she said softly, making no move to cover her naked body as she stared at him with her hypnotic violet eyes.

'Perhaps you'd like to rest, or maybe take a shower?' he suggested, his voice shaking slightly, still acutely conscious of his own frustrations, his aching prick crudely distending his tight white trousers. He didn't want to leave her, yet he was desperate to find a private place and spend a few precious minutes masturbating himself to his long-needed climax.

'A cold shower?' she teased, sitting up and eyeing the bulge at his groin.

'I could obviously do with an ice-cold one.' He gave a twisted grin.

'Why waste *that* on a cold shower.' She wriggled to the side of the bed and lowered her feet to the floor. Her legs were wide open, and she seemed unconcerned by the fact that he got a perfect view of her delicious pink quim peeping out of its halo of golden curls. Colin swallowed hard, his heart beating out of control.

'Miss Dawn,' he weakly protested as she pulled him between her outstretched thighs.

'Don't you think you know me well enough now to call me Zara?' Colin couldn't believe this was happening as she eased down his elastic waisted trousers, followed by his brief white pants. 'Very impressive.' She stared at his rigid cock. 'You don't disappoint me, Colin.'

His belly was flat and firm. His cock large, pulsing with life, a dewdrop of fluid glinting on the tip of its head. A thatch of dark brown pubic hair surrounded the thick column, partially concealing his full balls as they dangled enticingly between his muscular thighs.

Zara curved her fingers around the base of his dick, her long red fingernails standing out vividly against his flesh. Slowly she slid her hand up and down the engorged shaft, exciting Colin beyond belief.

His legs trembled and the pace of her breathing increased as he watched her run her pink tongue slowly over her lower lip. Then, holding his cock just beneath the glans, she kissed the pulsing head, lapping up the dewdrop of clear fluid. She dug her tongue into the tiny slit, burrowing deeper until his dick twitched with pleasure and his balls automatically tightened, aching for their release. Pulling his cock-head into her mouth, she sucked on it hard, twining her tongue sensuously around the rim of the glans, while her hands sought his balls, cupping their heaviness, caressing them gently.

Colin struggled to constrain his response, his body so aroused he could hardly contain himself. The pleasure was rising steadily, threatening to burst free and spurt out of control. Yet, he was desperate to savour this moment, as he stared hungrily at Zara's pussy, the moist pink lips splaying out between her open thighs. Soon the constant pleasuring of hand and mouth, sent his senses spiralling. He was unable to hold back the steadily rising pressure building inside him, and he felt it burst free as he pumped his seed deep inside Zara's willing throat.

She swallowed the salty emanations, then released his dick from the hot wet cavern of her mouth. Daintily she licked her lips. 'They say that spunk is the best beauty treatment a woman can have,' she said, smiling up at Colin.

His legs still shaking from the strength of his orgasm, he pulled up his pants then his trousers, suddenly realising that he'd lost all sense of time and space. One of the nurses could walk in at any moment. 'I don't know what to say.' He looked down at her beautiful body, her skin still slick and shiny with oil placed there with his own hands.

'Then don't say anything.'

As he stepped back, she took hold of her nightgown and slipped it over her head. She stood up, letting it fall over her body. 'In future, Colin, I would prefer it if you could attend to me personally. Is that allowed?'

'My patient's needs always come first,' he told her, hardly able to believe his luck.

'I'm glad to hear that. I think I'll be needing your attention on a regular basis while I'm here,' she added, a warm smile lighting up her face.

Chapter Four

When Sandra entered Christopher's room, she found him sitting in an armchair by the window wearing a thick, white towelling robe.

'You've not touched your meal, you naughty boy,' she admonished, looking at the tray placed on a nearby table.

'I wasn't hungry.' His voiced sounded a little strained. He pulled apart his robe to reveal his reddened, swollen penis, the flesh looked shiny and impossibly hard. 'My cock feels close to bursting,' he groaned stiffening anxiously as the slight movement he made put even greater pressure on his over-full anus. 'It's deliciously uncomfortable.'

'Has the waiting been good?' she asked.

'Yes,' he confirmed. 'Agonising.'

'I'm pleased to hear that.'

Sandra still wore her crisp navy-blue uniform with its starched collar and tight cuffs. Slowly she undid the garment, taking her time, knowing that Christopher was desperate to see what she was wearing underneath. Hearing his indrawn hiss of breath, she knew she hadn't disappointed him, as she dropped the dress on the floor.

'You look gorgeous,' Christopher muttered, two spots of colour appearing high on his cheeks.

She stood in front of him wearing only the tight, black rubber corset, hold-up stockings, and impossibly high black stiletto-heeled shoes. The corset had been a gift from him, when he'd arrived at the hospital over a week ago, and it was the first time Sandra had chosen to wear it. The rubber was firm and thick enough to be incredibly constricting, giving her an even more accentuated hour-glass shape. When she had first tried to put it on she'd been surprised; it proved so tight around her waist that she'd been forced to ask her erstwhile lover, Justin, to help fasten the clips at the back. The garment cupped her breasts, holding them out at an impossibly sharp angle to her body. In the centre of each cup was a small round hole, only a few inches across in size, allowing her nipples and a little of the surrounding flesh to bulge out of the opening. Her nipples were made to look larger, even more pronounced. The only other opening was a narrow slit extending from just above her pussy lips, to halfway up her buttocks, allowing access to both orifices at the same time.

The rubber had a strong odour and Christopher sniffed appreciatively as he stared in awe at the vision of delight. 'I've never seen you look more sexy,' he confessed, as he ran hungry eyes over her voluptuous form clad in the obscenely attractive rubber corset. 'Or more dangerous,' he added, glancing at the small whip she held in her hand. Its short leather strands were tipped by tiny gold beads that would deliver a stinging agony to his already abused flesh.

'There's more.' She cracked the whip against her hip, and opened her legs wide so that he could see her shaved pussy in all its naked glory. Sandra's inner labial lips were extraordinarily large, and the pink frill peeped decoratively out of the narrow slit of her sex.

'Wonderful,' he groaned, clearly unable to tear his eyes from the delectable sight. Christopher's breathing quickened as Sandra lifted one foot and rested it on the arm of his chair. The tight rubber pressed deeply into her pussy lips, and her pink purse gaped crudely open exposing all its treasures to Christopher's gaze.

'You promise to do exactly as you are told?' she asked as he stared transfixed at her open quim.

'Of course, matron,' he agreed enthusiastically.

Sandra took him by the hand and led him to a wooden, straight-backed, armless chair which she kept in his room just for this specific purpose. 'Sit,' she curtly commended.

Christopher sat tentatively down, the hard seat deliberately chosen to put even more pressure on the white plug still filling his anus. Sandra smiled cruelly as she straddled his legs, pulling apart her pussy lips with her fingers. Slowly she shafted herself on his rigid cock, and as her hot moistness engulfed him Christopher gave a strangled groan.

'Now touch my tits,' she ordered, allowing her full weight to rest on his trembling legs.

Christopher leaned forwards, eager to please Sandra. He pulled and tweaked her nipples, pinching them hard until she reached the plateau where pain and pleasure intertwined. In response, Sandra tensed, squeezing his aching cock with her hot moist flesh, bringing him painfully close to the climax he craved, but which she knew he'd never achieve. His balls were bound far too firmly to his body, the rubber too tight around the base of his cock.

She was certain his tortuous agony was reaching its point of perfection as he sucked hungrily on her left nipple, attempting to force more of her breast out of the tight opening. The teat and surrounding flesh turned a deep ruby red, and her nipple felt as though it might burst with pleasure.

'Greedy boy,' she gasped, lifting her hips, half unsheathing his cock, then pressing herself down hard again, grinding her pelvis against the smooth rubber. She began to move, bouncing up and down until Christopher winced in pain, finding the intense friction almost unbearable as his body cried out for its release.

'Let me come soon,' he pleaded, his senses now aroused to fever pitch.

'Poor baby,' Sandra mocked in a voice so wicked it made him shiver with pleasure.

'I beg of you, matron,' he whimpered, 'You don't usually force me to wait this long.'

Sandra laughed softly, and stood up very, very slowly. His cock reappeared, achingly hard still, and now shiny with her juices.

'Don't move yet,' she snapped. Stepping back she flicked the whip, caressing him with the gold-tipped strands. The tiny gold balls inflicted a stinging agony that excited Christopher beyond belief. Expertly she applied the whip again, three times in all, until every inch of his cock had been touched by the scalding bliss.

Christopher shuddered, and uttered a plaintive moan. 'I beg of you, I can't stand any more.'

He slid to his knees in front of her, looking so appealing and submissive that she almost felt pity for her adoring slave. 'First you must kiss my pussy, slide your tongue deep inside my cunt,' she said, flicking the strands of the whip across his back.

Christopher lifted his head, pressing his cheeks against her shaved pussy, eagerly sliding his tongue between her rosy lips, running it caressingly along the moist pink valley. He lapped hungrily at her clitoris, sending a shaft of pleasure through her entire sex. Then he pursed his lips, pulling her clit inside his mouth and sucking on it hard.

'I said put your tongue in my cunt,' she said sternly, repressing a shiver as his tongue slid deep inside her vagina, searching and probing like a live slippery snake. Christopher's face was pressed hard against her vulva, his breathing restricted, but still he did as he was ordered, twisting and pressing, caressing her vagina in a smooth swirling motion until she felt the inescapable pleasure starting to well up inside her.

Christopher knew very well how close she was to coming as he boldly lifted his hand and pinched her clitoris between his fingertips. Sandra stiffened and immediately forced herself to pull away. Her sudden movement surprised Christopher, obliging him to put his hands to the floor to prevent himself from falling over. 'Have I displeased you, matron?'

'You didn't do exactly as you were told, did you, Christopher?' she said coldly as she perched her buttocks on the side of the bed. Opening her thighs, she trailed the strands of the whip across her open pussy, expertly flicking the lash so that the tiny beads kissed her open quim. Sharp needles of pain increased the pressure inside her sex, and she gave a soft, sobbing sigh. Inverting the whip, she slid the thick leather-covered handle deep inside her body, thrusting it in and out, hard and fast, while Christopher stared at her, not daring to say a word.

It felt good, but the handle was way too small to give Sandra the complete stimulation she craved. Lifting her hand, she beckoned to Christopher. 'Come here.'

He struggle to his feet, his straining cock beating rapid tattoo against his rubber pants as he stepped towards her. 'Can I take them off now?' he begged.

'Be quick about it,' she snapped, dropping the whip on the carpet.

Christopher never took his eyes off her as he struggled to remove the constricting pants, moving quite stiffly as the dildo remained in his anus. He rolled the rubber downwards like a snake slowly shedding its skin, leaving his flesh pink and shiny, scored in places by the tightness of the rubber. He threw the sweat-stained garment on to the floor and rubbed his crushed balls with the palm of his hand.

'Do you want to remove the plug?' Sandra asked, already knowing his answer. Christopher enjoyed the intrusion, the ever present sensation of fullness, the constant internal chafing that acted like an aphrodisiac on his senses.

'No,' he said stepping hesitantly towards her.

Sandra let herself fall back across the bed. Her corset

was laced so tight that in this position she could only take shallow breaths. But she found the constriction pleasing, and it seemed to make every facet of her senses even more acute.

She felt Christopher grab hold of her thighs and thrust his cock inside her with a satisfied grunt. Reaching downwards she captured his wrists and placed his hands where she wanted them, on her breasts. He knew exactly what she wanted, and immediately grabbed her nipples, twisting and compressing them until the discomfort became almost unbearable. All the time his thrusts were growing more vigorous, more urgent, increasing the heat inside her quim. Christopher's pounding cock was inflicting his own erotic punishment on her, retaliation for the many tortuous hours he'd spent waiting for this one exquisite moment.

Sandra surrendered herself to the pain-tinged bliss she craved so much. Lifting her legs, she twined them around Christopher's sturdy waist. At once the open edges of the corset gusset dug deeper into her, and the hairy root of his penis ground against her aching clit. She felt the pleasure rise up inside her, spiralling out of control as the crushing pleasure overwhelmed her senses.

Ben Taylor proved to be a pleasant surprise for Helen. He was a charming young man, about the same age as her, who'd been working at the hospital for almost eighteen months. Ben was barely two inches taller than her, with well-defined features, a slightly overlarge Roman nose, and soft brown hair which almost reached to his shoulders. He looked more like an aspiring hippie than a doctor.

His manner was gentle, and he appeared to be well liked by everyone. Helen thought that in time they could become good friends. She found Ben attractive, although he wasn't the kind of guy she usually went for. His looks and gentle manner were a total contrast to Max's aggressive masculinity. Working with someone like Ben would prove to be a pleasant change.

After sharing a couple of drinks with him in the staff bar, and meeting some of the other hospital employees, Helen went to bed early. The next day she accompanied Ben on rounds, familiarising herself with the layout and routine of the hospital. None of the patients were desperately ill, most had come in for plastic surgery or relatively minor complaints. In contrast to her previous position, Helen felt that her work-load here would be extraordinarily light.

They were just finishing rounds, when Ben invited her to accompany him to a dinner party that evening. Helen would have said yes straightaway if she hadn't then been told that the party was being held by Sandra Pope. At first she was tempted to refuse, but she thought that might make her appear unfriendly and stand-offish, so she steeled herself to accept the invitation. Nevertheless, she was rather relieved when Ben happened to reveal that Sandra's boyfriend Justin Masterson, the hospital pathologist, would also be present.

Later that day Helen found herself sitting at a table in Sandra's apartment, still not sure if she should have come. Initially there were supposed to be three couples for dinner. But Gillian, a senior sister at the Princess Beatrice and her boyfriend Henry, were both unwell and had been forced to cancel at the last minute.

'That was delicious,' Helen said brightly. 'But I couldn't eat another thing,' she added, refusing a second helping of lemon mousse.

The evening had been pleasant enough and reasonably uneventful so far, but Helen had been hard pressed to prevent herself from spending most of the time staring curiously at Justin. She had never seen anyone who looked less like a pathologist. Usually they tended to be earnest, middle-aged doctors. Justin, however, was much younger, probably in his early thirties. He was tall and slim with a very dark complexion that bespoke some kind of Mediterranean heritage. His hair was cropped so short it was barely visible, and he wore tight, black leather trousers, and a matching, very brief waistcoat. Elaborate tattoos covered both his arms, and he reminded Helen of the bikers she'd seen portrayed in American 'B' movies. It didn't stop there though – Justin was also into body piercing in a big way. He had a silver ring through one eyebrow, a silver stud in his nose, and a number of silver hoops decorating each ear lobe. There was also a silver stud in his tongue, which was highly visible when he spoke.

'You'll enjoy working here, Helen.' Contrary to his appearance, Justin's accent could be described as cut glass, which made Helen think he'd probably been to public school.

She found him a contradiction in every way. All through dinner he'd been pointedly caressing Sandra's tits, trailing his fingers across her thighs, pressing them against her pussy, then against his own bulging crotch. Helen did her best to ignore his crude behaviour, but strangely enough she also found it rather stimulating.

In contrast to Sandra, Helen was very overdressed in her smart black crepe trouser suit. Sandra wore nothing but a flimsy black lace dress which barely covered her full breasts or her obviously shaved pussy. During dinner one of her hard brown nipples had become entangled in the open weave lace and was now on permanent show. Sandra must have known it was visible, but she made no attempt to cover herself, and was perhaps amused by the thought that it might be embarrassing Helen and Ben.

Justin smiled, absentmindedly lifting his hand to play with Sandra's pert little teat as Helen replied, 'I'm sure I'll enjoy it here, Justin.'

'More wine?' Ben asked, diverting Helen's attention for a moment.

'Yes, please,' she replied. The wine was quite delicious with a pleasant bouquet, and an innocuous fruity taste which had persuaded Helen to drink far more than she should. Her overindulgence and the warm sensual atmosphere had left her feeling light-headed, and slightly detached from reality.

'We are all very close here,' Justin said, draining his glass of red wine.

'So Sandra told me.' As his waistcoat swung open, Helen tried to keep from staring at Justin. She could see his flat copper-coloured nipples surrounded by small tufts of dark body hair. Each nipple was pierced at its base by a silver ring and, hanging from the rings, were thin silver chains that trailed across his tight midriff.

'Great, aren't they?' Sandra touched the chains. 'They were my idea, weren't they, Justin?'

'Yes,' he confirmed, staring thoughtfully at Helen. 'Sandra tells me that you and she were close as teenagers.'

'We were friends for a time,' Helen conceded cautiously.

'Helen was embarrassed when we were discovered naked in bed together at school. She had her tongue in my cunt when the teacher found us.'

'Did she?' Justin chuckled. 'And I bet you were enjoying it, my greedy little bitch.'

'I don't remember it like that at all,' Helen said stiffly.

'Perhaps it was Sandra who had her tongue in your cunt?' Justin slipped off his waistcoat, giving Helen an even better view of his unusual body jewellery. 'She loves cunt licking.'

'Helen really doesn't like discussing it at all,' Sandra interjected with a soft, sexy chuckle. She ran her fingers over Justin's chest, tugging gently at the chains, then trailing them teasingly over his bulging groin. 'She'd rather forget what happened in the past. But she's not too prudish to be fascinated by these.' Sandra pulled harder at the chains, stretching Justin's nipples until he gave a ragged groan of pleasure.

Helen was indeed fascinated, unable to tear her eyes from Justin's pierced nipples as she felt the heat growing in the depth of her sex.

'Do you like them?' Ben asked.

'I've never seen anything like that before,' Helen admitted, longing to touch them herself, and wondering what it would feel like to wear such bizarre decorations through her own nipples.

'Most people find body piercing compellingly sexy.' Justin smiled as he ran his hand possessively up Sandra's leg, gradually easing up her lacy skirt until it lay around her upper thighs. He slid his hands between her legs, and stroked her shaved quim. 'Should we have your clit pierced, Sandra, or your pussy lips?'

'Why not both?' Sandra splayed open her legs and gave a soft moan as Justin's fingers slid inside her.

Helen pressed her legs together, turned on by the sight, wishing his fingers were sliding smoothly inside her instead of Sandra. Lascivious thoughts filled her head, and she experienced a strong surge of sexual desire that left her weak and breathless for a moment. Lowering her lashes, she glanced over at Ben. He was staring intently at Justin and Sandra, and judging by his expression, he was just as turned on as she was.

'Perhaps we should be leaving?' she asked Ben, as his attraction for her suddenly increased.

'Why pretend to be such a prude,' Sandra teased, 'when I know damn well you're not.' She laughed. 'Let me show you the rest of Justin's jewellery.'

Deftly she undid his leather trousers, and slid down the zip. As his hardening cock sprang from the opening, Helen's eyes widened in amazement. She had expected something like a Prince Albert; she'd heard of guys having rings through their cock heads but never this! Either side of his glans was a silver ball – at least the size of a pea.

'Isn't that uncomfortable?' Helen couldn't help asking, her head throbbing with excitement. How would it feel to have Justin's cock inside her, the smooth, cold silver balls rubbing and chafing her. Her knees grew weak with the thought.

'Not uncomfortable. Wonderful,' Sandra replied. 'It's

called an Ampallang.' Then, to Helen's amazement, she suddenly hiked her shirt around her waist and straddled Justin's legs. Her pale buttocks were a shade fleshy and dimpled, while her hairless slit gaped open, revealing a delicious frill of shiny pink flesh. This was just too much for Helen to contend with. Her chair made a loud scraping sound on the parquet floor as she stood up.

'Do you want to leave?' Ben asked, as Sandra positioned herself over Justin's superbly decorated prick, and sank slowly down on to the rigid shaft.

'Yes,' Helen said shakily, watching mesmerised as Justin's cock gradually disappeared between Sandra's plump thighs.

Helen's eyes grew hazy with lust as Justin grabbed hold of Sandra's hips and pushed her down hard against him. Her heart beating out of control, Helen pulled her gaze from the rutting couple. Part of her wanted to tear off her clothes, shove Sandra aside, and straddle Justin – she longed to experience the bizarre pleasures of his pierced dick for herself.

Sandra moaned, her large breasts bouncing up and down in time to her vigorous thrusts. The sounds and smells of animal pleasure arousing her senses, Helen almost ran to the door. She had to leave before she lost control of herself. She reached the silent sanctuary of the corridor, relieved to find that Ben had followed her. As he slammed the front door shut behind him, Helen leaned limply against the cool corridor wall. Her head whirled, and she was consumed by unfulfilled longing, ready and eager for sex.

Her gaze rested on Ben, his attractions increasing by the moment.

'Are you OK?' Ben took hold of her arms. His face was level with hers, as he stared into her eyes. 'Don't worry. Justin likes to shock people.'

'That's obvious.' Helen's head spun, and she couldn't ignore the simmering heat between her thighs. Ben looked so sweet and concerned, and he smelled so good, of virile masculinity and lemon-scented cologne.

Acting quite out of character, Helen grabbed hold of Ben's shoulders, and pulled him close, twining her arms around his neck. Then she kissed him with lustful passion, thrusting her tongue deep inside his mouth. Ben responded immediately, kissing her back with equal vigour, grinding his pelvis hard against hers.

Helen was filled with such need, such wanting that she could scarcely breathe. 'Let's go to my place,' she suggested.

'Why not?' Seeming all too eager to comply, Ben took hold of her arm.

Helen's head was still spinning and her legs felt weak as Ben led her along the corridor and into her apartment. She was still in a semi-euphoric state as she walked into the lounge and sank down on to the blue velvet couch.

Ben kneeled down in front of her, the bulge in his trousers all too visible. 'Justin's pierced prick turned you on, didn't it?' he whispered in her ear, as he lifted her black crepe tunic, sliding it off over her head.

Helen giggled. 'I wanted to know what it would feel like inside me.'

Ben's lips felt warm and moist as he pressed tiny butterfly kisses across her bare breasts, then sucked her aching nipples. His fingers brushed her midriff as he expertly undressed her, divesting her of both trousers and panties. Helen felt the warm night breeze, from the open window, caress her bare skin. Her senses now were so finely tuned, she savoured everything – Ben's wine-tainted breath, the heat of his flesh, and the soft velvet, smooth and silky against her naked buttocks.

'So piercing turns you on,' he said as he slipped off his blue cotton shirt.

Helen gave an exclamation of surprise as she spotted the thin gold ring threaded through Ben's left nipple. 'You too?' She felt a sudden compulsion to touch it. Following the urge, she pulled gently at the ring, feeling his flesh stretch. Very carefully she twisted it just a little, putting pressure on the flat brown nipple until she heard Ben's indrawn hiss of breath. 'Does that feel good?'

75

Ben sighed. 'It feels great,' he murmured, his hands sliding between her thighs.

As he explored the hot moistness of her pussy, she arched her back. 'That's great also,' she gasped. Ben circled her throbbing clit, briskly rubbing the swollen flesh until she could bear it no longer and cried out, 'Please, fuck me, Ben!'

'Soon, baby,' he promised, sliding his fingers deep inside her. He held his palm against her vulva, and the pressure served to heighten the sweet torture as he began to move his fingers in a smooth circular motion.

After her strange experience in Sandra's apartment she found the pleasure was almost too much for her to bear. 'I'm so close,' she gasped, lifting her hips as the sensations built swiftly inside her.

'Come,' he urged, his fingers moving faster as he circled her clitoris, pressing and teasing. Then he leaned forwards to grasp one of her nipples between his teeth. The pleasure/pain drove her over the edge, and she climaxed, her quim clamping hard against his invading fingers, her body quivering with bliss.

Helen was still shivering in the aftermath of her orgasm, when Ben stood up to slide off his trousers. He stepped out of the pool of light coming from the table lamp. With the rest of the room in virtual darkness, she could only see a dark shadow at his groin. When he moved towards her again, she caught sight of his cock for the first time. It was hard, and large enough not to be a disappointment as it curved rigidly upwards towards his slim belly. Taking hold of her shoulders he eased down on to the carpet, and it was then that she got close enough to his cock to see the rounded nodules marring the shaft. They reminded Helen of the raised tattoos she'd seen in pictures of some ancient African tribe.

'Go on, touch it,' Ben urged with a smile as he straddled her hips with his thighs. He sunk lower until his cock was level with her face, and she could clearly see the round lumps under the smooth skin surface. 'There's nothing wrong with me, Helen,' he said with a chuckle.

'I had it done in LA; it's all the rage there. It's less ostentatious than Justin's Ampallang but is designed to cause similar heightened pleasure.' As she frowned in confusion he added, 'They put tiny silver ball-bearings under the cock-skin to increase stimulation during sex.'

'Ball-bearings?' she repeated, finding even the sight of the strange knobbly texture highly arousing. Intrigued by the idea, she touched the smooth baubles, running her fingertips gently over them, feeling the balls move slightly under the taut skin. During her medical career she'd seem some sights, but never anything like this. Ben's shaft was hard, the tiny metal balls even harder, and she could hardly wait to have this outlandish cock thrusting inside her. She was eager for the singular pleasure of experiencing the contrasting texture of silver, and hard male flesh.

As Ben kneeled between her thighs, she trembled with excitement, juices flowing freely from her hungry pussy. Lifting her legs, he placed her calves atop his shoulders, and stared down at her exposed sex. Grabbing hold of her buttocks, he pulled her closer, the roughness of the carpet scraping the tender skin of her back.

Positioning himself, Ben slowly eased his swollen cock-head inside her, and almost immediately Helen could determine the difference in textures. She felt the nodules brushed teasingly against her internal walls, and she instinctively clenched her muscles, overcome by the delicious shivers of excitement flooding her sex. It was exciting beyond belief, another dimension to pleasure as Ben, knowing exactly what to do to ensure total stimulation, began to move his hips in a smooth rotating motion. His strangely decorated shaft put pressure on every internal nerve-ending as he increased the pace of his thrusts.

Helen gave a sobbing cry as the fire inside her vagina increased to unimaginable proportions. She couldn't resist the temptation to rub herself while these phenomenal sensations were rioting through her. Then she felt one of his fingers wriggling its way into her anus and the combined intensity of the experience made her belly tremble and her hips twitch as orgasmic spasms flooded her body.

When Helen awoke next morning, Ben was gone. He was on duty first thing, while she wasn't due to start work until after lunch.

Without a doubt she'd had far too much to drink, she decided, as she reflected on the sensual pleasures of the previous night. Yet she didn't regret what had happened between her and Ben. In fact she hoped their liaison could continue on a purely casual basis. A meeting of two bodies to sate sexual desire, nothing more, nothing less. It would be nice to have a pleasant undemanding relationship after her emotionally charged roller coaster liaison with Max. Ben was a sweet uncomplicated guy, with an unusually interesting prick, who was extraordinarily good at fucking.

Helen felt she had changed since she'd arrived at the Princess Beatrice. There was something strange about this place, a sensuality lingering under the surface that prompted her to break free of previous sexual constraints.

Wanting to pass the time and clear her head, she took a long walk around the hospital grounds. She found a helicopter pad quite close to the main building, along with a large black helicopter stored in an adjoining hangar. It seemed a little odd to keep such a mode of transport at a hospital, she considered, as she continued her tour of the grounds.

After lunch she did her rounds, checking on a number of patients, most recovering from plastic surgery, or relatively minor operations. There were also a number of patients who didn't seem ill at all, but she felt she had no right to question their reasons for being there, as they were paying exorbitant sums for the privilege and probably greatly contributing to her inflated salary.

Helen wasn't looking forward to facing Sandra again after last night. Usually matron did her rounds of the hospital soon after lunch, but to Helen's relief there had been no sign of her today.

'There's one more patient for you to see,' the duty staff nurse said, as Helen filled in the last of her reports. 'He was operated on this morning, and has just come down from post-op intensive care.'

'I didn't know there was any surgery scheduled for today,' Helen replied. She had checked late last night, before she went to Sandra's and there was nothing more at all on this week's operating list.

'It was an emergency admission this morning.'

'Emergency?' Helen frowned – there was no A & E at the Princess Beatrice. Normally private hospitals tended to concentrate their efforts on routine operations and long-term illnesses.

'I admit it's unusual,' staff nurse Jones agreed. 'Apparently a film crew was working on location close by. There was an accident while filming a stunt or something, and the patient was brought here. They called in an orthopaedic surgeon, Mr Hyatt. Assisted by Dr Taylor, he operated straightaway. The patient's ankle was broken in a couple of places, and he had a slight concussion.'

'And Dr Taylor wants me to keep an eye on his vitals?' Helen said. It would be a change to have a proper patient to care for; she hadn't yet become accustomed to having such an undemanding work-load.

'Yes, he does. I'm told that the patient is a friend of our director, Professor Fenton. I presume that's why he was brought straight here.' Staff nurse Jones smiled. 'You should have seen the commotion when the man was brought in, he was accompanied by half the film crew and the director – an over-excited Italian guy who wouldn't stop talking. It was he who insisted we call in Mr Hyatt. Luckily for us he lives close by.'

'Who exactly is this patient?' Helen asked, wondering if she knew him too.

Staff nurse Jones handed Helen a chart. 'The actor,

Duncan Paul. All the nurses went mad when they heard it was him. Lots of them fancy the guy.'

'Including you?' Helen enquired, managing to appear cool and in control, while her heart raced.

Staff nurse Jones blushed. 'He is my favourite actor, and I've now discovered that he's even more gorgeous in the flesh than he is on the movie screen.'

'I know.' Helen flipped through Duncan's records, relieved to see that there appeared to be nothing seriously wrong with him. Mr Hyatt had pinned his broken ankle, while X-rays and a CAT scan had shown that the slight concussion didn't appear to herald anything more serious.

'You know him?'

'I met him briefly not long ago,' Helen replied casually. 'He seemed very pleasant.'

'Lucky you. He'll probably be pleased to see a familiar face,' the nurse commented. 'By the way, don't expect him to be awake. As you can see by the drug chart, I've just administered his last injection. Dr Taylor wants to keep him sedated for a few hours more.'

'Judging by what you've said it's the nurses who need sedating round here, not Mr Paul,' Helen joked. 'Now where is he?'

'The Rochester Suite,' staff nurse Jones told her. This was one of the most expensive suites in the hospital, with its own lounge as well as the mandatory private bathroom.

'I'll call you if I need you.' Helen moved over to the door of Duncan's suite, taking a deep breath before she stepped inside. It was odd how out of control she suddenly felt just because Duncan's name was mentioned.

This was the first time she had been inside the Rochester Suite. With its thick cream carpets, lush window dressing, antique furniture and expensive entertainment equipment, it seemed more like a high-class hotel suite – only the hospital bed in the adjoining room betrayed its true origins.

Duncan's eyes were closed, his long lashes brushing his tanned cheeks. His dark, almost black, hair was in ruffled disarray, making him look younger than when they had last met. For the very first time, Helen could stare at him without interruption, and it struck her that he really was the most good-looking guy she had ever come across. He was very masculine, yet his full bottom lip gave him a faint air of vulnerability that his female fans found most appealing. He always played the ultimate hero – macho and yet tender-hearted when the need arose.

If only she hadn't been with Max when she and Duncan had last met, she thought selfishly. She would have liked the opportunity to get to know him. Duncan had seemed to be attracted to her at the time but, on the other hand, perhaps he was just being polite; she couldn't know for sure.

She took hold of Duncan's hand and checked his pulse – a shade abnormal but that was to be expected after surgery. He didn't appear to have a fever, although his breathing was slightly uneven. Gently she brushed her fingers across his forehead, smoothing his ruffled hair.

He was still wearing a blue gingham hospital gown. His black silk pyjamas lay folded on a chair, ready for when he awoke. The nurses would have strict instructions not to disturb him for some time yet.

There was a small cage covering his damaged ankle to prevent the bedclothes from pressing down on his leg. Everything looked all right and so far there was no sign of any infection developing, but she had to check his ankle so she pulled down the sheet covering the lower half of his body.

To be truthful Helen was acting out of curiosity as well as concern for the patient. However, she saw far more than she had expected. Duncan's hospital gown was rucked up around his waist, and she found herself faced with a part of his anatomy she'd fantasised about for years.

His stomach was flat, firm and as deeply tanned as the

rest of his skin, so he must sunbathe in the nude, she considered, as she stared at the arrow of dark hair running from belly button to groin. His thick, deliciously large penis lay in repose on its bed of black pubic curls. Below lay the soft, hairy cushion of his balls.

Helen felt a stab of longing, as a thousand lustful thoughts consumed her senses. She wanted to press her hand against her pussy to relieve the sudden heat in her groin, as a shameful dampness formed between her thighs.

For the very first time in her career she acted in a purely unprofessional manner. She touched his prick, watching it immediately twitch and unconsciously stiffen as her fingers gently stroked the thick shaft. Duncan gave a faint groan and moved restlessly on the bed, still under the control of the strong sedative. She could do anything she liked to him and he still wouldn't wake.

Helen curled her fingers around the base of his cock, feeling her cunt tighten at the thought of masturbating it to perfect hardness. It would be so easy to pull up her skirt, straddle his muscular thighs and slide his prick smoothly into her hungry sex. Why shouldn't she take what she had secretly craved from this gorgeous man? Duncan was an integral part of her perfect fantasy. He was the image that filled her head when she was alone in her bed, pleasuring herself with her own hands.

She was all too conscious of the power she held over his helpless form at this moment in time. Her senses spun out of control as she allowed herself to be consumed by her lustful thoughts. She would never have contemplated anything as outrageous as this in the past, even if the opportunity had presented itself, but now she had changed.

Who would know, she asked herself, her hands trembling, sweat breaking out on her forehead. The aching need in her pussy increased as she looked down at Duncan, controlled by the drug, having no say in whatever she chose to do to him. Power was an aphrodisiac, yet if she did what she was tempted to do, she would be breaking the Hippocratic oath.

Steeling herself to resist temptation, Helen pulled down his gown, then covered his sleeping form with his sheet and blanket. She took a deep unsteady breath, feeling a little guilty for even considering such a move. Then she reminded herself that officially he wasn't even her patient. Duncan had been admitted under the care of Dr Taylor. In the truest sense of the words she wouldn't have been committing an offence against medical council regulations – sexually consorting with one's patient was a striking-off offence. Nevertheless, what she'd just contemplated could never be justified under any circumstances.

On the other hand, he was bound to be here for at least a few days, so there was nothing stopping her from getting to know him better now. There was even the faint chance that she might eventually get to act out her fantasies after all. She was still staring thoughtfully at Duncan when staff nurse Jones entered the room seconds later. Helen wasn't doing anything untoward, but she still jumped guiltily.

'Everything OK, doctor?'

'Fine, he's sleeping peacefully,' Helen replied, clipping the notes to the end of the bed. 'I'll check back on him in an hour or so. He shouldn't wake for some time yet. Leave instructions with the night staff to help him wash and change when he does.'

Staff nurse Jones smiled. 'The blue gingham gown does look rather incongruous on such a macho guy.'

'I suppose it does. If you need me I'll be in the staff restaurant,' Helen replied, now wanting to get out of the room as soon as possible. 'I feel in need of a strong cup of tea.'

'A gin and tonic wouldn't go amiss with me,' Jones joked. 'But if you're going to the restaurant, Dr Dawson, could you do me a favour? I've got some urgent samples for the lab. I've been ringing for a porter for half an hour, but they're all tied up at the moment.'

* * *

The path lab was on the ground floor, only a short walk from the staff restaurant. Helen had visited it briefly on her initial tour with Max, but that seemed ages ago now. She had been surprised at the time to discover how extensive the laboratories were. Most private hospitals shipped the majority of their samples out to large industrial laboratories. It proved way too expensive to have all the up-to-date equipment, and experienced staff, for what was essentially only a small amount of work compared to the NHS. However, the Princess Beatrice had haematology, biochemistry, histology and bacteriology departments.

She entered the unit, surprised to find it empty, totally deserted, and it was only four in the afternoon. First she tried the office door – the samples were usually dropped off there to be catalogued and labelled – but that was locked.

Helen wasn't sure what to do with her urgent samples. She glance down at the three plastic bags she held in her hand. One contained vials of blood, the two others post-op wound swabs. She didn't want the samples to be overlooked – they needed to be worked on straight-away.

'Hello,' she called. 'Is anyone here?' Her voice echoed eerily around the empty labs.

She pulled open the door of the nearest refrigerator; there was usually one set aside for out-of-hours samples, but this one was full of agar plates. She would have to check out the other labs; there must be someone here. All she found at first were gently humming machines and tidy benches, no sign of any staff. Then she heard the whirring noise of a centrifuge coming from a small room set between the bacteriology and haematology laboratories.

Making her way into the small laboratory, she found a white-coated Justin sitting at a bench working intently. 'Hi,' she said, feeling a little awkward about seeing him again, her mind suddenly filled with erotic visions of his embellished cock.

'Helen.' He swung round his chair and smiled at her. 'What brings you here?'

'This.' She placed the bag of samples in an empty space on his cluttered work bench. 'I'm told they're urgent.'

'Doctors don't usually run errands round here. That's the porters' job,' Justin remarked wryly. Despite the pristine white coat, the thought struck her that he still didn't look in the least like a doctor.

'The porters were all busy. I was passing the lab, I didn't mind,' she replied. The way Justin was looking at her made her feel uneasy.

She paused to wonder for a moment how he had ever managed to get a job here. Knowing Max, he would never have agreed to employ someone so disreputable looking. Max was a stickler for upholding convention, and wouldn't have approved of visible tattoos and body piercing. Of course, he wasn't averse to what could be hidden beneath clothing – that was an entirely different matter.

'I hear that you and Ben got on well,' Justin commented. 'Extremely well, according to what Ben told me this morning.'

'You shouldn't believe all you hear,' she said stiffly, wondering how much Ben had told Justin.

'Ben doesn't tend to exaggerate,' Justin pointed out.

'Where are all your staff?' she asked, wanting to change the subject.

'One of my senior technicians, Harry, is getting married on Saturday. They are all going out for the evening, so I let them off early. I'm a surprisingly easy-going boss, Helen. Very easy-going.'

'Then I suppose you're finishing up all the work they didn't get through,' she said teasingly, as she looked down at the cluttered bench.

'Something like that. Nothing urgent, just routine blood tests on our maternity patients. Now that the new unit is about to open, we've started up the maternity clinic again.' He rose to his feet and picked up the bags of samples she'd left on his bench. 'I'll pop these in the office. Get them registered and bar-coded. We wouldn't want anything to go wrong with them.'

'No, of course not.' Helen smiled politely. 'I should be leaving, I want to grab a quick cuppa before finishing my own work.'

'Seeing Ben tonight?'

'We haven't made any plans.' They'd not got around to talking after they'd retired to her bed. They'd just had sex for the second time and both fallen asleep straight afterwards.

'Perhaps we could all meet up in the bar for a drink later?'

'Perhaps,' she said cautiously, thinking it might not be a good idea to make a habit of spending time with Justin and Sandra.

'See you, then.' Justin wandered off in the direction of the office.

Helen was about to follow him, when her natural curiosity prompted her to first try and find out exactly what Justin had been working on, mainly because she was more than certain he had lied to her. She'd done her stint in pathology and knew the difference between routine blood tests for pregnant women and cross-matching blood for transfusion. Ben had already told her that the maternity patients were mostly in their second trimester. None had complications, and they weren't due to give birth for many weeks. There was no way any of them would require a transfusion at present.

She glanced down at the paperwork. Justin was cross-matching three units of B negative, ready for an operation. This struck her as strange. She knew full well there was no surgery planned for at least a week and blood was never cross-matched that far in advance, certainly not in an underworked laboratory such as this. She turned to check that there was no sign of Justin returning yet, then she began to quickly shuffle through the rest of the paperwork. What she discovered surprised her even more. The patient's name wasn't mentioned at all – he was continually referred to as Mr X.

The forms had been signed by Ralph Kalowski, a renowned plastic surgeon and a close friend and colleague of Max. Ralph was in the States with Max working on setting up the new clinics. Neither of them were due back in England for a number of weeks. Surely Ralph wouldn't return just for this one operation?

If Ralph did turn up here in the next few days, she might be able to find out what was happening. Ralph was a charming man, and she knew him reasonably well; she certainly trusted him far more than she did Justin. After visiting the restaurant she decided to check the operating lists again. Perhaps they had been changed to accommodate the mysterious Mr X.

Deciding it might be better to avoid Justin on her way out, she walked towards histology. There was a door at the far end of the lab that led straight into the corridor close to the staff restaurant. The histology lab was totally silent, with an overpowering odour of disinfectant and formalin. Helen had hated the pervasive smell of formalin ever since she'd done human dissection in her first years of training.

Doctors couldn't afford to be squeamish, but Helen still felt there was something unsettling about histology. She hated the sight of organs, from long dead patients, preserved for posterity in the bottles ranged along shelves. She walked towards the door, starting rather nervously, when she heard someone shout her name.

She didn't recognise the voice at first and thought it was Justin. When she turned she saw to her relief that it was Ben striding towards her, his white coat flapping untidily around his legs.

'I saw Justin in the office. He said you were following him, so I waited for you, but you never appeared.'

'I thought this way would be quicker. I was going to the staff restaurant.'

'It would be. But after hours, Justin keeps it locked. You can't leave that way.' Ben took hold of her and pushed her gently back against a bench. 'I was hoping to catch you alone.'

'Why?' she asked stupidly, her mind still semi-distracted by the puzzle of the cross-matched blood, and Justin's unnecessary lies.

'Why do you think?' Ben nuzzled her ear with his lips, while he lifted her skirt and slid his hands between her thighs. 'I couldn't wait until tonight.' He pressed his fingers against her panty gusset, finding it still slightly damp from her encounter with Duncan. 'Neither it seems can you.'

'I didn't know we were planning to see each other,' she said breathlessly as his fingers rubbed her pussy, then wriggled their way beneath her panties.

'Why not?' he asked, sucking on her ear-lobe while his fingers explored the moist valley of her quim.

'I didn't expect anything permanent. It was just . . .'

'Fucking,' he concluded for her. 'But such sweet fucking I had to have you again.'

'You're a greedy boy,' she gasped, as his fingers circled her clit, teasing the aching root. 'But we can't do it here, can we?' She felt her nipples harden, her breasts throb, and she wanted to beg him to fuck her here and now, even as she spoke.

'Why not? Justin won't disturb us, and there's no one else around.' His fingers worked their way in ever decreasing circles driving her insane with longing. She needed to feel those sweetly teasing digits sliding deep inside her.

'That's so good.' She opened her legs wider and moved her hand restlessly across the bulge at his groin, feeling incredibly horny and eager to savour his unusual cock again.

'Do you really want to go somewhere more private?' Ben asked.

'No.' She rubbed urgent fingers across the fabric of his trousers, smiling to herself as she felt him immediately harden.

Ben gave a low growling laugh and spun her around

so that she was facing the bench, and pushed her forwards until the rolled edge of the bench dug into her
belly. For a moment Helen tried to resist, the submissive
pose reminding her too much of Max. However, Ben
was far stronger than he looked. He held her imprisoned
there while he pulled up her white coat, followed by her
skirt, leaving them rucked untidily around her waist.

'Don't fight me,' he whispered, kissing the nape of her
neck. While on duty she always wore her long blonde
hair up in a French pleat. When he stroked the sensitive
spot with the moist tip of his tongue Helen shivered
with desire, filled with an unquenchable need he could
easily satisfy.

She could feel his bulge pressing against her buttocks.
Her cunt was wet and hungry for invasion, so aroused
she wanted him even if half the hospital was watching.

Ben jerked down her panties, letting them fall in a
flimsy heap around her ankles, while he gently forced
her upper body down across the bench. She heard the
hiss of his zipper, then felt the hot smooth head of his
cock slide intrusively between her buttock cheeks, and
tenderly rim the tight entrance to her anus. She tensed,
half fearing the invasion of the sensitive opening, yet
craving the painful intrusion, all at the same time.

'Relax, sweetheart,' Ben muttered, as his prick slid
lower, pushing its way between her eager pussy lips.
The warmth of her own fluid flooded her sex, as Ben's
beautifully adorned cock slid slowly inside her, delving
deeper until the root of his penis was jammed against
her buttock cheeks, the sac of his balls brushing heavily
against the back of her thighs.

'Tense now, tighten that pussy – feel my cock,' he
commanded, leaning forwards so that the weight of his
upper body held her pinned down.

She obeyed without thinking, her internal muscles
tightly embracing his rigid organ, feeling the line of hard
nodules. They pressed against the inside of her sex,
setting her senses alight with pleasure.

Ben began to thrust hard, grinding his belly against

her buttocks, and Helen instinctively stretched her arms forwards, gripping the back of the bench as he rode her in a wild gallop of lust. Her every nerve ending stretched taut as she writhed beneath him consumed by the absolute pleasure. Ben's body tensed and shuddered and he groaned loudly as he achieved his release.

For a moment they remained fused in a union of sated contentment, then very gently Ben withdrew and straightened. Too drained to move, Helen remained where she was for a moment, sprawled half naked across the laboratory bench, only half conscious of the faint rustle of fabric as Ben straightened his clothing. She lifted her head, just detecting a faint flicker of movement in the open doorway. As her eyes came into focus, she saw Justin standing there watching them, a leering, almost satanic grin on his face.

Helen straightened and pulled down her skirts, feeling awkward and exposed now that she knew Justin had been watching them. Too embarrassed to glance again in Justin's direction, she stepped out of her panties. She was about to reach down and stuff them in her pocket, but Ben got there first.

'These are mine,' he said with a chuckle. 'If you don't see me tonight, I'll have the second best thing. I can smell them, then wrap them around my cock and use them to wank myself.'

Helen gave an uneasy laugh, forcing herself to glance again at the open doorway. To her relief Justin was gone. 'You're sex mad, Ben.'

'We're all a little sex mad around here,' he said, grinning. 'Let's go to the restaurant, we can discuss what we plan to do later this evening.'

Chapter Five

*H*elen was approaching the nurses' station, in the East Wing, close to the Rochester Suite, when she overheard one of the junior nurses chatting to her colleague. 'He's gorgeous and so charming. I checked his pulse and touching him made me feel so horny. I swear my panty gusset got soaking wet.'

The nurse giggled, then coloured in embarrassment as she realised that Helen might have heard what she said.

'Can I do anything for you, Dr Dawson?' she asked, casting an uneasy glance at her friend, who had also gone pink.

'I've just examined Mrs Lichen,' Helen replied rather curtly. 'Her dressings need changing. They should have been done first thing this morning.' Despite feeling irritated, she consciously softened her expression. 'We all like a chat now and then, nurse Barker. But our patient's needs must come first,' she added, wanting to impress her authority without unnecessarily antagonising the staff working for her.

'Of course, Dr Dawson.' Nurse Barker nodded earnestly. 'I'll do the dressing straightaway.'

Helen dumped the papers she was carrying on the counter as the young nurse hurried off, while her companion moved over to the medicine trolley. Helen had deliberately left Duncan until last, but she could prevaricate no longer; she had to check up on him now. Mr Hyatt, accompanied by Ben, had seen Duncan earlier that morning, and the records showed he was recovering well from his surgery.

It would be the first time she had faced him while he was awake and alert. After her encounter with Ben in histology, she'd checked up on Duncan twice before going off duty. Both times he'd been asleep, and Helen had kept the visits brief and very professional – she'd not allowed temptation to overcome her again.

Part of her regretted that lost opportunity, while logic told her that her decision to desist had been correct. What she'd contemplated would have in a way been akin to rape. A pang of conscience overcame her and she felt more than a little nervous as she walked over to Duncan's room. Of course he would never know what happened, but she did and her heart began to beat a shade faster, her mouth growing dry with apprehension as she pushed open the door. She found Duncan sitting up in bed, leafing through a magazine, looking incredibly tasty in his black silk pyjamas. He looked to be in the best of health, but after such accidents appearances could be deceptive.

'Helen,' Duncan said, seeming to be pleased to see her.

'So you remember me,' she said, smiling.

'Who could forget someone like you.' His smile made her heart do a nervous somersault, and her knees tremble. 'I didn't know you worked here.'

'A short-term assignment only,' she explained. 'Max arranged for me to come here after our NHS hospital closed.'

'Why not? After all, he is the major shareholder here, so I'm reliably informed. You decided not to accompany him to the States, then?'

'I may join him eventually, if everything works out OK,' she replied cautiously. 'But nothing's set in stone.'

'Come to think of it I had the weirdest dream last night,' Duncan said thoughtfully, as he put down his magazine. 'I dreamed an angel came to care for me. She looked just like you, Helen.'

'Really?' She laughed. 'And I think you should get a new scriptwriter, Duncan.' She picked up his chart and perused it, doing her best to appear cool and unconcerned.

'Sounds pretty corny, I admit.' He shrugged his shoulders and grinned. 'I wasn't lying. I did have a weird dream and the woman in it looked just like you – perhaps not in the guise of an angel though.' He looked pointedly at her white coat. 'But she was wearing white.'

'Drugs do strange things to the mind,' she said dismissively, trying not to think that her actions might have had something to do with his dream.

The way Duncan was looking at her made her feel unsettled and slightly out of control. She fancied him like crazy, more than she'd ever fancied Max, or any other guy for that matter.

Helen could understand why the nurses had been so overcome by his looks and charm. All the celebrities she had ever come across had been somewhat of a disappointment, but not Duncan. He was even better looking in the flesh and was quite charming, not at all big-headed like most of the famous actors she had met. Perhaps she was being a bit harsh on the others she decided, after all she had looked in on Zara Dawn last night. She had proved to be very beautiful and far more pleasant and friendly than Helen had expected her to be.

'How are you feeling, today?' Helen asked.

'Not bad, considering.' Duncan looked down at the wire cage protecting his damaged foot. 'My ankle aches and I've still got a headache. The nurse gave me some pills but they haven't worked completely. There's still a slight throbbing pain at the back of my head.'

'You hit it pretty hard I understand. You were lucky to escape more serious injury. The headache is to be expected after a concussion,' she told him as she clipped his chart to the foot of his bed. 'If the pain in your head gets worse or you feel dizzy, or have any problems with

93

your vision, tell the nurse at once. All the tests show you are fine, but with head injuries we can never be too careful.'

'I feel so bloody stupid,' he admitted, smiling wryly. 'I mistimed a perfectly simple move and ended up in hospital, like this!'

'A stunt, I understand?'

Duncan nodded. 'Yeah.'

'I didn't think high-profile movie stars did their own stunts.'

'Some do, some don't. I do as much as our insurers and the director will let me. I feel I'm cheating the moviegoers if I don't.' He ran a hand through his hair. 'To be honest I enjoy it – the rush – the brief moment of fear.'

'And your public love you for it. Your movies always seem to be high in the popularity stakes,' she commented, trying to retain her professional manner as she moved to the side of the bed.

'Yeah, I suppose they do.' Duncan seemed almost embarrassed to admit it as he added, 'The powers that be reckon I can open a movie. That means if my name's on the credits it's more or less bound to do well at the box office. I think it's because the male punters love the spectacular action sequences.'

'And the ladies?'

'They are supposed to prefer the romantic bits – the sex scenes,' he added with a faint grin. 'To be honest I quite enjoy those myself. Most actors are lying if they say they don't.'

'And how does it feel to be every woman's fantasy?' she teased.

'Am I your fantasy?' he asked, his voice taking on a deeper seductive note.

'I never said that.' Her heart was now racing out of control, every fibre of her being conscious of his close proximity as the heat inside her pussy increased.

Helen noticed that his eyelashes were incredibly long as he stared at her with his beautiful dark brown eyes.

Her quim suddenly began to feel even hotter and incredibly moist as she noticed the way the thin silk of his pyjamas clung to his chest, revealing the muscular lines of his well-developed physique. She knew all too well what was hidden by his bedclothes, and as she recalled the sight of him helpless and naked, she began to feel a trace light-headed almost as if she were intoxicated by his presence.

'You said every woman,' Duncan reminded her.

'I meant most,' she amended, rather unconvincingly, as her mind was wracked by erotic thoughts. Sex seemed to be continually on her mind these days, and however much she had it never seemed enough.

'Now you've disappointed me,' he teased, his eyes sparkling. 'Do you know I've always had a thing about lady doctors?'

'Have you? So you like to see women in positions of authority?'

'They fascinate me,' he confessed. 'Probably because I so often portray the dominant aggressive male.'

'And would you like to be dominated, Duncan?' Helen felt she was playing with fire as she leaned towards him and smiled suggestively.

'I've not thought about it. I suppose the idea is titillating. Maybe I would find it a turn on – who knows?' His expression held the hint of a challenge as he added, 'Have dinner with me tonight, Helen. We can discuss it in more detail then. I'm told the food here is as good as any high-class restaurant, and I can promise you that the company will be stimulating.'

Beneath the handsome movie star image there lurked an intelligent, very interesting man. Helen would love to get to know him better in any number of ways, but she didn't want to appear too eager. 'I don't know,' she said cautiously. 'You're supposed to be resting.'

'You're a refreshing change. Most women jump at my invitations, but only because I'm famous, not because they want to get to know who I really am. To be honest I'm just a regular guy who wants to enjoy the company of a charming, intelligent woman –' he paused '– who also happens to be incredibly beautiful.'

'You think flattery will convince me to say yes?'

'I doubt that it would,' he replied. 'You strike me as very self-assured. I should guess once you've made up your mind nothing will change it.'

That didn't sound much like the person she'd been in the past, but since coming here, away from Max's influence, she had started to change. 'You may be right, Duncan. But as it happens, I've decided to say yes.'

Helen was feeling restless and a little up-tight. She longed for the evening to come as she was looking forward to spending time with Duncan. But, despite the fact that he'd said she was beautiful and clearly wanted to spend time with her, she was still feeling incredibly nervous and insecure. She had not felt like this since she was a teenager, anticipating her first date. She had forgotten how stimulating and nerve-wracking such emotions could be.

In the circumstances she decided to go down to the pool for a swim. Exercise calmed and relaxed her, and she'd taken none since being here, apart from her sexual athletics with Ben. Unfortunately all she had was a skimpy bikini that she used for sunbathing. During vigorous swimming the top had a tendency to slip off. However, it was doubtful that at this time of the day the pool would be crowded.

The indoor swimming pool was Olympic size and very impressive. It was surrounded by palm trees and other exotic plants. Helen stripped off in one of the changing rooms and padded across the smooth marble floor towards the inviting blue water. The place was very warm, the atmosphere sultry and sub-tropical, and as far as she could see the pool area was totally deserted. To her right was a large alcove containing couches and loungers, along with a limited range of lightweight exercise equipment. The more complex machines were next door, in the gym.

96

Helen heard a faint sound. She turned, glancing past a thick row of greenery and saw Ben standing by one of the couches in the alcove. To her amazement he was totally naked. Helen paused, and smiled, thinking that Ben had a rather cute bum; small but perfectly formed. It was then that she discovered Ben wasn't alone, as another naked man strolled into her line of vision. This time she wasn't surprised to see it was Justin. Looking at him totally nude for the first time, she discovered that Justin had a more well-developed physique than Ben's, but he was still quite skinny compared to the muscular build of Duncan Paul.

There was something very arousing about the sight of two naked men standing together, one so pale skinned, the other with a dark Mediterranean complexion. She had always been turned on by the sight of a good pair of masculine buttocks, and Justin's were curvier, more well defined than Ben's. Her excitement increased as Justin moved, and she caught sight of the chains on his nipples, his black pubic curls, and his flaccid, silver-decorated cock swinging enticingly between his slim thighs.

Did they always swim in the nude? she wondered. She found that idea a tad surprising as patients used the pool as well. Some of the female patients might be shocked, while others might enjoy it, she thought smiling to herself.

Helen paused for a moment, hidden from their sight by the row of plants, unsure whether to make her presence known to them or creep quietly away. However, something about their position, the way they were looking at each other incited her curiosity, making her decide to stay and watch. Justin spoke softly to Ben, then put his arm around his shoulders to pull him close. Tenderly Justin stroked and caressed Ben, sliding his hands downwards to cup his buttocks. His fingers kneaded and squeezed the firm flesh until Ben gave a faint groan of pleasure.

She could barely believe her eyes as she watched

Justin's hand slip between Ben's bum cheeks. Then she heard Ben's gasp of delight as Justin's fingers continued their even more intimate exploration, sliding teasingly inside his anus. Before this it had never crossed Helen's mind that Ben might be bisexual, let alone that he and Justin were lovers. She watched transfixed as Ben responded by stroking Justin's cock, gently caressing the shaft and the domed head, running his fingers teasingly around the base until the organ visibly stiffened.

Justin turned so that they were belly to belly and took possession of Ben's lips, kissing him passionately. This prequel to further intimacy stirred Helen, arousing previously unbidden erotic thoughts, wild lustful desires. She felt she was intruding on something private, but that only served to increase her need to stay.

She crouched silently behind her veil of plants eager to see what would happen next as Justin led Ben to a low couch. Ben lay down on his back and Justin straddled his head, facing down towards his belly. Justin, his sexual organs dangling invitingly down over his companion's face, stretched forwards until his head was level with Ben's pelvis and they were in the perfect position to perform mutual fellatio. Helen waited with bated breath, her pussy hot and aching, aroused by the eroticism of the moment.

Ben took hold of Justin's cock and guided it between his lips, just as Justin pulled Ben's penis deep inside his mouth. The two men were fused together in a tableaux of lust, their bodies held stretched and tautly perfect as they started to performed their rite of worshipful intimacy.

Helen watched with hungry concentration as Justin's lips slid up and down Ben's fat prick, leaving it slick and shiny, moistened by its coating of saliva. At the other end of the couch, Ben energetically sucked and licked Justin's cock and Helen felt her quim tingle with excitement as a warm wetness seeped into her bikini bottoms. She had to stay and witness the conclusion, wishing she could fling off her own clothes and join in this supremely masculine act of pleasure.

Helen had never witnessed two men having sex before; had never imagined it in her wildest fantasies. The sight was so arousing, so erotic, she was filled with the need to quell the steadily rising pressure building in her own sex. She pressed her hand against her aching pussy, grinding her palm against it, while her ears were assailed by the soft sounds of licking and sucking, interspersed by deep moans of bliss.

Straining forwards, not wanting to miss a moment, she slid her fingers inside her pants burrowing into the hot dampness. Eagerly she stroked her clit, then slipped her fingers inside herself, feeling the moist velvety flesh embrace the invading digits. It felt good, but rather insubstantial and she wished she had access to the generously sized dildo hidden in her bedside drawer. Suddenly Justin pulled away from Ben, making him groan with frustration, and she got her first full glimpse of the cocks in all their naked glory – both standing stiffly erect, both shining slickly in the subdued light.

Justin swung round as he moved down the couch, then kneeled between Ben's open thighs. 'Oh, yes,' Ben gasped, lifting his pelvis up towards Justin.

Reaching to his left, Justin picked up a tube of lubricating jelly. Reverently he smoothed it around Ben's anus before sliding a rubber over himself, while Helen waited with bated breath. Leaning forwards, Justin grasped the base of his penis and began lovingly to rim Ben's anal opening, slowly easing the swollen head inside his friend, stretching the tender flesh until Ben gave a whimper of painful bliss.

Helen burrowed her own fingers deeper, urgently rubbed her aching clit, as Justin gave a sudden unexpected thrust, burying his cock fully inside Ben with a satisfied grunt. He jammed his pelvis hard against Ben's cheeks. Then, not moving his hips, he ran his hands gently over his companion's stomach, being extra careful not to touch the rigid cock that cried out for the caressing pleasure of his fingertips.

Placing his hands either side of Ben's slim hips, Justin began to thrust, gradually increasing the pace, settling into an unrelenting rhythm, with movements so violent that Ben's twitching cock beat a rapid tattoo against his stomach. Justin was arse-fucking the man who had made love to her last night, and Helen's entire body tingled at that thought. Her head spun and she was filled by the pain of wanting as she watched the thrusting heap of male testosterone straining towards a mutual climax.

Then Justin curved his hand around Ben's prick, wanking it roughly in time to the movements of his hips. The most primitive of emotions stirred within her as she heard Ben's cry of total abandonment. She saw both men shudder as a fountain of white spunk spurted from Ben's prick, covering his chest and neck in a sparkling array of creamy droplets.

Helen frantically rubbed her burning clit, straining towards her own climax. She was agonisingly close but no matter how hard she tried it just wouldn't come. Shivering with frustration, wanting to scream aloud in vexation, she saw the two men disentangle their bodies and relax on the couch together in a loving embrace.

Envying them their satisfaction, she turned away and hurried quietly towards the shelter of the pool. Trying not to even ripple the still surface, she moved down the steps into the cool embrace of the water. It brushed tantalisingly against her throbbing breasts, and her inflamed pussy as she forced herself to swim the length of the pool with smooth regular strokes. The harmonious movements gradually began to soothe her, and calm the agitated beating of her heart, but still the aching sexual hunger remained.

Somewhere along the way she felt the insubstantial bikini top slide from her breasts. She was past caring, and actually the cool water brushing against her erect nipples felt surprisingly good. She continued to swim up and down, her long blonde hair splaying out behind her in the water, willing the fire in her loins to subside. Gradually she allowed herself to become mesmerised by the repetitive movements, as she concentrated on swimming length after length. She never heard the splash of someone else diving into the pool, never realised she was no longer alone.

Helen came back to reality with a start as she felt strong arms grab hold of her. She was pulled back against a hard male body and dragged to the shallow end of the pool. Stunned by the assault she struggled to pull away from her captor, splashing agitatedly around in the water.

'Don't panic, Helen,' she heard Ben say, just as she blinked the water from her eyes, and saw him swimming towards her.

Helen now knew without a doubt who was holding on to her. 'Let go of me, Justin,' she shouted furiously. 'Leave me alone.'

'Calm down,' he said soothingly, holding on to her determinedly as she wriggled about, trying to get away from him.

He clamped a hand over her right breast, holding her even closer so that she could feel the hardness of his belly against her upper buttocks and his nipple chains grazing her back, while the agitated movements of the water made his balls slap loosely against her thighs. Judging by the hardness of his dick, digging in the groove between her bottom cheeks, her struggles were arousing him no end.

'And you get your bloody hands off me,' she hissed, trying to ignore the rising tide of lust which threatened to consume her senses.

'You don't really want me to,' Justin said, just as Ben reached them and stood up, the surface of the water lapping lazily around his chest, the droplets on his gold nipple ring making it sparkle.

'How did you know it was me, Helen?' Justin added huskily, his warm breath brushing her water-splashed cheek.

101

'It was bloody obvious.' She gave up the fight, relaxing against him, secretly enjoying the feel of his hard body, and the sensation of his fingers rubbing and squeezing her nipple.

Ben stepped closer, so that she was neatly sandwiched between two naked male bodies. 'Did you see us together, Helen?' he asked, cupping her chin with his hands, forcing her to look deep into his eyes.

'So what if I did?'

She could still detect the odour of spent sex clinging to him, even though it was half masked by the smell of the chlorinated water. Helen shivered as Ben leaned forwards and ran the tip of his tongue over her damp cheeks and the trembling fullness of her lower lip.

'Did it turn you on, seeing us fucking?' Justin said softly as his teeth closed around her ear-lobe, nibbling and sucking, while he continued to stroke and caress her breast.

'Maybe,' she gasped, as Ben plunged his hand inside her bikini bottom, cupping her pussy, putting pressure on her aching sex.

'Now you'd like to play too, wouldn't you, Helen?' Justin growled.

Helen didn't answer, just moaned softly and closed her eyes as Ben slid beneath the water to ease off her bikini bottoms. The garment fell away from her as Ben slowly raised her legs, until they were floating on the surface, her thighs splayed wide apart.

Justin whispered filthy words of encouragement as he cradled her shoulders with one arm, letting her half drift on the surface, the water lapping gently at her bare flesh. Ben moved closer, forcing her legs wide apart, while Justin stroked her breasts and took possession of her mouth. As Justin thrust his tongue between Helen's lips, exploring the interior with strong stabbing movements, his tongue stud clicked around her teeth. Ben lifted her buttocks out of the water and pressed his face to her open quim.

Ben's mouth eagerly explored her, his lips tugging at

her clit, his tongue lapping and probing before he pushed it into the wet slit of her vagina. The sensation was familiar, yet like nothing she'd ever known – two sets of hands on her body, two men kissing and devouring her with tongues and lips, while she floated on the cool water in this exotic semi-tropical cavern.

She savoured the delicious feel of Ben's tongue as it burrowed into her, while Justin pulled one of her nipples into his mouth rubbing the tiny metal ball over sensitive flesh. The sensations were gloriously wicked, and she abandoned herself to the bliss, the soft sounds of her moans echoing eerily around the pool. The pleasure was inescapable as it built swiftly, and Helen bucked her hips, thrashing around in the water as her climax consumed her senses.

Before she had time to recover, she was pulled to the edge of the pool and lifted from the water to be deposited on a soft white towel. Naked, apart from the crumpled remains of her bikini top, she shivered, feeling suddenly cold, her hair plastered wetly around her shoulders and back.

Justin stood over her, his cock now hard and ready. Helen stared up at him, overcome by the fact that she'd so enjoyed being pleasured by two men at the same time, eagerly waiting for Justin to crouch down and thrust into her with his magnificent dick. Helen wanted to climax again, this time with a firm cock powering boldly inside her.

She was destined to be disappointed. At that moment Ben distracted Justin by touching his shoulder. Immediately Justin lost interest in her and turned towards him. The two men embraced, running hungry hands over each other's bodies, and as she watched them kiss Helen was consumed by jealousy. It was obvious that they wanted each other far more than they did her. She felt deflated, used; they had both been playing with her emotions, toying with her senses, nothing more. Disappointed with Ben, and resenting Justin, she struggled to her feet. Wrapping the towel around her naked body, she hurried towards the changing rooms. She looked back only once. Ben and Justin hadn't even noticed she'd left, so engrossed were they in each other. Ben was kneeling submissively in front of his companion, just about to take Justin's cock into his mouth.

By the time Helen had showered and changed ready for the evening ahead, she had managed to push her interlude with Ben and Justin to the back of her mind. She had to admit that she'd enjoyed the unusual pleasures, regardless of how it had all eventually ended. There was certainly something very erotic about watching two men make love, and she would like to witness it again. The hospital was saturated with a sordid sensuality that was quite addictive. She felt she should try and keep her distance from Ben and Justin in future. She didn't want their behaviour to affect her emotions or her judgement, but she feared she would not be able to resist their powerful pull on her senses.

Filling her mind with images of Duncan, she dressed carefully in a form-fitting black crepe dress, sheer black hold-up stockings and high black court shoes. She decided not to pin up her hair and instead wore it in loose waves around her shoulders.

When she arrived at the Rochester Suite, Duncan looked pleased to see her. He was sitting in the lounge area in a large leather armchair, wearing a black silk robe over his pyjamas, his cast-covered ankle resting on a low stool.

'Hi!' He smiled warmly. 'Glad you could make it.'

Duncan was the famous movie star, a fantasy figure for most of his fans, yet tonight he seemed so ordinary and conventional in comparison to Justin and Ben.

'So am I,' she said, sitting down in the chair opposite his. To her left a table was elegantly set with delicate china, silver cutlery and tall crystal glasses.

'I'll call for the food now that you're here. I hope you don't mind, I took a chance and just ordered a variety of different things. This place isn't quite as flexible as a normal restaurant; they needed to know what we wanted in advance.' He pressed the call button at his side. 'I'm famished, how about you?'

'So am I,' she agreed. Her eyes drank in his perfect physique, and handsome face, hardly ably to believe she was here with the man she most desired. 'Absolutely famished,' she added, pressing her thighs together, all too conscious of the heat still simmering inside her quim.

The door opened and a waiter carefully pushed in a heavily laden trolley. 'Do you wish me to serve, Mr Paul?' he asked, placing the trolley beside the table.

'Just the champagne for now. We can serve ourselves later.' Duncan looked enquiringly at Helen. 'You can drink, can't you?'

She nodded. 'I'm off duty tonight, and not on call.'

The waiter handed Helen a tall glass. 'It's good,' Duncan announced as he took a sip of his champagne. 'I wasn't sure how comprehensive their wine list was here, so I sent for a supply from my own private cellar.'

'Are you a connoisseur of wine?' Helen asked as the waiter departed.

'I try to be.' His dark eyes were compelling as he stared thoughtfully at her. 'Of many things,' he added in a low husky voice, which sent shivers of desire spiralling up her spine.

Helen took an extra large gulp of her champagne, all too conscious that her earlier climax had left her feeling surprisingly unfulfilled. She lusted after Duncan, fancied him like crazy, and she didn't think she was misreading the signals he was sending her. She was certain he was feeling as horny as she was. It appeared that she could have everything she had ever desired, sex with the leading man in her own perfect fantasy. She found the thought of what was to come stimulated her senses even more. Her breathing quickened and her skin tingled with excitement.

'That was delicious,' she said, putting down her glass, as Duncan placed his half-finished drink on the floor beside his chair. The food on the trolley was all cold –

fresh lobster, cuts of meat, salad, fresh fruit and a couple of luxurious desserts. 'Do you want to eat now?'

'Do you?' His eyes slid downwards until they were resting on her bosom.

'You did say you were famished.'

'I did.' Duncan grinned. 'But famished for what? One could interpret the remark in a number of different ways.'

Helen enjoyed flirting, but she was determined not to give in too quickly to his considerable charms. He couldn't move about easily with his cast-covered foot, which left her in virtual control of the situation. 'I'll dish up yours. You aren't supposed to be putting any weight on that leg just yet. Lobster and salad, OK?'

'Whatever you say, doc. After all, you're the one in charge of me.' His mouth twitched slightly as he tried to suppress a rather provocative smile.

'If we are going to be precise, Ben Taylor is officially your doctor, not me,' she countered rising to her feet, and filling a plate for Duncan.

'Now I feel disappointed,' he teased, watching her every movement. She turned, the crepe dress clinging to her body, the skirt riding up almost to her stocking tops, and placed his plate on the table.

'I thought our intention was to discuss in more detail your thoughts about women being in positions of authority.' She filled a plate for herself, even though her appetite had totally disappeared.

'So we were.' He grinned wickedly. 'Although if I recall correctly wasn't the exact wording, "women dominating men"?'

'Exercise total control is the dictionary definition.'

'Would you enjoy exercising total control over a man, Helen?'

The undercurrent of sexual desire was a tangible entity, thickening the warm evening air. 'I've never really tried it, yet,' she replied, popping a fresh strawberry into her mouth. She approached Duncan, holding

106

the choicest of the ruby-red fruit. 'Do you want one of these?'

Duncan gave a lazy smile. 'You tell me. You're the one in control here.'

She bent forwards, so that he got a good view of her bare bosom as the low neckline of her dress gaped open, and placed the strawberry in his mouth. 'Quite delightful,' he said as he chewed and swallowed the fruit. 'Speaking of control, you claim you've never tried it, but that's not true. Don't you exercise control over your patients?'

'Medically, yes,' she agreed, moving to stand astride his cast-covered foot. 'For instance, I could arrange to prescribe a drug for you that would make you utterly helpless within seconds, unable to move even a muscle.'

'Then you could do anything you wanted with me,' he said, his voice thick with passion.

'Would you like that? To lie helpless on your bed, while I assumed total control over your naked body?' Helen ran her tongue slowly over her lower lip as she selected a long stemmed rose from the vase in the middle of the dinner table. 'Did your girlfriend send you these?'

'No.' He gave a low, rich chuckle. 'My fan club as it happens. I don't have a girlfriend. Speaking of partners, what about Max?'

'Max isn't here, is he?' She brushed his cheek with the sweet-smelling head of the rose, trailing it slowly downwards over his corded neck. The velvety petals caressed the narrow V of skin revealed by his open-necked robe and, as the petals became bruised, the heady scent grew stronger. 'Our relationship isn't that serious, Duncan,' she said, realising that she had managed to break free from the ties that had previously bound her to Max. 'There's no commitment on either side,' she added, certain that Max's feelings were based more on a sense of possession than anything else.

Duncan didn't speak or move a muscle as Helen pulled apart his robe and slowly unbuttoned his pyjama jacket. She jerked the black silk apart, exposing his tanned chest to her gaze. Duncan's pecs were well developed, the skin below it stretched taut over a mesh of hard muscle, so tight she could see the lines of his ribcage beneath the smooth skin.

Helen felt the sudden surging pleasure of holding sway over another's senses as she leaned forwards and took possession of his lips. She kissed Duncan, thrusting her tongue into his strawberry-scented mouth, while she ran her hands downwards, feeling the engorged hardness of his cock trapped beneath the fine silk. It was rigid, straining against the waistband of his pyjama trousers. Her clit hardened in response, and fluid bathed her pussy, as she imagined how good it would feel thrusting inside her.

Duncan lifted his hand to touch her, but she slapped his arm with the stem of the rose, hearing his soft gasp of surprise as the thorns seared his skin. 'You do as I say tonight.'

He placed his hands back on the arms of the chair, clutching them extra tightly as Helen unfastened his pyjama trousers. She jerked them open, freeing his cock, and it reared away from his flat belly, deliciously hard. Ripe and juicy, ready for plucking, Duncan's cock drew her gaze like a magnet. Helen's head spun with excitement, but she wasn't quite finished teasing Duncan as she slowly ran the velvety head of the rose up and down his large shaft. She heard his indrawn hiss of breath, watching his cock twitch and tighten in response.

Gently she pulled the clothing away from his body until the entire front of his torso was exposed, then she dragged the head of the bloom over each nipple, teasingly brushing his belly, and the shaft of his dick, until he groaned in hungry agitation.

Helen saw by the expression in his eyes how horny and frustrated he felt, but Duncan still kept his lips clamped determinedly together, not saying a word. She was equally determined to hear him beg, to force those pleading words from his mouth. She stood astride both his legs, her thighs wide apart, and slowly eased up her skirt. Tantalising his senses with the sight of her lacy stocking tops and the pale skin of her upper thighs, she managed to arouse him even more when he saw that she wasn't wearing panties.

Duncan stayed silent, his breathing heavy and laboured as he stared intently at the tangle of golden curls covering her pubis.

'You have to ask,' she prompted, running the rose over her open pussy lips, anointing her sex with the strong perfume seeping from the bruised petals.

'And if I don't?' There was a stubborn expression on his handsome face, yet she knew he was enjoying every moment of this sweet torment.

'I could deny you what you so clearly want,' she teased, staring at his cock. 'Or I could punish you in some way.' She brushed the flower against his throbbing dick, making it twitch.

'Are you sure you haven't done this before? If not you should know that torture is definitely your forté.' His voice sounded tight and strained, but still he didn't move a muscle.

'You are remarkably resilient,' she taunted. 'Perhaps you've indulged in such games before?' Helen stroked his belly and chest with the flower head, then tossed the rose aside and leaned forwards to tweak his copper-coloured nipples, pulling at them with her fingertips until they darkened and hardened even more.

By now Duncan's breathing had become laboured and his cock looked ready to explode. 'I've always been a man of action, relished being in control. This situation is unique – I've never been hampered by a broken limb before. If I wasn't, I'd lift you into my arms, carry you to the bed – '

'And fuck me until I begged for mercy?' she interjected, laughing softly. 'But you're the invalid, Duncan, and I'm the doctor, so you must do as I say.'

He watched mesmerised as she slid her fingers

between her pussy lips, running them along the damp slit. Once they were liberally anointed with her juices, she stroked them across the head of his cock. Duncan uttered a faint groan, and dug his hands into the leather-covered arms of his chair, holding on as if his life depended on it. 'This is agony.'

'All you have to do is say please,' Helen murmured, her fingers teasing the root of his cock, circling it slowly, but never taking hold of the shaft.

'Please, Helen.' Duncan exhaled loudly, his penis aching with excitement.

'Almost there.' She wanked him with long smooth strokes. 'What else should you say?'

Duncan strained his pelvis upwards. 'Please let me come inside you?' he begged, as she felt the juices seep out of her pussy and coat her inner thighs.

However much she wanted to prolong Duncan's agony, she knew she couldn't wait a moment longer; she had to have him now. She crouched over his thighs, kneeling on the leather seat, as she eased her body downwards until her open quim was poised above his rearing cock. Duncan gasped as his cock head touched the moist entrance, jerking his pelvis upwards so that it slid part-way inside her. Unable to wait a moment longer, she slowly sheathed herself on to him, shafting downwards until she felt the root of his penis jam hard against her pelvic bone.

Helen paused, accustoming herself to the wonderful sensations of fullness, then she began to rock her hips.

'So good,' Duncan groaned, as she started to clench and release her interior muscles, exciting them both beyond awareness.

Lust overtook her completely. Placing her hands on Duncan's wide shoulders, she lifted her hips, almost releasing her hold on his cock, before easing her body down again. The sensations were sweetly perfect as she increased the pace and pressure of her movements, until she was breathing heavily and a veil of sweat covered her brow. The thrusting pleasure, the feeling of total power over Duncan's senses, was so overwhelming, so intense, that she almost lost control.

She bit back her moans as she concentrated on her rapid, rhythmic movements. She felt the pressure building inside her, and at that very moment, Duncan let go of the chair arm and slid his fingers in the slit of her sex. Lights danced before her eyes as he took hold of her clit, pulling on it roughly so that the painful pleasure pushed her over the edge into a gut-wrenching climax.

As the intense sensations died away, she leaned limply against Duncan's muscular chest. He kissed her tenderly while he stroked and caressed her trembling body. Helen could still smell the scent of the rose, now tinged with the sweaty odour of sex. It was the sweetest perfume she had ever known.

When Helen eventually left Duncan it was almost 2 a.m. After their sexual encounter, they had drunk, eaten, and then talked for ages. She was feeling extraordinarily happy as she walked along the almost deserted corridors of the hospital. The night staff were seated at their desks, yawning, reading or drinking coffee, while their patients slept undisturbed.

She could hear nothing, not even the sound of her own footsteps on the thickly carpeted floor, then the silence was suddenly broken by the distant sound of spinning rotor blades. As the helicopter drew closer, Helen thought it would pass on by, but the sounds grew steadily louder and she realised it must be landing in the hospital grounds. 'Who would be arriving here in the dead of night?' she asked herself.

She was on the ground floor, making for the rear entrance of the hospital, when she heard the noise increase again as the helicopter took off. By the time she reached the open courtyard the helicopter would be far out of sight. Helen turned into the corridor that led to the rear doors.

Helen paused as she saw tall forms through the dimpled glass, then the swing doors were pushed open.

Something, she didn't know what, told her to step back into the shadows and avoid being seen. She slipped into a small unused examination room, just off the corridor. The room was pitch black as the blinds were tightly drawn. She would be able to hide and see into the corridor as the new arrivals passed by.

There was the rattle of a trolley and the sound of gruff male voices coming closer. Illuminated in the doorway she saw the trolley. The patient, a middle-aged man with a prominent hooked nose, had a face that seemed familiar, although she had no idea who he was. He was accompanied by three bulky looking men in dark suits, and Ben Taylor, dressed casually in jeans and T-shirt.

Helen didn't know what to think, but it did cross her mind that this might be the mysterious Mr X. Yet there were still no procedures officially scheduled for a number of days. Why was this man's identity being kept so secret, and what was so strange about his intended operation? The staff were loyal enough to keep quiet whatever happened, even if Mr X were famous and they were to be besieged by the press, so what reason could there be?

Helen chanced a furtive peek into the corridor, just in time to see the small group turning left. Curiosity prompted her to follow them. Taking off her high-heeled shoes, she tiptoed forwards. When she reached the intersection, she saw the group piling into a newly installed lift. This lift went straight to the new maternity unit, and the West Wing annex, which was currently being refurbished. None of the new rooms were due to be finished for a month or even more.

Certain that she wouldn't be able to relax until she learned more about the new arrival, she hurried up the stairs to the first floor. Curiously she peered through the glass panel in the stairwell door, and saw the patient being pushed through the double doors, to the right of maternity, which led into the annex and nowhere else. Rumour had it that these rooms would be even more expensive than those in the West Wing, or the Rochester Suite, but they were far from finished, certainly not ready for occupation. What the hell was Ben doing putting one of his patients in there?

Chapter Six

*T*he first thing Helen did when coming on duty the following morning was to check the operating lists. Why wasn't she surprised to discover nothing had been added? Frankly she had suspected as much, concluding that if Ben and Ralph Kalowski had taken so much trouble to hide the patient's name even from hospital staff, then they were not likely to broadcast it for all to see on the surgery schedules. Nevertheless, this conclusion did make her wonder exactly how many of the staff members were in on this weird conspiracy.

On the other hand, perhaps she was being totally paranoid. There could be some perfectly reasonable explanation for concealing this patient's identity. She tried unsuccessfully to put the puzzle to the back of her mind as she went about her work.

She would have been tempted to speak to Ben, if she hadn't discovered just how close he was to Justin. There was something about Justin Masterson that made her distrust him, a suspicion that there was far more to him than met the eye. Of one thing Helen was certain, he was a manipulative bastard, who probably used everyone to his own ends. Strange, she considered; she didn't usually make snap judgements about people, but she had with Justin.

Duncan wasn't on her morning list, but she intended to pop in and see him after she had finished her rounds. She had enjoyed herself more than she cared to admit last night, and she was looking forward to seeing him again.

The majority of Helen's patients were in the East Wing of the hospital, where the staff were pleasant, friendly and very approachable. Since she'd been here she'd rarely had cause to go to the West Wing. The patients there were almost exclusively attended by their respective consultants, or just admitted for rest and relaxation, with little need to see the duty registrar.

Helen had found most of the staff in the West Wing a little weird. They acted as though she was intruding on their territory, and for some reason appeared suspicious of her presence. Also, Helen had discovered that Sandra seemed to exert greater control over the West Wing than she did any other part of the hospital.

Eager to spend some time with Duncan, Helen completed her rounds as swiftly as she could. She had only one patient left to check on – Miss Zara Dawn. As she approached her room, there seemed to be an inordinate number of people milling about, none of them members of staff.

'What's going on, nurse Barker?' Helen addressed the nurse who had been talking about Duncan yesterday.

'It is a little chaotic,' nurse Barker agreed, 'But Miss Dawn's consultant said it would be OK.'

'What would be OK?'

'Miss Dawn is scheduled to appear in a TV mini-series soon after she leaves here. Apparently it's a historical one, and wardrobe and make-up are here, fitting her for some of the costumes. Isn't it exciting?'

'Perhaps a tad too exciting for some of our other patients,' Helen said, as she saw a couple of women chatting by the nurses' station, one of them lighting a cigarette.

Helen stormed over to them. 'This hospital has a no smoking policy. Put that out at once.'

The heavily made-up young woman, dressed entirely in black leather, stared at Helen. 'Says who?'

'I do,' Helen replied. 'No smoking, and tell the rest of your people to be a little quieter. They mustn't get in the way of hospital staff. If you don't follow the rules, I'll have you all thrown out.'

As Helen turned away she heard the woman mutter something derogatory about her under her breath. 'Nurse Barker,' she said. 'If there's any trouble call security and eject the lot of them. I'm going to get a cup of coffee and let this hubbub die down. I'll come back later to see Miss Dawn.'

'Yes.' The nurse looked at her rather curiously.

'Is something wrong?' Helen asked her.

'If you don't mind me asking, doctor,' the nurse replied hesitantly. 'My friend told me that you dined with Duncan Paul last night.'

'That's correct.' Even the mention of his name made Helen smile with secret pleasure. 'I've met Duncan before as it happens. We have a close mutual acquaintance.'

'You are so lucky,' nurse Barker said breathlessly. 'I'm a really big fan. I know there are rules laid down about troubling patients, purely for their protection. It stops them being harassed, but I wondered, as you know him so well – '

'What exactly are you getting at?'

'His autograph, personalised, maybe even saying something like "With love"?' nurse Barker said, turning a little misty-eyed.

Helen gave a soft laugh. 'Is that all? I'm sure he wouldn't mind. I'll mention it when I see him later.'

'That's so good of you, Dr Dawson,' nurse Barker said. 'I'd be so grateful.'

'In the meantime, keep a close eye on these people,' Helen said, as the leather-clad woman left Zara's room, banging the door nosily behind her. 'Please ensure they don't disturb the other patients.'

'Yes,' nurse Barker agreed, smiling.

Helen turned, intending to go down to the staff restaurant, grab a quick coffee, and perhaps a bite to eat, but when she caught sight of Ben Taylor she changed her mind. He didn't stop to speak to her as he strode past, after just having exited a little-used corridor which led only to maternity and the uncompleted annex.

She decided it wouldn't hurt to take a quick peek in that direction. If Ben had been to the annex it was likely that the mysterious patient was still in residence. Helen turned and walked swiftly along the same corridor, realising almost immediately that something was different about the place. Usually there were a number of workmen around, but the area was totally deserted. It wasn't the weekend, and she could think of no other reason why the men shouldn't be working today.

As she reached the end of the corridor she turned sharp right, passing the stairwell she'd hidden in last night. A thick, heavy piece of plastic sheeting had been fitted across the annex entrance a few feet in front of the double entrance doors. Helen brushed impatiently past it, letting it snap back in place with a loud rustle as she caught sight of the burly, dark-suited man sitting on an upright chair just in front of the annex doors. She was almost certain that she recognised him from last night.

He uncoiled his bulk from the chair and stood up as she approached. 'No one allowed here,' he said in a thick foreign accent, towering menacingly over her.

Helen pretended to examine the papers on her clipboard. 'I'm the duty registrar. According to my records I've a patient to see here. A gentleman who's about to undergo surgery.'

'No one allowed,' the man repeated, shaking his head.

'Get out of my way.' Helen tried to push past him, but he grabbed hold of her, digging his thick, meaty fingers into her upper arms.

'No!' he growled, as Helen uttered a loud cry of indignation.

'What's going on?' The accent was upper-class English, but the new arrival looked foreign; Spanish or South

117

American. Helen didn't recognise the man who stepped out of the annex, letting the door swing silently shut behind him. Dark complexioned, with black hair smarmed severely back from his hard face, he wore an expensive pale-grey suit, and an elegant cream silk shirt and matching tie.

'That's what I'd like to know,' Helen said angrily, trying to shake off the brute who had accosted her. The swarthy stranger spoke sharply to her assailant in Spanish. He immediately let go of Helen as she added, 'I'm a senior registrar at this hospital.'

The swarthy man raised his finely arched eyebrows. 'Then you should have already been informed, doctor, that this part of the building is off limits to all staff.'

'I've heard nothing of the kind,' Helen responded, irritated by the man's superiority as he stared scathingly at her. 'On whose authority, may I ask?'

He shrugged his shoulders. 'The hospital board I suppose.' He smiled coldly. 'This gentleman has been posted here to prevent anyone entering.'

'There was no need for him to use such force on me,' she complained as she rubbed her bruised arms.

'I regret he was rather overzealous, but he was acting purely out of concern for your safety.'

'My safety?'

'Yes.' The man waved his hand in the direction of the annex. 'The architect has discovered a fault in the structural integrity of one of the rooms. It needs to be dealt with immediately. This part of the building is very old, and specialists have to be brought in to solve the problem.'

Helen knew without a doubt that he was lying, such information would have been broadcast all around the hospital by now. While this unintelligible brute wouldn't have been posted here to stop people entering, that job would have been assigned to hospital security. This was all a lie to prevent her getting inside the annex, discovering the mysterious patient's identity.

'Then why are you here?' she asked.

'I'm a representative of one of the specialist companies,' he lied smoothly.

'I happen to know that there is a patient in one of the rooms,' she countered defiantly.

'You are mistaken, doctor.' He stepped back a pace, so that he was standing directly in front of the doors. 'Your information is incorrect. There are no patients in this part of the hospital. I should warn you that if you even try to enter you will be putting yourself in considerable jeopardy.'

The threatening note in his voice was obvious, and Helen knew she would never get into the annex at this point in time. 'Then perhaps you are right, perhaps I have been misinformed,' she agreed calmly, trying not to show how uneasy he made her feel. 'The records I have must be wrong.'

'Indeed they must,' he agreed, stepping forwards to take hold of her arm, and leading her very gently past the plastic, back into the main corridor.

'I hope this matter will soon be sorted. I wouldn't like to think that it might delay the opening of the maternity unit.'

'I am certain it won't come to that,' he replied, his gaze following Helen as she reluctantly turned around and began to retrace her steps back to the East Wing.

Zara looked at her reflection in the mirror, greatly pleased by what she saw. Her bruises were disappearing, and she felt much better, mainly because of the constant attentions of Colin. She had only known him a couple of days, but in that short time they had become close. There was something so genuine and trustworthy about Colin that she had found herself speaking to him very frankly, telling him things she had never told anyone else.

Colin wasn't on duty until later, but she was hoping he would stop by soon, after his regular exercise session in the gym.

'It looks great,' Betsy said enthusiastically. She was a skinny, quite unattractive young woman, but Zara liked her because she was sweet-natured and a brilliant costume designer.

The dress was made of pink duchess satin, liberally embroidered with gold and decorated with fake gems. Combined with its petticoats and the rigidly boned corset it was uncomfortable and very weighty. Nevertheless it pulled in Zara's waist, thrust up her bosom and gave her an even more incredible looking figure than usual. In order to provide a more complete picture, make-up had piled Zara's hair on top of her head. When filming began she would wear wigs althought none of them were finished yet.

'I love it, Betsy, just love it.' Zara smiled as Betsy snapped a couple of Polaroids of her in the outfit. 'Although I can barely breathe.'

This was the first time that Zara had worked on a historical series, the first time she'd worn quite such restrictive clothing. She had worked on a sci-fi picture which had come close. There had been no satin and jewels then, just skin-tight spandex, PVC and leather.

'You look so regal, just like a queen,' Betsy said, as she bent to rearrange the voluminous skirt.

Zara laughed. 'Considering the fact that I'm playing a queen that sounds OK to me –' She faltered as the door opened and Colin entered in tight-fitting pale-blue jeans and a white singlet, which showed off his muscular arms and pecs to perfection.

He gave a low whistle of approval. 'You look amazing, incredible,' said Colin. The way he was looking at her made Zara feel gloriously happy, sexy and very horny.

'So this is the gorgeous guy you were talking about,' Betsy said, looking him up and down as if she wanted to leap into bed with him. 'Zara's told me all about you.'

'No, I haven't.' It had been a long time since Zara had blushed quite so obviously . 'She's fibbing, Colin. I just happened to mention how nice you were.'

'But what she didn't say spoke volumes,' Betsy added with a trilling laugh. 'She definitely underplayed your considerable charms.'

Colin shuffled his feet appearing faintly uncomfortable. 'Should I leave?'

'No,' Zara said firmly. 'Betsy's just teasing. Actually she was just going to gather up the others and go down to the restaurant for coffee.' She looked pointedly at the young designer.

'Sure.' Betsy nodded. 'Coffee it is. Do you want me to help you out of the costume first?'

'I'll keep it on for a while. I've got to wear it, or something similar on set for hours, so I may as well try and accustom myself to the discomfort.'

'Whatever you say.' Betsy cast one long, lingering, hungry glance at Colin as she left the room.

Colin didn't even seem to have noticed Betsy's interest in him as he stepped closer to Zara. 'I wasn't exaggerating,' he said softly. 'You look wonderful. Every inch the famous movie star.'

He twined his arm around her waist and looked at their joint reflections in the mirror, appearing a little out of place in his modern clothing next to Zara in her elaborate eighteenth century costume. 'I could just picture you in a billowing white shirt slashed to the waist, wearing tight knee-breeches, a sword at your side. Ever thought of taking up acting?' she teased, smiling at his reflection.

'I'd be terrible at it.' He loosened his hold on her waist and she turned to face him, her satin skirts rustling.

'But you'd look gorgeous. Your physique would be perfect for period drama. I'd make sure your knee-breeches were even tighter than those jeans,' she said, eyeing the considerable bulge at his crotch.

'I might be able to look the part, but I'd never be able to act. I'm no good at faking it.'

'Thank goodness.' She smiled provocatively as she ran her hands down his chest, to press her palm gently against his tightly restrained cock.

'I feel horny every time I lay eyes on you,' he groaned. 'But dressed like this you look so unapproachable. It reminds me so much of the wide gulf there is between us.'

'There is no gulf as far as I'm concerned,' Zara insisted, pressing her hand harder against his groin, as she stretched up on tiptoe, kissing him lovingly.

Colin returned the kiss with restrained passion. 'If only I could believe that.'

'Believe,' she insisted, stepping away from him, her heart beating faster. 'I may look unapproachable on the outside. But do you know what women of this time wore under their dresses?'

'Corsets?' he suggested, watching the swelling rise of her bosom as she tried to breath in her restrictive garments. The bodice was cut so low that he could see the dark aureoles of her nipples peeping out of the pink satin.

'Very tight corsets,' she amended, 'but underneath their skirts and petticoats they wore nothing at all.' She gradually lifted the heavy satin so that he could see the white silk stockings, held up by pink satin garters just above her knee. Colin watched in silence as she pulled the skirts higher, slowly baring her thighs.

'I want you right now,' he gasped, as she exposed her naked sex to his hungry gaze.

He sank to his knees, ducked under her heavy skirts and parted her thighs. Zara's senses spiralled out of control as she felt the heat of his breath on her pussy. He spread her labial lips, holding them open with his fingers, and blew softly on her throbbing clit.

'Touch it,' Zara pleaded.

Colin ran his tongue slowly along her moist slit, and as his lips closed lovingly around her clitoris, she gave a soft mewling sigh. He tugged at the tiny bud, sucking eagerly as he pulled it into his mouth. The sensation was delicious and Zara closed her eyes. She relaxed letting the pleasure wash over her, forgetting about everything else but the feel of Colin's hands and lips.

The sudden sound of the door opening brought her back to reality with a nervous start. Acting instinctively

122

she tossed her full skirts over Colin's kneeling form. 'What is it?' she snapped, glancing angrily at the nurse who had intruded on her privacy and now hovered awkwardly in the open doorway.

'Sorry to disturb you, Miss Dawn,' the nurse said apologetically. 'The kitchen wanted to know if you wished to delay lunch until after your costume fittings?'

'Of course, delay it,' Zara snapped. 'I'm very busy.'

She wasn't usually rude to the other staff, but she could hardly contain herself at present. Colin, hidden in the warm cave of her skirt, was busy nibbling and sucking, inciting her senses to fever pitch. She put her hand out to grasp the back of a chair, just to help her stay upright as Colin bit gently down on her aching clit. Zara clenched her lips, trying to remain composed as she struggled to hold back her moan of bliss.

'I'll leave,' the nurse muttered, pulling the door shut with a loud bang.

Zara didn't care if she'd seen Colin crouched under her skirt, as she felt his hard tongue wiggle its way teasingly into her vagina. She opened her thighs as wide as she could, pressing urgently against his head through the bulky layers of fabric, trying to force his tongue even deeper as it writhed and twisted its way inside her.

Moisture bathed her pussy, mingling with Colin's saliva as he captured her clitoris again, pulling it so hard into his mouth that she lost control completely. Zara climaxed, barely able to remain standing as the sweet pleasure consumed her senses.

Justin pulled off Sandra's clothes, almost ripping them in his haste. Then he pushed her down on to the bed, just as Ben dived towards her. They landed in a tangled heap of naked flesh. Sandra immediately tried to pull away, but Justin jerked her back with a cruel chuckle of amusement, and held her trapped against his chest.

'Damn you,' she squealed. 'I invited you both here for a serious discussion.'

'What could be more important than fucking?' Justin growled.

Sandra had some urgent matters to talk about so she'd invited Justin and Ben to lunch. The food had been ready on the table when they arrived. Instead of eating, they'd laughingly thrown of their clothes and dragged her into the bedroom. This was the first time they had acted like this and ganged up on her, although she'd been aware that Justin was also fucking Ben on a regular basis. In fact she had already begun to form plans for a pleasant threesome, but not like this! Sandra's scenario had involved her being in total charge of the situation, while here they were treating her as the helpless victim.

Sandra knew they were only playing but, to her surprise, she did feel a little scared by their rough behaviour. They were obviously prepared to use force and instinctively she had resisted. Turned on by their brutality, yet also apprehensive, she savoured the strong frisson of fear that suddenly flooded her senses.

She struggled to get away again, but Justin pinned her down, roughly kneading her large breasts, while Ben forced open her legs. Justin had a thing about breasts, and he rubbed and squeezed her lush flesh, pulling and twisting her nipples until Sandra moaned with pain, while Ben buried his head between her thighs, pressing his face to her pussy. Moisture flooded her quim, lust quelling any further thought of resistance. She wanted them both, was hungry to feel their hands roughly abusing her defenceless flesh.

Justin took possession of her mouth, pushing his tongue between her lips, while Ben plunged his tongue deep inside her. Sandra gasped as Ben's questing tongue squirmed deeper, just as Justin's mouth slid down to her breasts. He sucked hard on one nipple while he cruelly dug his nails into the other. Sandra closed her eyes, wallowing in pleasure, but they flew open again as she felt Justin attach a nipple clamp to her left breast. The cold metal teeth dug into her puckered teat, further abusing the already inflamed flesh. The pain set her nerve endings alight, and the tingling bliss radiated down towards her groin.

'Please,' she begged, as the tantalising sensations shot down to her belly, further inciting the heat in her quim, while all the time Ben's tongue wriggled and squirmed inside her. 'Fuck me!' she shouted. 'Now!'

Strong male arms immediately manhandled her body, until she was left lying atop Ben's naked form. Then Justin hooked his hands under her arms and pulled her to her knees. She was forced to squat astride Ben's hips and her legs trembled as she looked down at his rigid dick, ready to thrust its way inside her. She'd seen it before, but only when it was flaccid. The buried ballbearings were even more noticeable now it was erect, and she admired the tightly distended flesh, with its random display of hard pellets. Tiny bullets of bliss, she thought distractedly, as Justin dug his fingers into her fleshy hips, pushing her down on to Ben's waiting cock. It slid smoothly inside her, filling the aching void. She gasped with pleasure as Justin thrust her down so firmly that her pelvis ground against Ben's, while his cock head brushed the neck of her womb.

Sandra started to move, half-lifting herself, allowing the rigid dick to nearly slide out of her, before thrusting down again. She didn't consciously compare sensation, but his shaft felt different to Justin's. The protrusion caused far less intense pressure on her sensitive internal walls than Justin's silver balls, but the sensations were deliciously good all the same. She ground her open pussy against Ben's silky pubic hair, while with each lift and violent thrust her full breasts bounced up and down. Her left nipple, still tightly enclosed in the clamp, screamed for its release as the flesh around it turned numb. The pleasure-pain it caused contributed to the tight waves of bliss that assailed her quim as she rode Ben with wild abandon, galloping closer and closer to her climax.

Before she could reach the pinnacle of pleasure, Justin

grabbed her from behind, stopping her suddenly in mid-movement. He pushed her forwards until her full breasts were crushed against Ben's chest. She wanted to protest, to tell Justin that penetration was less deep this way, but she stayed silent as she felt him part her buttock cheeks. The lubricating jelly felt icy cold on her exposed arse-hole, and when he squeezed a mass of it into the tight opening she gave a soft moan of surrender, knowing full well what would happen next.

'Ben and I are gonna fuck you so hard that you'll pass out with pleasure,' Justin promised her, as she heard the familiar sound of a foil packet being torn open.

Sandra held her breath, anticipating an action so delicious she could hardly bear to wait. She wanted it so much, yet she still shivered nervously as Justin's cock probed her buttock cheeks. He rimmed the entrance, protected by her tightly closed sphincter muscle, forcing it to relax and open as he eased his cock head inside.

As his cock slid deeper, Sandra gave a sobbing sigh, her body expanding to accommodate the bulky organ. Justin buried himself to the last final inch, until his balls slapped warmly against her trembling buttocks. Sandra had been arse-fucked on many occasions, but never as completely as this. She savoured the utterly sublime sensation of having both intimate orifices stuffed full of pulsing male flesh.

Justin paused, breathing deeply, then took a firm hold on Ben's slim waist, sandwiching Sandra between them. He started to move, rocking his hips and she felt the studs tenderly chafe her inside. Gradually Justin altered the angle of penetration, so that his cock pressed against the thin, sensitive barrier that separated his penis from Ben's.

The hot pleasure was blissfully perfect, and as Justin thrust harder Sandra was so overwhelmed that the sensations blocked out all conscious thought. All three bodies rocked in unison, the throbbing rhythm transmitting itself from Justin, through Sandra to Ben.

Sandra's nerve endings contracted, spiralling out of

control. As she climaxed, she felt Ben and Justin's cocks pulse in mutual orgasmic waves. She felt blackness beckon as she almost passed out with pleasure.

Slowly she regained her senses. Both men were still buried inside her, but Justin was now supporting his body weight with his arms in order to prevent their combined weight from crushing Ben. Sandra had never felt so close to them both, and she pressed her lips to Ben, kissing him with great tenderness, while Justin slowly eased his body from hers.

She felt weak, as though she'd just completed the most punishing physical exercise, as she flopped down on to the bed next to Ben. Justin lay down on the other side of her and removed the clamp from her nipple. Her breast tingled with an angry fire as it slowly came back to life, and she couldn't suppress a whimper as Justin bent forwards to tenderly suck her tortured flesh.

'That was amazing,' Ben gasped.

'Told you it would be.' Justin chuckled. 'Next time we could find someone a little less willing than our darling Sandra.'

'Are you referring to Helen?' Sandra asked, as a knowing look passed between the two men. 'It's her I want to discuss.'

'Why?' Justin asked. 'Can't you lure the bitch into your bed?'

'It's nothing like that,' Sandra said in irritation. 'Her behaviour is troubling me.'

'She doesn't trouble me at all.' Justin grinned at his friend. 'Ben's already discovered that there is a randy little bitch hidden under that icy exterior. In fact I can vouch for that myself. Give me a week or so and she'll do anything we want. Then if you have a fancy to play girlie games with her, Sandra, you can.'

'It's not sex I'm referring to, Justin,' Sandra exclaimed.

'What's she been doing that troubles you so bloody much?' he asked, idly playing with her nipples.

'She's started sticking her nose into matters that don't concern her.' Sandra pushed Justin's hand away and sat up. 'For instance, Ben, did you know that Helen was spying on you last night?'

'Spying?' Ben questioned.

'Yeah. She saw you bring in our special patient, then followed you all up to the annex.'

'What was she doing in the hospital at that time of night when she wasn't on duty?' Ben asked.

'I'm told that she dined with Duncan Paul. She stayed in his room until two in the morning.'

'Do you think she was fucking him?' Justin asked, grinning.

'Quite probably,' Sandra replied. 'He's a great-looking guy. I wouldn't mind a piece of him. I've frigged myself a few times while watching one of his torrid scenes on TV.'

'I fancy him as well; he's fucking gorgeous,' Ben said, grinning lasciviously. 'Unfortunately I hear he's a committed heterosexual – what a waste!'

'One can never really tell with someone like him. Image is everything, maybe he keeps his true persuasions hidden,' Justin commented casually.

'We digress here, guys,' Sandra, interjected. 'Do you know Helen went to the annex this morning, and tried to get in to see our new patient?'

'She did what?' At last Sandra had got Justin's full attention. 'Why the hell did she do that?'

'Because she's a nosy bitch. Frankly I'd probably do the same if I saw a patient arrive in the dead of night and saw him being taken to a part of the hospital which is ostensibly closed. Helen is the registrar on duty today, and there's no mention of a new patient on her lists. What would you do in the circumstances, guys?'

'She didn't get to see him, did she?' Justin asked anxiously.

'Of course she didn't,' Sandra retorted. 'But she spoke to his aide, Mendoza. He gave her some bullshit story about structural problems in the building just to fob her off.'

'Did she believe him?' Ben asked.

Sandra shrugged her shoulders. 'Who knows? If she didn't then it will all depend on how persistent she turns out to be. She may choose to forget about it, she may not.'

'Perhaps we should make efforts to back up this story – arrange to have the staff notified officially that the area is off-limits. Use the same bullshit Mendoza dreamed up.'

'Has anyone considered that Helen might have recognised our patient?' Ben asked.

'I doubt it. He's not widely known over here,' Sandra said confidently.

'Not yet,' Justin pointed out. 'But soon it's likely his picture will be plastered all over the papers.'

'We'll have to cross that bridge when we come to it,' Sandra replied. 'If needs be we'll have to find ways to keep Helen quiet.'

'At the moment all she knows for sure is that a patient has been put in the annex, even though the rooms aren't ready yet.' Justin looked thoughtfully at his two companions. 'We just wait and see what Helen does next. If she backs off that's fine.'

'And if she continues to nose about?' Ben queried.

'The saying is, keep your friends close, your enemies even closer. So we draw her into our intimate circle. She's ripe, we know that, and soon she'll be ready for plucking. If we play our cards right, she'll be so involved she'll do anything we tell her to.'

'You sound confident.' Sandra wasn't so sure about Helen as Justin was.

'Why shouldn't I be? I am the master in sexual matters; I'll soon teach that little whore subservience.'

'Careful, Justin, don't overestimate your abilities,' Sandra warned.

'I never do,' he said with a confident laugh. 'Now we came here for lunch, didn't we? And I'm famished.'

'The food's on the table,' Sandra pointed out. 'The steak will be cold by now of course.'

'Who wants steak when we can have pussy?' Justin

jerked apart her thighs and buried his face between her legs.

Helen had been trying since lunch time to contact Max in New York. It was five hours earlier there, so he should be in his office, but every time she phoned he was either out or involved in meetings. She had been planning to casually mention Ralph Kalowski. Max was bound to know if Ralph was returning to England, he might even have some information on the operation and Ralph's mysterious patient.

She had visited Duncan for a short time after she'd returned from the annex, but she hadn't told him about her suspicions or what she'd seen. She wasn't sure she knew him well enough to burden him with her concerns. Duncan was more mobile now and managing to get about on crutches, but the insurers of his movie had insisted he stay at the Princess Beatrice for at least a few more days. Helen was rather pleased to learn that news and she had promised to spend this evening with him.

Fortunately Helen had not found cause to speak to Ben. In fact, she had made a conscious effort to avoid him. She didn't want to have to answer any awkward questions about why she'd been trying to get into the annex.

Deep in thought, she wandered along the corridor and almost walked straight into a tall man dressed in a dark blue suit. 'Ralph!' she exclaimed. 'I never expected to see you here. I thought you were still in New York with Max.'

'So I was. I flew in last night.' Ralph smiled warmly at Helen. 'Max told me you were working here. I was hoping to bump into you. By the way, he sends his love.'

Ralph looked as elegant as usual in a Savile Row suit. His slightly greying hair was immaculately coiffured, and his face was tanned. He looked fit and well. Helen had always been a little curious about Ralph's sexuality. She had never seen him with a lady friend, and he had an abnormal interest in clothes and the way he looked, while his features had a soft femininity about them. His interest in physical perfection was a tad extreme. Yet that made him a great plastic surgeon, because he could understand why his patients were so hung up on the most minor imperfections. Like Max, even his private clinics were booked up for months ahead.

'What brings you here?' Helen asked casually.

'Just checking up on a few things,' he replied dismissively. 'I had a couple of important financial matters to settle here in the UK. Nothing very serious, they just couldn't wait.'

'It's good to see you, Ralph. Have you time for coffee and a chat?

He glanced at his watch. 'Not really, I am in rather a rush.'

'Could I ask you something before you leave?'

'Anything, Helen.' He looked at her enquiringly.

'My position here doesn't involve surgery, of course. But I'd like to keep my hand in. I was hoping, if you had any surgery planned here, that I could scrub-in, maybe help out?'

'By all means,' he agreed enthusiastically. 'It'll be a pleasure to work with you, Helen. Unfortunately, I've nothing scheduled for quite some time.'

'Nothing at all?'

'Nothing,' he confirmed. 'I made a point of keeping my schedules free and clear while Max and I were engaged in setting everything up in the States. Nevertheless, when I do operate here again you are very welcome to assist.'

'That's kind of you,' Helen replied. 'Are you returning to New York soon?'

'Almost immediately,' he confirmed. 'My flight leaves Heathrow first thing tomorrow.'

'Could you please tell Max I've been trying to contact him, but he's never available when I phone.'

'It'll be my pleasure.' Ralph made an obvious point of looking at his watch again. 'Now I really must go.' He leaned forwards and gave Helen a chaste kiss on the cheek. 'I look forward to seeing you in the States. You and Max must come for the weekend. I've just bought a place on Rhode Island. It's delightful, you'll love it.'

Christopher stiffened, feeling nervous yet excited as Sandra walked into his room. She looked very smart and officious in her severe navy-blue dress with its white collar and cuffs. On her head was a starched frilly cap, just like matrons in the old days used to wear. She reminded Christopher of the stern English nanny who had looked after him as a child. Every time he was naughty nanny would pull down his trousers and spank him on his bare buttocks. She had continued to punish him like that until he was well into his teens.

Eventually Christopher had come to look forward to such spankings, and he'd been bad purely so that nanny would punish him again and again. Afterwards he had always gone to his room and masturbated himself to a climax, all the while imagining that it was nanny's hands wanking his cock.

'Have you been good today?' Sandra asked, her expression hard and unrelenting. Her dark eyes stared at him as if he were the lowest of the low.

Christopher swallowed nervously and shook his head. 'I don't think so, matron.'

'Should you be punished?' She placed the cardboard box she was carrying in front of him. 'Open it!'

With shaking hands he pulled off the lid, his excitement increasing when he caught sight of the contents; a large flesh-coloured dildo attached to a leather harness. It had another penile projection on the inside so that the wearer would be equally stimulated when using it on a victim. 'Punished, with this?' he asked.

'Yes,' she confirmed, snapping on a pair of thin latex gloves.

'Thank you,' he mumbled, reverently removing the contraption and running admiring hands over the cold

132

plastic cock that would soon be thrust inside him. He was so excited he could hardly contain himself.

Sandra lifted her skirt, and Christopher gave an ecstatic sigh as he caught sight of her freshly shaved pussy. The neat pink inner frill peeped tantalisingly out of her fleshy labial lips. 'Strap the dildo on me,' she commanded.

Christopher removed his robe and kneeled naked in front of her. Trembling with anticipation, he slipped each foot in turn through the elaborate leather straps, and eased the contraption upwards until the domed head of the inner protrusion pressed against her quim. Without saying a word, she opened her thighs wider. She was already wet and as he gave a gentle push the dildo slid smoothly inside her. Soon it was fully sheathed and the padded leather cup was pressed close to her pussy. Christopher fastened all the straps tightly so that the narrow bands dug in her fleshy hips, then kissed the head of the dildo, before shuffling back a pace to admire his handiwork.

From head to waist Sandra was every inch the stern matron, while from hips downwards she was a harlot; naked apart from suspenders, black stockings, and the huge flesh-coloured dildo standing lewdly out from her shaved quim. 'Beautiful,' Christopher groaned, feeling his prick stir with excitement.

'Move!' Sandra commanded curtly. 'Bend over that chair.'

Christopher stood up and scurried over to the hard-backed chair Sandra nearly always used during her sessions with him. He bent forwards, butt stuck up in the air, palms balanced on the hard seat, shivering with pleasure at the first stinging pain as her rubber-gloved palm made contact with his buttock cheek.

Sandra worked swiftly. Covering his buttocks with firm slaps until the skin turned crimson, burning as if it were on fire. Then Christopher felt the delicious sensation of cool oil trickling over his abused flesh. He lifted his buttocks so that viscous liquid seeped between his arse cheeks, settling in a greasy pool around his anus.

Sandra massaged the puckered opening, relaxing the muscles until she could easily slide her fingers inside. 'You're nice and tight today.' She placed the huge head of the dildo against the trembling ring and slowly she began to push it inside Christopher's anus. He couldn't repress a faint moan, it was larger than anything she had used on him before, and he doubted he would be able to accommodate the entire bulk. Yet he savoured the tightly stretched pleasure as the cool plastic gradually filled him to the absolute limit. The delicious sensation of fullness increased the pressure in his groin and he felt his own cock harden and grow.

Sandra began to move her hips, thrusting in and out very slowly, rotating her pelvis, drawing inscribed circles with the bulbous end of the dildo. It was so painfully pleasurable that Christopher could hardly contain his loud moans of bliss.

His cock twitched, tightening even more as Sandra sweated and heaved above him. A tiny dewdrop of liquid seeped from the narrow opening, and Christopher wanted to reach back, stroke his throbbing balls and curve his fingers around his penis. He was desperate to wank it to a climax while Sandra kept up the unrelenting rhythmic thrusts. Yet he could do nothing, one arm alone was not strong enough to hold him in this position of submission.

'Is that good?' Sandra asked breathlessly, as she paused for a moment, her warm stomach pressed against his buttock cheeks, the dildo remaining buried deep inside his anus.

'Yes, matron,' he groaned, lights dancing before his eyes as she moved her body from side to side, putting even more pressure on his extended flesh.

It felt so good, Christopher could barely draw breath. He gave a strangled groan as she brushed teasing fingers over his penis, then cupped his balls in her sweaty palm. She gently squeezed the sensitive flesh, increasing the pressure building inside him. Christopher felt his consciousness shrink until it was concentrated on that one portion of his body where every sensation in the universe was centred. Pain and pleasure lanced through him as Sandra started to push into him again, wanking his dick in time to her thrusts. The forceful sensations spiralled out of control as his orgasm came.

Chapter Seven

The warm water of the shower sprayed Zara's naked form. The jets were set on *pulse*, making her skin tingle and her body feel alive as she washed the remnants of shampoo from her hair. Zara's thoughts, however, were far away as she considered what the future now held for her.

Barbara Worth, her manager, had already arranged to have Warren ejected from Zara's large house in Weybridge. Now that Warren was out of her life, she had no wish ever to see him again. Whatever happened, of one thing she was certain: Warren would never achieve the stardom he craved. Most likely he would drink himself into oblivion, surrounded by hookers and hangers-on.

Now Zara could concentrate on sorting her life out, and the first and most important decision she had made concerned Colin. They had only got to know each other a few days ago, but somehow she felt as if they had been together for years. She trusted Colin far more than she had any other man. He appeared to care for her deeply, but she still wasn't totally certain he would agree to what she had in mind.

Colin loved nursing, but his abilities were virtually wasted in a place like this. Wages were so bad in the public sector he could never afford to return to the NHS.

Zara wanted him to leave the Princess Beatrice and work for her instead. She planned to offer Colin the position of personal trainer, health adviser, and lover, all rolled into one.

Most movie stars had large retinues of people who travelled with them all the time, so no-one would think it strange if Colin was always by her side. He wasn't the kind of guy who would enjoy being considered her gigolo, and Zara didn't want to short-change Colin by taking him completely away from the career he loved. That was why she had persuaded the producers of her new mini-series to give him the job of running the project's medical facility.

Zara smiled, heartened by the thought of having Colin close, living in her home, sharing her bed. She was nuts about Colin; he was the best thing that had happened to her for years, and the age difference between them didn't matter one iota.

She reached out to the shower controls, humming happily to herself. Before she could turn off the water, the shower door opened, strong arms pulled her out of the cubicle and wrapped her in a warm fluffy towel.

'You almost gave me a heart attack,' she squealed, as Colin held her close.

'Once I caught sight of your naked body through the door of the shower, I couldn't contain myself a moment longer,' he said, holding her tightly as he covered her lips with his.

Zara returned the passionate kiss, then pulled breathlessly away. 'I'm making you all wet,' she said, seeing the damp patches on his white uniform.

'Who cares?'

As she let the towel drop to the floor, he hungrily eyed her naked form. Zara instinctively sucked in her stomach and thrust out her bosom, her body tingling with excitement. She cupped her full breasts, rotated her hips teasingly, then plucked at her nipples, making them harden into firm peaks. Colin loved such provocative behaviour and she saw the growing bulge in his groin, enjoying the way she could so easily turn him on. 'Fuck me, now,' she begged.

Colin turned to lock the door, then pulled off his white cotton top. Colin's chest was virtually hairless, his smooth honey-coloured skin blemish free. Zara admired his wide chest, flat belly and muscular arms, while below, distending the thin trousers, she could see the huge line of his dick. She shivered, watching eagerly as he flung off his shoes and rolled down his trousers. The pants he wore were little more than a triangle of white fabric which barely cupped his penis and balls, with a narrow strip at the back neatly bisecting his buttock cheeks.

'You look good,' she said, smiling. 'Good enough to eat.'

'I'm nothing compared to those handsome actors you mix with,' he said with a self-deprecating grin, as he kicked off his underpants.

'You're better than all of them,' she insisted unable to tear her gaze from his impressive sexual organs. 'You are real; they are a product of the scriptwriters' fantasies. Most of them are pretty unexciting in the flesh,' she added, pushing him down on to the closed toilet seat.

Colin sat with his legs parted, and his balls resting on the white plastic, while his semi-erect cock lay angled across one muscular thigh. Zara kneeled down in front of him and reverently curved her fingers around the base of his penis, stroking it gently, watching it stiffen into perfect hardness. As her fingers worked their swift magic, drawing the flesh of his shaft rhythmically up and down, she felt her juices start to flow and her sex grow wet.

She leaned forwards, intending to pull the bulging head into her mouth, but Colin moved faster than her. Sliding his hands under Zara's arms, he pulled her upright and towards him in one smooth movement. 'God, how I want you,' Colin groaned as she stood astride his legs, her open pussy poised above him.

Hungrily he eased her hips downwards until their

bodies met, and his cock head pressed teasingly against her. Zara trembled with excitement as she slowly speared herself on its length, savouring the feel of the hot, deliciously hard shaft sliding deeper and deeper.

'I've never wanted any guy quite as much as you,' she confessed, sitting splayed across his thighs, his cock buried securely inside her.

'And I can't believe I'm actually fucking the famous Zara Dawn.' Colin smiled lovingly at her as he began to rock his hips, his cock shaft gently masturbating her inner flesh.

Zara placed her hands on his wide shoulders and raised her hips, letting his cock slide part-way out of her. 'Then feel it,' she murmured, pumping downwards, grinding her pelvis against his. Keeping her body stable by pressing her feet to the floor, she gradually increased the pace and pressure of her thrusts, feeling the pleasure begin to build inside her sex.

Her wild movements made her breasts bounce up and down. Colin just managed to grab hold of one rosy nipple, squeezing it tenderly, while his other hand delved between her open thighs. He searched her damp quim, and when he touched her clit she wriggled and squirmed with pleasure, still managing to keep up the pace of her rhythmic pumping.

Colin had the ability to turn her on just with his mere presence, but touching him aroused her even more, and the fucking was the best she'd ever had. Now the feel of his cock sliding smoothly in and out of her, coupled with the sweet sensations of his fingers touching her clit, incited her beyond awareness. She was achingly close to coming, and she felt her body start to contract around his cock as Colin squeezed her clit hard between finger and thumb, taking her up and over the edge. The orgasm exploded inside her in a glorious rush, while at the same time Zara felt the pulsing sensation as Colin came at exactly the same moment.

She collapsed limply against Colin's chest, gulping for

air. 'You're unbelievable,' she managed to gasp while covering his face with kisses.

'So are you,' he growled, kissing her back with equal passion. He didn't even pull his mouth from hers as he cupped her buttocks with his strong hands and stood up. With his cock still embedded deep inside Zara, he carried her over to the shower, moving easily as though she weighed little more than a few pounds. Colin stepped into the cubicle, directly under the spray, and stood there letting water stream over them as his erection slowly subsided. As his cock slipped smoothly out of Zara, Colin gently lowered her until her feet were resting on the tiled floor.

He took a handful of scented gel and smoothed it reverently over her body, one large hand tenderly rubbing her breasts while the other strayed downwards, slipping between her open thighs. His fingers burrowed between her legs, gradually invading her soft, wet depths, anointing them with the sweet-smelling gel.

Zara strained forwards, pressing herself against Colin's hard body. 'Deeper,' she begged.

Colin complied, thrusting two then three fingers into her hungry cunt. 'That's so good,' she gasped.

She lifted her face to the water as Colin bent his knees, forcing yet another finger inside her. Zara moaned, splaying her hands across his chest, digging her nails into his hard muscles, while Colin's bunched fingers thrust deeper, stretching her so completely that she could hardly bear the blissful torment. All the while he rubbed his fleshy thumb over her still-sensitive bud.

Water streamed across her face, dribbling into her half-open mouth as the muscles in her pelvis began to clench spasmodically. Zara's orgasm consumed her senses, and she felt as if the cubicle was rocking wildly around her as she clung on to Colin. He held her trembling body close until the violent spasms slowly subsided, and Zara became acutely conscious of his steadily growing erection as it dug into her trembling stomach. She wondered how he could recover so quickly. Some of her other lovers had been much younger than him, yet all had far less stamina than Colin.

'Are you OK?' he asked, looking down at her lovingly.

'Fine,' she replied, her voice a little shaky. 'That was amazing. We should do it all over again, but first we need to talk.'

'About what?' he asked, pulling her out of the direct spray of the water, tenderly smoothing her wet hair away from her face.

Zara wasn't quite sure how to set about broaching the subject of Colin leaving the Princess Beatrice. She was just about to speak when a light tap on the bathroom door disturbed her train of thought.

'Miss Dawn,' said a male voice. 'This is Dr Taylor. Are you all right?'

'Fine,' she half-shouted. 'I was just taking a shower.'

'Nurse Barker was worried. She seems to think you've been in there rather a long time.'

Zara resented the disturbance, the intrusion on her privacy. 'I'm OK,' she insisted, running her fingers over Colin's hardening shaft, feeling it jerk excitedly in her hands.

'I just need a quick word if you wouldn't mind,' Ben shouted through the door again. 'If you need help I can send nurse Barker in.'

'They have a key to unlock the door from the outside,' Colin mouthed a little anxiously.

'That won't be necessary, I'm coming out.' Zara cast a regretful glance at Colin's erect prick. 'I'll be back,' she whispered. 'Keep it hard and ready for me.'

She stepped from the shower and slipped on her white bathrobe. Zara's knees felt weak, her pussy ached and she had no desire to be with anyone but Colin as she tightened the belt of the robe and unlocked the bathroom door. She stepped into her room, pulling the door firmly shut behind her, having no wish for Colin's presence to be discovered by Dr Taylor or anyone else for that matter.

'What did you want, Dr Taylor?' she asked, making it

141

obvious she was unhappy at being disturbed, as she sat down at her dressing table to comb her damp hair.

'It's about your depression.' He moved a chair and sat down beside her.

Rather reluctantly she turned to face him. 'It's gone,' she pointed out. 'I'm fine as you can see.'

'The surgery has made you feel better, I can understand that,' he agreed. 'And you look wonderful, but it's likely your chronic condition may return again in the future. Depression as severe as yours isn't just a mental state, it's a malfunction of your brain chemistry.'

'I've been told that before, doctor. If it returns again, I'm certain I can handle it,' she insisted confidently.

'And if you don't?'

'Then I'll go back on the drugs.'

'What would you say if I told you that I could cure it for good?' he asked, staring at her intently. 'There's a new drug – called *Ampesoman*. It works in a similar way to *Prozac*, stimulating the serotonin levels, but with this drug the results appear to be permanent.'

'And you think I should try it?'

'Yes,' he confirmed. 'I can confidently say that if you do, you'll never have to face depression again.'

It had just started to drizzle with rain as Helen walked swiftly across the paved courtyard and into the main building. She was on her way to see Duncan, the third straight evening they had spent together.

Last night she had dined in his room, and they spent the rest of the time having sex and talking for ages. Once again she'd been the dominant partner. Despite the fact that Duncan was gradually becoming more mobile, he seemed to enjoy letting Helen be in charge and taking the lead in their lovemaking – although he had teasingly promised Helen, when they'd spoken earlier, that he intended to get his own back on her tonight.

As far as Helen knew, after she had spoken to Ralph the previous afternoon, he'd left the hospital and was by now back in New York. The fact that he had left confused her, because she was certain there was still a patient lodged in the annex. The place had now been declared off limits to most of the staff, with the same explanation she'd been given: there were problems with the structural integrity of one of the rooms. If Ralph wasn't going to operate, why was the man still being kept here? If he was just unwell, there was surely no need to go to such trouble to conceal his presence from the staff.

Tonight she had on a skimpy, provocative dress, chosen to incite Duncan, but to walk through the hospital she had covered it with her white doctor's coat. She didn't want her many visits to Duncan becoming too obvious. She wanted the staff to think that she was on call tonight and this was a professional visit.

There were a number of different ways to reach the East Wing, including the corridor which passed the annex. Helen's continued curiosity prompted her to choose that route. She climbed the stairs and paused in the stairwell, first peering cautiously through the glass panel of the door, mainly because she didn't want to be seen checking the place out again. The sheet of plastic was still stretched across the entrance to the annex. Then she saw it brushed aside by an orderly pushing a trolley, containing a number of trays of half-eaten food. As the orderly left the annex, he was followed by two men: Ben Taylor and Ralph Kalowski. Deep in conversation the two doctors turned into the corridor that led to the East Wing. Helen waited for a few minutes then followed them, all the time asking herself if Ralph had lied to her? Had he ever intended to fly back to the States this morning?

Once she reached the East Wing, she spotted Ben in the distance striding away from her, while Ralph was perched on a desk at the nurses' station, leafing through a patient's record file. 'Ralph,' Helen exclaimed, doing her best to sound surprised and pleased at the same time.

Ralph glanced up, appearing a little uncomfortable on

seeing her. 'Helen,' he acknowledged awkwardly, snapping the file shut. Before she could see the patient's name on the front he quickly stuffed it in his briefcase.

'I thought you were planning to fly back to New York this morning?'

'Something came up, and I had to delay my flight,' he said as he stood up.

'Nothing serious, I hope?' she asked in all innocence.

'No, not too serious,' he assured her. 'A minor financial matter cropped up that couldn't wait until my return. As I was passing the hospital, I just popped in to sort out a couple of billing problems with the accounts department.'

'They must be working late.' She glanced at the clock, knowing full well accounts closed at 5 p.m. and it was now well past eight.

'Overtime, I presume,' he said, looking as though his mind wasn't fully focused on their conversation. 'You're working late also?'

'Actually I'm not on duty,' she confessed. 'I'm on my way to visit a relative of Max's. His cousin was brought in a few days ago.'

'You mean that actor fellow?'

She nodded. 'Yes, Duncan Paul. Max and I ran into him in London recently. I don't know many people here yet, so we've been keeping each other company for an hour or so in the evenings.'

'Max will appreciate your kindness.'

Helen thought that most unlikely. 'I'm sure he will,' she replied. 'When will you be returning to the States then?'

'Probably tomorrow.' Ralph glanced pointedly up at the clock.

'Am I keeping you from an appointment?'

'It's a long drive back to town, and I have to pop into see my solicitor to sign some important papers. He's cancelled a personal engagement just to see me, so I can't be too late.' Ralph frowned, then clicked open his briefcase and brought out a small gold-wrapped package. 'I almost forgot. Max asked me to give this to you. I neglected to bring it with me yesterday, so I was planning to leave it for you at reception.'

'That's kind of you. Thank Max for me, will you, Ralph?' She didn't open the package, just slipped it in her pocket.

'Now, I really must be leaving,' Ralph said briskly.

'Well, drive carefully,' she said with a smile.

'I always do,' Ralph replied. 'Goodbye, Helen.'

'Bye, Ralph,' she echoed as he walked towards the lifts.

After Ralph had disappeared, Helen entered Duncan's suite. She found him sitting in one of the armchairs appearing every inch the handsome movie star in black designer trousers and a blue silk shirt. The deep colour accentuated his tan and he looked extraordinarily fit and well, not at all as if he should still be here in hospital.

'You're late,' he commented. 'Not that I'm complaining,' he added, placing a sheaf of papers on top of the pile already on the coffee table. 'You were probably busy working.'

'You're busy too, by the look of it,' Helen said, moving to stand beside his chair.

'Just trying to work a few things out. At present the crews are managing to shoot around me, but it's taking a lot of reorganisation. Because of my accident, all the action sequences not done by the stuntmen are having to be moved to the end of the shooting schedule. However, by that time we're supposed to be at Shepperton studios working on the interiors. It's as complicated as hell.'

'It must be,' she agreed. The only time Helen had been to a movie set she had thought that most of the people there seemed to spend all their time standing around doing virtually nothing. But she could appreciate how difficult it must be to have the star of the film out of action. 'Are you in most of the scenes then?'

'Luckily only about fifty per cent,' Duncan replied. 'I'm taking more of a back seat on this one. Let's forget about work though. I thought we'd eat a little later tonight, if you don't mind?'

'What do you want to do now?' she asked, although she knew by his wicked grin exactly what he had in mind. Casually she ran her fingers through his dark hair, caressing the nape of his neck. Just touching Duncan made her pulse race and her knees feel weak.

Duncan turned to look at her, still grinning cheekily. 'I've always fancied making love to you while you're wearing your white coat, doc –' he paused, then added '– and nothing else.'

'Really?' She laughed.

'Yeah. So why don't you strip right now. Take off everything but the coat and fulfil my fantasy.'

'Maybe I don't want to,' she challenged, jumping back a couple of paces as he rose swiftly to his feet.

'May I remind you that I'm in the driving seat tonight.' He moved very nimbly, considering his ankle was still in plaster, catching her before she had a chance to step teasingly away from him.

'I might not let you be,' she countered, as he jerked her close. Duncan smelled of expensive cologne and she could see the tiny pulse beating at the base of his neck. 'Careful,' she warned, 'You're still officially classed as an invalid.'

'Says who?'

Duncan slid her white coat from one lightly tanned shoulder and bent to kiss her smooth skin. The neckline of her strappy dress was low, half revealing her breasts, and the garment was held up by two of the thinnest of thin shoestring straps.

As Duncan pulled gently at the flimsy strap, she replied, 'Says your doctor, and most probably the company insuring your movie. You did say their terms were very precise.'

'Too damn precise. To hell with them.' He pulled at the strap until the fabric started to tear at the seam that attached it to the front bodice of her dress. 'Forgive me,' he added, ripping it away so that the silky fabric slid

146

downwards to expose one breast. 'I hope the dress wasn't too expensive.'

'Who cares,' she said dismissively. 'It doesn't matter anyway,' she added, only interested in the thought of imminent sex. He ripped the other strap and the dress slid smoothly downwards, landing in a pool around her feet. Helen was left wearing only a brief pair of lemon lace panties and her white coat.

'I now have every intention of demonstrating to my bossy doctor how well I actually am!' Duncan growled as he cupped her naked breasts, stroking and kneading them with the palms of his hands, rubbing her nipples hard with his thumbs until her entire bosom throbbed with delight.

'Do you?' Her eyes glazed over as he pressed the heel of his hand against her pubis. 'If you're turned on by the sight of the white coat, perhaps you'd like me to hang a stethoscope around my neck as well?' she teased, as he dug his fingers into the gusset of her panties, pressing the thin cotton between the lips of her sex.

'I can't think of anything erotic to do with a stethoscope,' he countered, easing down her panties, letting them drop to the floor. 'Can you?'

'Not off hand,' she managed to say. By now he was stroking her naked pussy, his fingers delving in the crack of her sex. She gave a moan of pleasure as he ran them along the moist channel until he reached her clit, pausing to rub it gently until she moaned again.

Duncan kissed her with passion, while his fingers strayed further, teasingly stroking the paper-thin skin between her vagina and anus. The tickling bliss sent her senses spiralling out of control. 'You'll let me do anything I want?' he whispered, pulling his hand back to burrow his fingers in the soft wet depths of her cunt.

'Yes.' She bore down against his fingers, her senses so titillated, her need for him so strong that she would agree to any demands he made of her.

Duncan jerked her close, grinding his pelvis against

her naked belly. She could feel the strength and size of his erection as he held her hard against him, his hands cupping her arse cheeks through the thick cotton of her white coat.

'A hospital bed isn't my idea of absolute comfort,' he commented, gradually leading her into the adjoining room. 'Apologies for not swinging you into my arms and carrying you, à la Richard Gere, but I doubt my ankle would stand up to that just yet.'

'I'll take a rain-check on that then,' she said, suddenly finding herself sprawled across his bed, Duncan staring down at her with his compelling dark eyes.

'You'd get loads more patients if you carried out all your consultations dressed like this,' Duncan teased, joining her on the mattress.

'You think so?' She laughed, hardly able to believe she could feel so happy. 'Ouch,' she exclaimed as he pulled her close, and her hip made contact with a hard object in her coat pocket.

'What's wrong?'

'This,' she replied, removing the package Max had sent her.

'A present for me, perchance?' Duncan asked, smiling expectantly. 'You shouldn't have, Helen.'

'I didn't,' she replied rather awkwardly.

'I was just teasing, I wasn't really expecting it to be for me,' he said. 'Don't forget, I'm supposed to be an actor.'

'It's from Max. A colleague of his brought it over from the States.'

'And you haven't opened it yet?' Duncan took the package and placed it on her stomach, watching it rise and fall with each breath she took. 'Why not? After all he wrapped it very prettily.'

She knew he was still teasing but that didn't help. 'Duncan, I just don't want to be reminded of Max tonight.'

She had already decided to break off her relationship with Max as soon as she saw him again. It was only now that she had come to realise how much she'd let Max rule her life in the past.

'My poor cousin will be so disappointed,' Duncan said, a rather cynical smile hovering on his lips as he looked thoughtfully at the package.

'He won't know.'

'I reckon Max is pretty much in the dark about a lot of things at present.' Duncan idly played with her pubic curls. 'For instance, I doubt he'd ever guess what you're doing right now.'

'I don't care if he knows everything,' she said, desperate to feel those teasing fingers sliding between the lips of her sex. 'Max and I are over and done with, I just haven't got around to telling him yet. Frankly I'm not sure he'll care overmuch. He doesn't think of me as a person, he just likes to control people.'

'So you've figured him out at last,' Duncan replied. 'Don't get me wrong, I'm fond of the guy. But he's got a propensity to use people, and he can be pretty selfish about his own needs, leaving little consideration for others.'

'You're probably right,' she agreed, eyeing the enticing bulge at his crotch, wanting to forget completely about Max and his stupid present. 'If you're so keen to know what's inside, then open it yourself.'

'I was always like this about presents. I remember being so excited at Christmas, when I was a kid,' he said, grinning. 'There's something exciting about not knowing what's inside,' he added, picking up the package and shaking it.

As Duncan stripped off the stiff gold paper, Helen concentrated her attentions on unbuttoning his shirt, far more interested in unwrapping this male package than the one sent by Max.

Opening the box, Duncan pulled out small silver clips from which dangled delicate filigree flowers. 'Earrings?' she exclaimed. 'That's odd, Max knows I rarely wear them.'

'Not earrings.' Duncan gave a throaty chuckle. 'I know

Max all too well – these are far more his style. They are nipple clamps, my sweet.'

'Nipple clamps!' Helen recalled Max's promise to her before he'd left, and her stomach contracted with nervous excitement as she stared at the surprisingly pretty objects. 'I've never seen any before.'

'What an innocent you are,' Duncan teased, bending forwards to concentrate his attentions on her left nipple, rubbing it and squeezing it into a firm peak. 'Let's try one for size.' He pulled the tender flesh, stretching the teat, then fastened the clamp at its base.

Helen squeaked with surprise. It was the strangest of sensations; slightly uncomfortable, yet deliciously titillating, all at the same time.

The clamps were cleverly fashioned, designed to compress the nipple just enough, so that the wearer eventually reached the plateau where pleasure and pain intertwined. By now Duncan had imprisoned both her nipples in the decorative clamps and, as Helen moved, the delicate silver flowers brushed gently against her breasts.

'They feel strange,' she said. Judging by the way Duncan was looking at her, he found the decorations highly stimulating.

'I happen to know that Max frequents this particular jeweller quite often. He once told me that the guy makes clit clamps as well. They are cute little things, designed purely to keep a woman in a constant state of arousal.'

Helen couldn't even begin to imagine what that would feel like – the pulling sensation, the ever-present pressure. 'I don't think I could handle that. I'd never be able to concentrate on my work,' she admitted with an uneasy laugh. 'The thought is extremely titillating, but don't you think that's carrying things a bit too far?'

'Depends what turns you on, I suppose. Every person is different.' He flicked the filigree flowers, and the slight movement sent a shiver of pleasure coursing through her nipples and down her spine. Not surprisingly the sensations made her pussy grow wetter than ever.

'Looking at you naked turns me on,' she said, easing off his shirt. 'The sight of your muscular chest is very stimulating. Who needs sex toys, when I have you around?'

'Kind of you to say so,' Duncan replied, sighing softly as she splayed her hands across his pecs, pinching his small flat nipples. 'It doesn't take much to please you then, does it?'

'I did say naked,' Helen reminded him. 'So take your trousers off as well,' she added, taking hold of the zip of his flies, and sliding it downwards, finding that every movement she made served to increase the pressure on her restrained teats.

Duncan needed no more prompting to slip off his trousers, and to her delight she discovered he'd not bothered with underwear. His cock was already rigid, rearing away from his flat belly. It looked so delicious she had to kiss it. Bending forwards, she tenderly mouthed the domed head, running her tongue round the edge of the glans. 'That feels good,' Duncan groaned, shuddering with bliss.

She ran her fingers slowly down the impressive shaft. 'I know a guy who's had his penis implanted with a line of silver balls. Do you fancy that, Duncan?'

'About as much as you fancy a clit clamp, I reckon,' he replied, with wry amusement. 'Some folks are way too keen on body piercing for my restrained tastes, although it's all the rage at present. Some of my close friends have opted for a neat Prince Albert, but even the thought of having a ring through the end of my dick sends shivers down my spine.'

'You're supposed to be the great macho hero,' she teased. 'You're not supposed to be afraid of anything.'

'We could come to an agreement,' he suggested with a wicked grin. 'You have your clit pierced, just here –' he demonstrated by gently squeezing the root of the sensitive peak '– with a neat gold ring, and I'll consider a Prince Albert.'

'I think I'll take a rain-check on that too,' she said,

running her hands upwards to tenderly caress his muscular stomach and chest.

'Well, what about a cast of my penis?' he suggested, his fingers continuing to tantalisingly stroke her pussy, feeling it grow wetter as her juices flowed.

'To use when I'm alone in bed?'

'Yeah. I could have it made up in latex, even have a vibrator inserted in the middle if you like. A good friend of mine keeps a cast of his dick on the mantelpiece in his rumpus room, along with casts of his girlfriends' pussies. He's managed to build up quite a collection.'

'I think I prefer the feel of your fingers to plaster of Paris,' she gasped as he continued to play with her clit.

'Why not my mouth?' he ran the tip of his tongue over the ends of each compressed nipple, anointing the teats with his saliva. 'Or my cock?'

'Both. Either. I don't care.' The tight-fitting clamps magnified the sensitivity of each nipple, and even the gentle brushing motion made them tingle with delight.

Helen groaned as Duncan pulled one throbbing teat into his mouth, sucking on it, his teeth grazing the hard metal. He slid his fingers inside her, making her wriggle and squirm with pleasure as they ventured even deeper. 'Ask me,' he urged. 'Beg me to fuck you.'

'Please,' she gasped, moving her hips with desperate urgency, wanting his finger to be replaced by the hardness of his cock. 'Fuck me now, Duncan.'

He moved to kneel between her open thighs, his powerful body looming over her. This magnificent man was just about to fuck her and she recognised one of the primary scenes in her own favourite fantasy. She had run it so many times in her mind that the reality of it now seemed somehow surreal, as if this were all still part of an erotic dream. Yet when Duncan thrust his cock deep into the aching emptiness of her sex, the blissful sensations were as real as real could be.

He tilted his hips, altering his angle of penetration, ensuring each loving thrust would further stimulate her clit. Then, never taking his eyes off her face, he began to move, settling into a smooth unrelenting rhythm. He fucked her so exquisitely that the pressure in her groin grew, mingling with the tortured bliss that assailed her breasts. Helen's pleasure magnified, merging into a sensation so strong that when her climax came it was the best she'd ever known.

Once again it was very late when Helen left Duncan. There had been no point in even attempting to repair her dress, so she'd left it with Duncan and just wore her white coat, tightly buttoned, with only her brief panties underneath. She felt sated and replete, her pussy aching pleasantly, as she walked along the deserted hospital corridors. Duncan had removed the clamps, but her breasts still felt engorged, and her nipples ached almost as if they were still confined. Tonight she had reached the ultimate pinnacle of pleasure, a sensation so complete she'd never achieved it with anyone else before.

Helen's medical training told her that sexual attraction hinged on a number of things – a physically appealing partner, pheromones, and most importantly what went on in the mind. The brain sent messages to the senses, sometimes turning pure lust into an emotion that was radically different and far more complex. She was intensely attracted to Duncan, but her desire for him was pure body chemistry, nothing else; she barely knew him as an individual. He was her ideal man in fantasy, if not in fact.

Perhaps one of these days she'd set herself the task of writing a theses on why people were attracted to one another. Of course she would need to do a massive amount of physical research, the thought of which titillated her. However, at present all her thoughts and needs were focused on Duncan Paul. She had a few days yet before he was due to leave the hospital, and she planned to put that time to good use, and forget about the future for now.

Helen knew that she would soon have to think about contacting Max to break off their relationship. She still hadn't decided if she would go and work in the States, which might be a good idea, as she would gain valuable experience there. Nevertheless, she had no intention now of working for Max when she got to America; she was not going to allow herself to get into the position where he had control over her life ever again.

This evening Helen had let herself forget about Ralph and his mysterious patient. She didn't even bother to attempt to return home via the annex, she just walked towards the main staircase and lifts. Her thoughts were on personal matters and she noticed very little. It didn't even strike her as odd that the corridor leading to the theatre suites was still brightly lit. Usually at night it was in pitch dark and the theatres were locked.

Helen probably wouldn't even have stopped to look, if she hadn't caught a brief glimpse, through the glass doors, of a man who looked just like Ralph. The man was wearing a green operating gown, and on closer examination it was definitely Ralph. He was just leaving the post-op recovery room; patients were kept there for some time after surgery, before being taken back to their rooms.

Ralph had lied, when she had spoken to him only a few hours ago. She could only presume he did have something to hide and his patient tonight was the mysterious Mr X. Then she saw Ben Taylor, wearing a white coat over his green scrubs, accompanying the patient out of post-op recovery.

The patient was lying prone on the trolley. She couldn't see who he was as his face was totally swathed in bandages, even his eyes were covered. Judging by the drips and drains that surrounded him, the surgery had been very extensive. Helen found that strange, because she knew that Ralph did not like carrying out more than one procedure at the same time – it was one of his idiosyncrasies. It was not his style to do such obviously extensive reconstruction work during one operation.

Not wanting to be seen, Helen looked round for a hiding place. The only refuge in sight was an unlocked linen closet. She slipped inside, pulling the door shut, leaving just a crack to peep through as she watched Ralph, Ben and the patient walk past her. It wasn't a regular porter pushing the trolley; it was one of the burly bodyguards dressed in a Princess Beatrice uniform.

Helen was now even more determined to discover what was actually going on around there, as well as the patient's true identity. Routine procedures were not done in the dead of night and patients were not hidden away from hospital staff.

She waited until everyone had disappeared from sight, then left the sanctuary of the linen cupboard and made her way down to the ground floor. As she walked back to her apartment, Helen's thoughts were in turmoil. She had to speak to someone about this and the only person she could chance trusting was Duncan. Helen decided that she would confide in him first thing in the morning.

When she reached the staff apartment block, she was surprised to hear a lot of noise coming from Sandra's flat. It sounded as though she was having a party, and the music and laughter were very loud considering it was late. Helen couldn't help wondering what was going on inside and she unconsciously slowed her pace as she walked past Sandra's front door.

'Going somewhere?' Ben's voice called from a distance. Helen jumped nervously and turned to watch him striding towards her, breathing heavily as if he had been running to catch up with her.

'Just to bed,' she replied trying to sound composed. 'Have you been operating?' she asked, eyeing his scrubs.

'Goodness, no,' Ben lied smoothly. 'I spilled some ether on my clothes. The smell was so bad I had to change and this was all the night nurse could come up with.'

'You couldn't exactly walk about the place in your underwear,' she said lightly, conscious of how little she had on under her white coat.

'No.' he smiled. 'Do you know, Helen, I get the feeling you're avoiding me.'

'Whatever made you think that?' she replied, trying to sound surprised.

'Was it what happened in the pool?' he asked, taking hold of her arm. 'Did Justin and I upset you? You ran off pretty quickly.'

'You were so busy, I'm surprised you noticed,' she countered dryly.

'Are you jealous?

'Of course I'm not jealous. I don't own you, Ben, and I wouldn't want to. What you choose to do with Justin is none of my business,' she said stiffly, suddenly unable to get the erotic vision of the two men together out of her mind.

'I could respond by saying I'm a tad jealous of your liaison with Duncan Paul,' Ben replied. 'Are you fucking him, perchance?'

She felt as though her cheeks had gone suddenly red, although she hoped they hadn't. 'Duncan and I share a mutual friend, that's why I'm visiting him.'

'You mean Max Fenton? Duncan is his cousin, so I'm reliably informed.'

She nodded. 'As you may know, Max and I worked together and – '

'You and he were lovers,' Ben interjected. 'Don't bother denying it. Sandra saw him arse-fucking you in maternity the first day you arrived.'

'Can't anyone have any privacy around here,' she complained indignantly, embarrassed by the thought that they had been spied on that afternoon.

'Sandra knows everything that goes on in this hospital, haven't you realised that yet?' Ben's expression became serious. 'Look, Helen, something's worrying me, and I think we should talk.'

'Talk about what, my sex life?'

'You know damn well I don't mean that,' he said. 'You're no fool, Helen. I'm certain that you've figured out there are some pretty heavy things going down here.'

'What do you mean by heavy?' she asked, knowing she had to proceed very cautiously. She didn't want to let on that she knew anything, but she was secretly hoping that Ben might be planning to confide in her. She was also aware that he was close to Sandra and Justin, as well as being up to his neck in most things that went on around there, including the tissue of lies surrounding tonight's operation. She had no idea why he was even attempting to speak to her now, and she knew she couldn't chance trusting him. Yet she still liked Ben, despite everything. She could be coming to totally the wrong conclusion, but she did pause to wonder if he was now regretting getting so involved in all the intrigue.

'We can't talk here, that's for certain.' Ben glanced up and down the corridor a little nervously as if concerned about being seen with her. 'Let's go inside, join the party.'

'If you want to speak about private matters, then surely it's a pretty silly place to go. We won't get any privacy, judging by the noise, and someone is bound to overhear anything you tell me,' she pointed out.

'It's a party, Helen. No one will be interested in us, they'll be too intent on getting drunk and enjoying themselves.'

Helen frowned. There was logic to his argument. If they didn't go to Sandra's she would have to invite Ben up to her apartment. Frankly she had no wish to be completely alone with him. At least in Sandra's flat there would be other people around. Nevertheless, she knew she couldn't let herself believe anything he told her – but there was a chance she might be able to garner at least a smattering of the truth from the conversation. Ben might let something drop, something minor that might help her put two and two together.

'I'll come,' she agreed. 'But I can't stay long.'

'This won't take that long, I promise,' he said, smiling in relief.

He pushed open Sandra's front door, and walked inside. Feeling nervous, and very reluctant, Helen followed him. The noise of music, talking and laughter grew considerably louder, and the whole place looked to be in semi-darkness. They went into the kitchen, which was brightly lit and devoid of partygoers. It was filled with mess and clutter, including lots of bottles of various drinks, half-empty glasses, overflowing ashtrays, spilled beer on the floor and piles of used crockery in the sink.

'Now, what did you want to tell me?' Helen turned, standing with her back to the kitchen table, as Ben leaned casually against a cluttered worktop.

'Ben wants to tell you that you shouldn't be pushing your pretty little nose into things that don't concern you,' Justin announced as he strolled into the kitchen, the sound of his voice making Helen stiffen nervously. He was wearing only a pair of tight-fitting leather trousers that amply served to emphasise the considerable bulge at his crotch.

'What things that don't concern me?' Helen sounded far bolder than she actually felt. She was tempted to try and make a run for it, but Justin was between her and the only door, and there was no other way of escape. Where Ben was concerned, she'd let her misguided emotions take precedent over her judgement. He wasn't Mr Nice Guy, of that she was certain: he'd set her up. All she could do now was pretend she didn't feel threatened or scared and try and brazen this out.

'You know what I'm talking about,' Justin sneered scathingly.

'I am a doctor at this hospital. The board therefore entrusted me with a certain amount of responsibility towards staff and patients,' she said, presuming he was referring to her efforts to gain entry to the annex. 'I have every right to know all that is going on around here,' she added, trying to hide her fearful apprehension as Justin moved closer. She felt like a rat in a trap.

'So you have a responsibility towards your patients, do you?' Justin was standing so close to her now that she could feel his wine-tainted breath on her cheek, and she was certain she could detect the odour of spent sex clinging to his body.

'Yes, I do,' she agreed, her heart pounding out of control.

'Towards Duncan Paul?' Ben asked.

'To all my patients,' she replied, not even looking at Ben, as she dare not take her eyes off Justin, who looked ready to pounce on her at any moment.

'Does that responsibility include fucking?' Justin asked with a cynical smile.

'Duncan and I are friends . . .' she faltered, as Justin reached out and jerked open the top of her white coat to reveal her naked breasts.

'Very close friends, it seems!' Justin raised his eyebrows enquiringly. 'And do you visit all your patients dressed like this?'

'Get your hands off me.' She tried to pull away from him, still regretting her desperately foolish decision to chance coming in here with Ben. But her retreat was brought short by the kitchen table, just behind her.

'Scared?' Justin taunted.

'Helen, we're not going to hurt you,' Ben said reassuringly. 'Are we, Justin?'

'Of course not.' Justin pulled open her coat completely, giving a low whistle of approval as he looked her up and down. 'Very nice. Did I neglect to mention in the pool that you've got a really great body, Helen.'

She tried to pull her coat together, but Justin stopped her, jerking the garment down her arms and away from her, leaving her clad in only her brief panties. Helen stiffened, acutely conscious of the way Justin and Ben were now staring at her, their desire all too obvious. Surprisingly that made her fear subside a little, there was a certain kind of power in knowing that they both wanted her, especially after they had so summarily rejected her by the pool side.

Very aware of the sudden change in mood between her and the two men, and the sudden wanton need that filled her body, she glanced down at her breasts. Her nipples still looked ripe and redly engorged as a direct result of the nipple clamps. For a moment she almost wished she'd left them on, imagining how much they would serve to arouse Justin and Ben. 'Did I happen to mention you were an arsehole, Justin.'

'Feisty as well now, are we?' Justin sneered. 'Who would have believed it. Sandra told me that not so long ago, when she watched Max arse-fucking you, Helen, that you were delightfully submissive.'

'If you know Max was fucking me, you must also know that we are involved. So you should be careful, shouldn't you, Justin,' she challenged. 'One word from me and Max will have you sacked.'

Justin clapped his hands slowly. 'Very clever, Helen. But threats of any kind won't wash with me. I'm pretty sure that Max doesn't know you're fucking his famous cousin. Max is a possessive kind of guy, isn't he? What say I let him know that his piece of pussy is fucking Duncan and anyone else she can lay her hands on.'

'Do it,' she hissed. 'I don't bloody care. Do anything you want, Justin!'

'Anything?' Justin thrust his hand into her panties and cupped her pubis, his fingers slowly easing their way inside the damp slit of her sex. Despite her fear and loathing the feel of his fingers exploring her quim inflamed her senses, and for a moment she almost wanted him. Helen tried to keep control of herself, telling herself not to give into the wild, illogical urges that suddenly consumed her thoughts.

'I don't blame you for wanting Duncan Paul.' Justin's fingers delved deeper. 'He's famous and fabulous looking. I wouldn't mind a piece of him myself. Does he have a big cock? Does it feel good when he shoves it inside you?'

'Go away and leave me alone,' she said, her voice trembling, while his burrowing fingers made her knees grow weaker and weaker with longing.

'But you don't want him to leave you alone, do you, Helen,' Ben taunted, watching them closely.

'That's right. Relax, sweetie, let's get to know each other better,' Justin purred soothingly. 'We can work this all out. You can become part of our special little group. Then we'll let you in on all our secrets,' he added, still continuing to frig her, his voice becoming almost hypnotic in its intensity.

'Secrets?' she asked tremulously.

'We all have secrets.' Justin ran the tip of his tongue across her bottom lip, and Helen fought the temptation to open her mouth, let him kiss her properly. She wanted to press herself closer to him and savour the alien feel of his pierced tongue. 'Some secrets are more interesting than others of course,' he continued in a mesmerising tone that made her head spin. 'If you come with me, I can show you,' he purred, keeping his hand pressed to her quim, as his other arm slid around her waist.

Chapter Eight

*F*eeling slightly detached from reality, Helen found herself letting Justin lead her into the elaborately decorated bedroom. The room was warm, the air thick with the odour of perfume and sex. Helen had eyes for only one thing as she stared in amazement at the woman on the bed – bound and blindfolded, she could neither move nor see.

It didn't even register for a moment that the woman was Sandra. Helen was so aroused, so overcome by the erotic vision that confronted her. She had never realised how uniquely stimulating and exciting bondage could be. She felt her pussy grow wetter and her heart rate increase as she looked at the lush, full-breasted female tied to the four-poster bed.

Thin ropes were looped around Sandra's ankles and wrists, then tied tightly to the four corner posts of the bed. Sandra could barely move, and her legs were held so wide apart that her sex gaped open. Helen was rooted to the spot, never even realising that Justin was locking the door as she stared at the vivid slash of Sandra's quim. Her flesh looked moist, rosy and engorged. Helen's head swum almost as if she were intoxicated.

Sandra's breasts were so huge that they spilled over the sides of her body, the nipples red and swollen, tightly compressed by evil-looking nipple clamps. They were a far cry from the dainty objects Max had sent to Helen. She pitied Sandra, and yet a part of her almost envied the captive's discomfort.

'Justin, is that you?' Sandra asked, restlessly moving her hips. The pink lighting in the room cast deeper crimson shadows on the valley of her sex, and Helen was filled with the sudden need to press her lips to the hot flesh, savour the musky odour of Sandra's sex. It was many years since she'd been with Sandra, and she couldn't even recall how it felt to pleasure a woman with her mouth.

'Someone has come to see you,' Justin teased, picking up a peacock feather, trailing it over her breasts, down her belly, across her shaved pelvis. The tickling sensations drove Sandra wild and when Justin drew the feather slowly between her legs, she was tantalised almost beyond endurance. 'Harder,' she pleaded.

Sandra's frustrated whimpers pierced Helen's belly, further inciting her senses. Lust filled the air, oozing thickly over Helen's bare skin, making her shiver with eager anticipation as she heard Ben moving behind her. She uttered not a word of protest as he eased off her panties.

'No one will do anything you don't want,' he promised her as he slid leather straps around her body, just below her bust.

Helen glanced down, watching with detached fascination as Ben cupped her breasts in an elaborate garment. It was fashioned out of strips of leather and chains, with silver rings that encircled her breasts, just a shade larger in circumference than her nipples. When Ben tightened the straps at the back, her breasts were tightly compressed by the garment pushing her nipples forwards until her flesh bulged lewdly though the confining rings.

'Pretty.' Justin tossed aside the feather and stepped over to Helen. 'When Ben is finished preparing you, I give you permission to do anything you like to Sandra.'

'Who will do anything they like to me?' Sandra asked agitatedly.

'You have to guess,' Justin replied. 'That's all part of the game.'

He turned back to help Ben finish dressing Helen. The bottom of the garment was similar to the top, all straps, buckles and chains. Her pussy was to be confined however by a one-and-a-half-inch-wide strip of leather, fastened at both the back and front by tiny buckles. Just before it was fastened at the front, Justin slipped a small pink object between Helen's legs, placing it directly over her clitoris. The objected reminded Helen of a sea anemone, with tiny pink pliable fronds that brushed against her sensitive flesh. When the buckles were tightened the fronds dug into her and the sensation was surprisingly pleasurable.

'Look at yourself,' Justin said, turning her towards the mirror.

She looked so unlike herself, her hair tangled and in disarray, her lips still semi-swollen by Duncan's kisses, her pale flesh criss-crossed by the leather straps of the erotic garment. Her breasts were so tightly confined, it made her nipples look even bigger, even more pronounced as they bulged obscenely out of the metal rings.

Justin held a small plastic object in his hand, and attached to it was a wire that ran down her back to the tickler lodged next to her clit. She wanted him to turn it on, to experience the teasing pressure, but he just slipped the battery holder under one of the straps strained tightly across her buttocks.

'You are beautiful.' Ben looked at her with admiration as if he desired her above all else. For a second she almost forgot his perfidy and the fact that he'd so recently rejected her in favour of Justin.

'Now for your outfit, Ben,' Justin prompted, watching Helen turn and walk, almost as if she were mesmerised, towards Sandra who was still lying helpless on the bed. Feeling aroused and excited, yet somehow detached from reality, Helen stared down at Sandra's huge nipples

164

tightly compressed by the clamps, the metal teeth biting visibly into her flesh.

Helen gently brushed her finger across the tip of one teat, and Sandra gave a pleading moan. Without saying a word, Helen forced open one of the clamps, releasing the abused nipple. It looked so sore, so tempting, that she couldn't resist pulling it into her mouth, sucking on it hard, making Sandra squirm with pleasure.

'The other one,' Sandra begged. 'Take it off, they are too tight. Justin knows how much pain they cause me.'

'But you adore pain,' Justin said to her, now wearing an equally outrageous garment. His penis and balls were cupped by a large ring, which pushed his sexual organs up and forwards so that they appeared even bigger.

He never took his eyes off Helen as she released Sandra's other tortured teat. Before she could bend down and take it in her mouth, Justin took hold of the red, angry nipple, twisting it cruelly while his mouth sought Helen's. As he kissed her, Helen pushed her tongue into his mouth, savouring the bizarre feel of the metal stud that punctured his tongue. Suddenly, Helen realised how easily Justin was managing to gain control of her senses. She pulled back and stared at him, hardly able to believe she had allowed this to happen. Helen despised Justin, but there was a cruel sensuality about him that she found utterly compelling.

Justin smiled, as if he knew exactly what she was thinking, and handed her a long, thin, leather-covered switch, with a handful of leather strands at its thinnest end. It was a cross between a whip and a riding crop. 'Sandra likes to be punished,' he explained, twisting one of her erstwhile girlfriend's sore nipples, until he forced a squeal of anguish from her.

'It turns her on even more. If you don't believe me look at her buttocks. I've already punished her quite thoroughly, but I think a few more strokes are needed to finish the job.'

Helen looked down at Sandra, trussed and totally

helpless, then at the instrument of agony she held in her hand. She suddenly had a compelling urge to use it, the need lancing through her like a physical pain. Despite all that had happened, all the years that had passed, a secret part of herself still lusted after Sandra's lush womanly curves. Perhaps deep down most people had bisexual urges that they kept buried until the perfect opportunity presented itself.

There was a faint line of a lash mark curving around Sandra's left hip, but her belly was still pale and unblemished. Helen gave an experimental flick of her wrist, and the strands of the whip brushed against Sandra's stomach, but the blow didn't even leave a mark. Clearly she had to put a little more effort behind it next time.

Helen pulled back and hit Sandra again straight across her belly and naked mound of Venus. The blow was much harder, and the strands left a faint red mark while Sandra's belly shuddered from the assault.

'Very good,' Justin said softly, like a teacher encouraging his pupil. 'Keep every blow separate, try not to hit her in the same place again.

Helen did as he suggested, laying the blows lower, until Sandra's bare pubis and thighs were criss-crossed by faint red wheals, and she moaned aloud from the painful pleasure.

'You've found your calling,' Justin teased, as Ben moved to stand beside him.

Watching Helen whip Sandra had turned Justin on even more. His prick was now rigidly distended, his balls tightly protruding from the metal ring. Ben now had on a similar style of garment, but his balls, and erect cock were covered by skin-tight thin black leather. The design made his penis look doubly menacing. Helen wondered if he had ever fucked anyone while his dick was sheathed in the leather. Her entire body felt weak as she imagined what it would feel like to have the leather-covered organ powering inside her.

'Sandra isn't quite ready yet,' Justin pointed out, still teasing and playing with his helpless victim's nipples.

He contrasted the pain with pleasure, leaning forwards to kiss her passionately now and then. 'Use the other end of the whip.'

Helen turned it in her hand. Holding the end decorated by the thin lash strands, she slapped the thin leather-bound handle across the inside of Sandra's thigh. It made a satisfying smacking sound as it seared her flesh. Remembering Max's erotic domination of her own body, Helen aimed the second blow across Sandra's open quim – driven on by Sandra's soft groans of anguish to repeat the blow again.

'Please,' Sandra begged. 'More.'

This time Helen aimed far more precisely, ensuring the tip of the switch caught Sandra's clit. It was already deep scarlet, and hugely swollen. Yet on receipt of the blow it appeared to stiffen even more, stimulated into life by pain.

'Doesn't that feel good?' Justin purred, moving behind Helen.

'Yes,' she replied in a low voice, trembling with excitement as she felt his pierced cock dig into the small of her back. She dare not admit it, but she would have given anything for him to bare her sex, and thrust his delicious organ deep inside her.

'Move round, position yourself between her thighs,' Justin urged. 'Just a few more strokes and she'll be ready for anything.'

Helen found herself obeying Justin, climbing on the bed to crouch between Sandra's open thighs. Helen smelled the strong odour emanating from Sandra's pussy; rich, spicy, intoxicating and familiar, even after all this time.

Employing great care, she punished Sandra with the pliable end of the switch. One blow across each fleshy labial lip, one straight down the line of her sex, and a final stinging slap across her hungry clit. Sandra sounded close to a climax as she gave a sobbing gasp of surrender.

'Now use this!' Justin thrust the most unexpected of

objects into her hand. Helen glanced down at it, almost laughing at the absurdity of the moment.

'Are you serious?'

'Deadly. It works, try it,' he told her. 'Use the head, press it down hard on her clitoris.'

Helen turned on the electric toothbrush, wincing slightly at the noisy buzz it made, watching the white and green head vibrate and rotate. Tentatively she applied the tips of the bristles to the sensitive hood of the tiny scarlet organ.

The sensations drove Sandra insane. She thrashed about the bed, straining against her bonds until the ropes dug cruelly into her skin. Helen wondered if it could really feel that good, and she was tempted to try the brush on herself – but not here in front of Ben and Justin, she wasn't ready for something that outrageous just yet. Nevertheless part of her longed to experience those sharp little bristles brushing her pussy, scrubbing teasingly against her clit.

The buzzing sound filled her ears, and Helen barely heard the sobbing moans of pleasure as she systematically applied the rotating bristles up and down Sandra's open quim. She appeared close to her climax, and the temptation grew inside Helen until it became an all-consuming need. She discarded all pretence as she threw away the toothbrush and buried her face in the alluringly moist slit of Sandra's pussy. It tasted musky and salty, acting like an aphrodisiac on her senses. Helen hungrily lapped at the dewy flesh, running the tip of her tongue up and down the narrow valley, before pausing to circle Sandra's pert little bud. It was amazingly large and it stiffened just like a tiny prick, welcoming the adoration of Helen's lips, as they encircled its root, nibbling and sucking until it grew even harder.

Sandra cried out, wildly bucking her hips. Helen forced her to keep still by digging her fingers deep into the flesh of her inner thighs. She pulled the swollen lips even wider apart, stabbing her tongue into Sandra's greedy cunt – teasing, circling, sucking, until her willing victim could hold back no longer.

Helen felt Sandra's stomach muscles contract as violent waves of ecstasy flooded her quim. It pulsed against Helen's mouth and she was filled with the need to experience the delicious pleasures for herself.

Justin seemed to sense what she was thinking immediately. Stepping behind Helen, he pressed the switch which turned on the tickler. The slender nodules of the sea anemone, which had been gently caressing her as she moved, burst into joyful life. The tiny fronds vibrated against her sensitive flesh with amazing speed, stimulating each nerve ending to its fullest extent. Helen was amazed that something so small could generate such blissful sensations.

She tensed, thrusting her buttocks upwards, moving her face from Sandra's pussy to press tender kisses on her still trembling stomach. Justin unbuckled the leather gusset, between Helen's thighs, that held the clit tickler in place. She moaned with distress, not wanting to be denied the pleasurable sensations even though she was desperate to feel him inside her. Justin curved his arm around her, holding the tickler firmly against her pussy, yet letting the strap fall away from her sex. Helen felt his cock-head press hard against the entrance to her vagina, as she shivered, anticipating the singular delight of being forced to accommodate his uniquely embellished organ.

The silver bars made the experience doubly delicious as he smoothly invaded her soft depths. His hot hardness, coupled with the cold bars, slid deeper, driving her wild with pleasure, while the little clit tickler buzzed relentlessly on and on.

Helen was beside herself as Justin rode her from behind, pounding his cock harder and harder into her willing flesh. His thrusts, and the sweetly throbbing assault on her clit continued as the pleasure grew inside her, then she lost control completely.

* * *

Colin lay on his side, knees slightly bent. Zara's buttocks were pressed close to his belly with his cock buried deep inside her. They lay there, not moving a muscle, just savouring the sensual sensations. 'Keep your breathing even,' Colin whispered in her ear. 'And try to work your internal muscles very slowly.'

They had both read about Tantric sex, how it was supposed to enhance and extend the pleasure. Masters of the art were said to spend hours making love, turning it into an almost religious experience.

Colin and Zara were trying it for the first time, discovering that it wasn't as easy as it appeared to be. It took enormous control to hold back on their orgasms, yet still retain the constant heightened state of pleasure. With his dick buried inside her the need to come was driving him insane, he doubted he could continue this for much longer, let alone almost indefinitely.

'Careful,' Colin groaned as Zara tensed her internal muscles, slowly milking his cock, appearing to have far more control over her body than he did over his. Zara gave a soft laugh and continued the erotic assault on his senses.

'Can't you hang on?'

'Not much longer,' he gasped, feeling her vagina tighten in waves around his engorged penis. In the past, some of his Army colleagues had told him of their visits to whores in exotic parts of the world. Some of these women could do amazing things with their vaginal muscles, and one guy even claimed to know a girl in Bangkok who could fire Ping-Pong balls from her cunt. Experiencing Zara's ability to arouse him just by the internal contractions of her vagina made Colin believe such amazing abilities might be perfectly possible.

'I can't hold back.'

'Then don't.' Zara took hold of his hand, which had been resting on her stomach, and placed it between her thighs. 'Touch me,' she begged.

As Colin's fingers started to explore her quim, Zara closed her eyes, while she focused her attention on relaxing and contracting her internal muscles in rhythmic waves. Colin took a deep breath and expelled it slowly, his fingers concentrating on stimulating Zara's clitoris, trying to give her as much pleasure as she was giving him. Zara's constant sexual contractions were imposing such pressure on his penis that it was driving him almost insane with delight. He hadn't needed to move a muscle himself, yet the sensations were astounding. The pleasure so all-encompassing that, almost without warning, his body was consumed by a powerful wrenching climax.

'That was amazing.' He nuzzled the nape of her neck, his body still shaking from the strength of his release.

As his heartbeat slowed down, and his body readjusted, Colin became even more conscious of the agitated beating of Zara's heart, and the need for her own fulfilment, as she pressed her buttocks into his stomach. He worked her clitoris harder, pulling it, teasing it just as he knew she liked it. Her body strained against his, then he felt her internal muscles spasm around his semierect cock shaft in wild pulsing waves.

She gave a soft moan, and relaxed against him. Not only was Colin sated, he was utterly content. He could think of nothing better than remaining just like this for the rest of his life; wrapped in a loving embrace with Zara, while their passion slowly dwindled and strength returned to their trembling limbs.

Zara turned to face Colin, twining her arms around his neck. 'We need lots more practice before we get the hang of this,' she said, smiling.

'And we have all the time in the world to do so,' he replied.

Colin had agreed at once to Zara's request that he work for her. He could think of nothing better than spending every moment with this fascinating woman, so he had given in his notice less than an hour after Zara had first made the suggestion. Taking into account the holidays he was owed, he would be leaving the Princess Beatrice in three weeks. Unfortunately, that didn't give him time to go to the Bahamas with Zara, but he would be ready to greet her when she returned and they would start work on her new mini-series together.

'I've never felt happier,' she confessed. 'And if you're that keen on getting a perfect grasp of Tantric sex, then we can find a teacher.'

'You're joking, surely?' he exclaimed. 'Do you really think we need someone to teach us how to have sex?'

'Perhaps it would just be better to keep practising a lot,' she said teasingly. 'On the set I'll have a very comfortable motor home, and there's loads of sitting around to do between takes . . .'

'I wish we were there right now.' Colin glanced at his watch. 'I really should be leaving. I'm on duty in a quarter of an hour, and I've a number of urgent matters to deal with.'

'And I wish you didn't have to go,' she said, pouting slightly.

'I'll second that.' He was conscious of Zara watching his every move as he stood up and stretched.

'You really do have a beautiful body, Colin,' she said, watching him slip on his underpants and trousers.

'So do you, my sweet.' Colin blew her a kiss, then stepped over to the dressing table to smooth back his ruffled hair. 'I haven't time for a shower. I hope I don't smell of sex.' He turned and grinned at her. 'Do you know I think some of the other nurses suspect something is going on between us.'

'They'd be pretty stupid if they didn't. You spend ages in here, even during your shift. Far too much time probably.' Zara sat up and leaned forwards to pick up her robe. Colin paused to admire the firmness of her breasts and the soft curve of her belly. 'Use some of my cologne,' she suggested. 'It's on the dressing table.'

'Won't I smell a little too exotic?'

'Not if you use the bottle on the far left, it's designed for both men and women,' she replied.

Colin went to pick up the cologne, but hesitated when he saw the brown plastic container sitting beside the assorted perfumes. 'Pills?' he queried with a frown, picking up and shaking the bottle. On admission, patients were required to hand in all medication. Every hospital, public or private, had exactly the same policy. Any medication needed was written up by the doctor in charge and dispensed by the nurses. 'Didn't they tell you to give these up when you checked in?'

'I didn't have those pills when I checked in,' she replied, fastening the front of her robe and walking over to Colin.

'Where did you get them?' he asked as he checked the label. It wasn't an official hospital prescription, and he didn't recognise the name *Ampesoman*.

'Is this the third degree?' she asked.

'I'm only concerned for your wellbeing.'

'I know that.' She put her hand on his arm. 'Don't worry. It's all above board. Dr Taylor gave them to me for my depression.' She gave a soft laugh. 'They are some sort of miracle cure. Not that I'll need them in future, I've never been happier. But I thought I ought to try them just to please him.'

'Dr Taylor shouldn't have left them with you, Zara. He should have given them to the nurses to dispense.' Colin put down the pills and pulled Zara into a loving embrace.

'So he went against hospital protocol? Perhaps he had his reasons. Who cares anyway?' She looked up at him. 'Does it really matter?'

'No,' Colin lied. 'Of course it doesn't.'

'Then forget about the pills.' She kissed his cheek. 'I don't want to push you away but you should be on duty in five minutes.'

'Yeah,' he agreed, reluctantly pulling away from her, and slipping on his top.

Helen couldn't even remember how she got back to her apartment, or into her bed. Her memories were pretty hazy from round about the time she had ended up in bed with Sandra, Justin and Ben. Somewhere along the way she'd had a couple of drinks and after that everything was blank. She could recall brief snatches – tangles of naked limbs, male and female bodies pressed close to hers, licking, sucking and fucking. Truthfully she preferred to forget it had ever happened, despite the fact she had found it all amazingly pleasurable at the time. On reflection, it had all been a little too extreme for her peace of mind and had a dreamlike quality about it that didn't equate with reality.

She was more than certain that Justin had planned the entire thing, perhaps thinking that as she became more involved in their devious sexual practices, she would give up poking her nose into matters he considered none of her business. However, Justin had no idea how stubborn Helen could be at times.

One thing she did know: she now totally distrusted all three of them. Justin was a strange, eminently sexual guy, with the unique ability to reach a part of her she hadn't known existed before. Justin was like a vampire preying on his victims, seducing them, clouding their perceptions with promises of mind-blowing sex. In future she would have to fight much harder to resist the temptation. Deep at the heart of this hospital was a swamp of sexual promiscuity that lured people towards it, and then swallowed them up completely.

There was only one answer, she decided, as she walked around the hospital the following morning, ever conscious of her sore muscles and aching pussy. She had to concentrate hard on discovering exactly what was going on around here, what dark secrets lingered under the facade of normality.

'Dr Dawson,' someone called out, just behind her.

Helen recognised the voice of Colin, one of the senior staff nurses. She liked Colin; there was something very straight and trustworthy about him. 'Is something wrong?' she asked, thinking he looked concerned, as she turned to face him.

'There is,' he confirmed in a low voice as if not wanting to be overheard. 'Could I speak to you in private?'

'Sure. Let's go into the staff room,' she suggested. 'There's unlikely to be anyone there at this time of day.' They found the small sitting room, which was set aside for staff, empty. Helen waited until Colin shut the door. 'Well?'

'This isn't easy for me. I don't like to question a doctor's treatment,' Colin said cautiously. 'I know if I have any problems I should theoretically go to a senior sister or matron.' He paused, and frowned. 'But I feel I can trust you, Dr Dawson, so I decided to come to you first.'

'I'm flattered.' She smiled encouragingly. 'Feel free to tell me anything you want, Colin. To be frank, I can understand why you don't want to approach your supervisors in an instance like this. I'm more than happy to give you some guidance if I can. Anything you say to me will be in the strictest confidence, I promise you that.'

He nodded. 'Thank you, Dr Dawson. I want to ask you about a drug Dr Taylor has prescribed for Miss Dawn. It's supposed to be a new treatment for acute depression but I've never heard of it.'

'There are new drugs coming on the market all the time, Colin,' she told him. 'The pharmaceutical companies sometimes come to us before they make any effort to publicise a new drug.'

'I appreciate that.' Colin stepped closer. 'But this is far more complicated. Not only is the drug unknown to me, but Dr Taylor has disregarded all hospital procedure.'

'In what way?' Helen asked in surprise.

'He has given Miss Dawn a supply of the tablets to keep in her room. There's no record of the prescription in her notes. As far as the hospital is concerned she's not even on any medication.'

'No record,' Helen repeated thoughtfully, wondering what Ben was up to. She had no intention of saying so to Colin as yet, but such behaviour by a physician was

175

unforgivable, and extremely dangerous. 'Do you know what this drug is called?'

Colin removed a piece of paper from his pocket and passed it to her. 'I wrote it down.'

'*Ampesoman*,' she read, 'I've not heard of it either. But I can easily make some calls, contact a few colleagues,' she said, having no intention of speaking to Ben as yet. 'I'll find out more about it, Colin. Will that at least put your mind at rest at present?'

'I'm sure it will,' Colin said with a grateful smile. 'I don't want Miss Dawn to come to any harm. You may not be aware of it, Dr Dawson, but Miss Dawn and I are involved. In fact I'm leaving the hospital to work for her,' he explained. 'She's a very special lady, and she is of paramount importance to me. Dr Taylor's behaviour really has me worried.'

Helen nodded. 'To be perfectly honest, Colin, there are a number of things going on around here that trouble me too.' She paused, then took a chance and decided to confide in Colin. Helen was certain that if he'd had any part in the conspiracy he wouldn't be questioning Ben's actions. 'Have you heard any rumours about a patient being lodged in the West Wing annex?' Colin looked at her in surprise. 'No – nothing. I was told, like everyone else, that there were some construction problems, and that the area was off limits to staff and patients alike.' He frowned. 'But then the West Wing is a pretty weird place. The staff keep themselves to themselves. They rarely mix with the rest of us. At times it's almost like we were two different hospitals.'

'I thought I was imagining their attitude towards me,' Helen admitted. 'I always feel that they consider me an intrusive outsider when I go to see a patient there.' She gave an awkward laugh. 'And that in itself is a pretty rare occurrence. So the two sets of staff don't mix at all?'

'Not even socially,' he replied. 'Haven't you noticed that in the restaurant and staff bar?'

'I've never really thought about it,' she said, shrugging

her shoulders. 'I haven't spent much time in the bar since I've been here.'

'Even the annual staff parties are held apart. We're having a barbecue in the grounds next Wednesday, while they are holding some elaborate fancy dress do. Rumour has it they are holding it in the ballroom, but they keep their plans pretty hush-hush,' Colin said.

'How strange,' Helen exclaimed. The ballroom of the former mansion was on the ground floor, situated directly beneath the West Wing annex. Helen had heard it hadn't been in use for years. 'Another thing, Colin. Did you know that Mr Kalowski operated on a patient late last night, round about midnight?'

'Midnight?' Colin echoed. 'All the theatre staff only work day shifts. The operating theatres close about six. Only a few emergency operations have ever been done here; the last was the one on Mr Paul.'

'And I suspect that this operation was no emergency.' Helen absentmindedly drummed her fingers on the files she was holding. 'There must have been a full compliment of theatre staff – any idea who might have been called in?'

'The regular theatre sister is on annual leave at present. Her usual replacement is matron's friend, Gillian Clark. She's one of the sisters from the West Wing. There's normally no crossover of staff; matron doesn't allow it. Yet funnily enough Gillian had been put on our rota to provide temporary cover in the East Wing last night. Then there was a last minute reshuffle, because Gillian was unavailable for some unknown reason.'

'Perhaps she'd been reassigned to theatre?' Helen suggested. 'Is there any way you could find out?'

'I can try.' Colin appeared confident. 'I recently went on an aromatherapy course. Fran, one of the former nurses from the West Wing, was also there. She left about six months ago after some sort of altercation with matron. Fran's boyfriend Jack is a theatre technician here, and I know for a fact that she still harbours some resentment about being forced to leave. I'll phone her, she may be able to tell me something.'

'Helen, there you are.' Duncan smiled at Helen as she entered his room. As usual the place was knee-deep in papers, and there were a couple of men with Duncan, presumably discussing the movie he was making. Judging by the description Duncan had previously given her, one of the guests was Paolo Barsini, the excitable director of his current project.

'We must leave.' Paolo spoke with a strong Italian accent. 'Is this your beautiful doctor?'

'Yeah,' Duncan confirmed, giving Helen a conspiratorial wink. 'Helen Dawson, may I introduce the great Paolo Barsini.'

'A pleasure,' Helen said as Paolo made a great show of kissing her hand, while he reeled off a long sentence in Italian which sounded enormously flattering.

'In his usually effusive way, Paolo is telling you how beautiful and charming you are, Helen,' Duncan explained as he stood up.

'*Ciao, bellisima,*' Paolo said, then waved his hand at Duncan.

'*Ciao, Paulo,*' Duncan said, adding a few more words in fluent-sounding Italian. Helen, who had never been much good at languages, was impressed. 'He's actually a nice guy,' Duncan remarked, after Paolo and his companion had left. 'But so excitable, it's quite exhausting.' He paused. 'What's wrong? You look worried.'

'I'm not sure.' Duncan pulled her into his arms, holding her close for a moment. 'There are some pretty strange things going on around here Duncan, and they worry me.'

'Sit down, tell me all about it.' He led her to the sofa, brushing a pile of papers on to the floor so that he could sit beside her.

Helen started by telling Duncan about the patient lodged in the annex, and Ralph's secrecy about the operation. Helen was certain the man he'd operated on had been Mr X because she'd checked up and none of the official patients in either wing had been taken to theatre last night. She knew that some of the other staff must be in on this as well, but apart from the sister Colin had spoken of, she had no idea who as yet.

'So why do you think they are keeping the identity of this patient so secret?' Duncan asked, his interest aroused.

Helen shrugged her shoulders. 'I don't know. The only logical explanation I can come up with is that he's here to have his appearance radically altered, and he doesn't want anyone to know about it.'

'So he's a fugitive from justice or something?'

'Sounds like a plot for a bad TV movie, doesn't it?' she said with a wry smile.

'A scriptwriter once told me that the most bizarre explanation is most probably the right one,' Duncan replied.

'What does he do? Write for the *X Files*?' Helen gave an uneasy laugh. 'That's not even the end of it, Duncan. You know Colin, the staff nurse?'

'Yeah,' Duncan confirmed. 'Nice guy.'

'He spoke to me in confidence this morning about one of his patients, Zara Dawn, the actress. Dr Taylor has prescribed a drug for her – *Ampesoman*. It's only just been developed in the States, and it's still experimental. The drug company has recently been give permission to set up initial trials on human patients, but it's still a long way from getting FDA approval and even further from being allowed into the UK.'

'You checked on this?' Duncan asked. Having lived in America for quite a while he knew that FDA were the controlling body for drugs in the States.

'Yes, after Colin told me he discovered the pills in Zara's room. Ben Taylor has given them to her, but there's no record of the treatment in her hospital files. As far as the Princess Beatrice is concerned Zara isn't even on the drug; if they don't know then neither will her GP.'

'Why would Dr Taylor do this?'

'Cold, hard cash I reckon,' she said with a sigh. I e-mailed my friend, Peter Caxton – he works for the FDA in Washington. He advised me in strictest confidence that the drug company who developed *Ampesoman* are carrying out limited trials. However, because of some perceived side-effects, they are paying every patient who goes on the trial a considerable sum of money. I think I could maybe understand Ben's actions if Zara had some terrible life-threatening disease, and the drug was her only chance of survival, but just for money, it's unforgivable.'

'How much money exactly?'

'$10,000 for each patient. I know for a fact that Zara doesn't know about the money, or anything else about the drug for that matter.'

'$10,000,' Duncan repeated. 'I realise that most British doctors are badly paid, but that's not enough to chance jeopardising a career.'

'Don't forget, Duncan, we are only talking about one patient here. What if Ben has twenty on the trial? That would give him $200,000 for little or no effort.'

'Sure, and from there on the sky's the limit?'

'It all depends how many he's supposed to have on this trial. My friend couldn't find that out. I don't know what's made him do it. He doesn't strike me as the kind of guy who would use his patients so cruelly. On the other hand it could be Justin's influence. He does seem to have a strong hold over Ben.'

'Justin doesn't sound the nicest of characters,' Duncan exclaimed sarcastically.

'I need you to exert all your considerable charms and keep the ladies in the Records Department fully occupied,' Helen told Duncan, as she pushed him along the corridor in a wheelchair. He'd wanted to walk, but she felt he would be infinitely more appealing to the female staff if he appeared to be more incapacitated than he actually was.

'I keep telling you that I can play the movie star part to perfection,' Duncan replied with a dry laugh.

'You don't have to act, just be your usual charming self; you know, the brave but injured hero,' she teased. 'The women will fall over themselves to get a glimpse of you, let alone talk to you,' she added, as she pushed him through the double doors into the Records Office.

The effect Duncan's unexpected appearance had on the entire staff, who were all female, was astounding. Their chattering ceased as they stared at him in stunned silence. Then, almost in unison, they rose to their feet and hurried over to him.

'Mr Paul,' one exclaimed excitedly.

'We love your movies,' another said, as they almost fell over each other in their haste.

Helen suddenly experienced a surge of jealousy as she watched the women crowding around Duncan. He appeared to be enjoying the adoration. Helen had never realised how complex it was to be involved with such a major celebrity. It had been bad enough with Max, while with Duncan it would likely be a million times worse.

The members of staff thronged excitedly around Duncan, but one woman held back. A middle-aged, over-weight lady with her hair confined in a tight bun. 'Can I help you, Dr Dawson?' she asked.

'I came in to look up a few things,' Helen told her. According to the woman's ID tag her name was Audrey and she was the office supervisor. 'I hope you'll forgive the intrusion. Mr Paul is a patient here and he expressed a wish to meet some of the other hospital staff – the behind-the-scenes people.'

'So thoughtful. Who would have expected it from such a star.' Audrey's stern expression softened as she glanced adoringly over at Duncan, still surrounded by her staff. 'He is one of my favourite actors. Isn't he good-looking?' she added in a conspiratorial whisper.

'Yes,' Helen agreed. 'He's brought some photos to sign for your ladies.'

'Do you think he'd sign one for me?' Audrey asked

with girlish excitement. 'My friend Elsie will be so jealous.'

'I'm certain he would,' Helen replied. 'There's no need for you to bother yourself looking up the information I need, Audrey. I can easily do it while you chat to Mr Paul.'

'Would you mind?' Audrey glanced back at Duncan, who was now putting personalised messages on all the photos, handing them with a flourish to each fan, and following that up with a kiss on the cheek. 'You can use any desk. All the girls are logged on to the system. Do you know how to use it?'

Helen had watched one of the clerks use the system when she was last there. 'Yes, I think so,' she confirmed confidently. 'However, some of the information I need isn't current. Dr Kalowski has asked me to do a study on the different plastic surgery procedures we carry out here. It means I'll have to cross-reference operating records, such as full face-lifts and breast augmentation.'

Audrey smiled. 'That's not too difficult, Dr Dawson. Just press F6, type in the name of the procedure, and the system will automatically bring up a list of all the patients who have had that specific procedure carried out at the Princess Beatrice.'

'That's great,' Helen replied. 'It'll make my task much easier than I expected it to be. Oh, one more thing – '

'Yes?' Audrey tried to conceal her frustration, glancing eagerly back at Duncan, who was now chatting casually to all the ladies.

'Are the entire hospital records available to me? Or do any of the staff keep their records in separate files.'

'Professor Fenton has a personal file, but most of his records are accessible if you need them. I know Dr Taylor and Dr Masterson both have files set up that can only be accessed by private passwords, but I'm not aware that they keep anything like that in them. All patients are listed in alphabetical order, and if you find any that don't have full up-to-date details let me know.

I'll find out who has them, and get the respective member of staff to provide hard copies for you.'

'You are most efficient, Audrey,' Helen said, sitting down at the nearest desk and watching Audrey hurry over to speak to Duncan.

Helen was used to a number of different computer systems, and this one proved to be very similar to the one they had at St Matthew's, but it was far more up to date, far more sophisticated. She decided to pull all the records for patients having had facial surgery. She suspected that Mr X wasn't the first patient secretly brought into the hospital for extensive facial reconstruction. In a way she hoped to be proved wrong; she wanted her suspicions about Ralph and the others to be untrue.

As quickly as she could, she brought up the lists of patients that she needed, scrolling swiftly through the many names. She would have to go through each file one by one to figure out the true extent of their surgery, so at first she just looked for anything that struck her out of the ordinary, something that might lead her to the truth.

She had almost come to the bottom of the list when one name caught her eye – Bruce Wayne. She only noticed it because Duncan had recently mentioned that he had once been approached to play Batman, soon after Val Kilmer declined to reprise his role in the next sequel. Poor bastard, she thought, imagine being lumbered with such a recognisable name. She wondered what the small asterisk beside the name meant, and when she tried to pull up Bruce Wayne's records she drew a blank. All she could find was the date the file had first been created, six months ago.

Helen back-tracked, finding a few more names with asterisks beside them. Oddly enough the names were all familiar – Barney Rubble, Lois Lane, Clark Kent. This was too much of a coincidence, she thought, and her suspicions were confirmed when she spotted the name Fred Flintstone with a neat asterisk beside it. Perhaps she had found something? Justin had a twisted sense of humour, twisted enough to give these secret patients names of cartoon characters. Could Mr X be a derivative of the *X men* – a children's cartoon character just like all the others?

She tried each name in turn, finding, just like the first one, that she couldn't pull up any records apart from the date the file was first created – all at fairly regular intervals over the last two years.

'Have you found everything you need?' Audrey asked, looking a little flushed as she clutched a signed picture of a bare-chested Duncan to her ample bosom.

'Some, but not all,' Helen said. 'I can't bring up the records for the asterisked names. Do you know if they are held by any of the doctors in the personal files?' she asked, pressing the button, so that the laser printer would churn out the lists she needed.

'Asterisks,' Audrey repeated with a smile. 'That's not surprising. Dr Taylor asked me to have all those names deleted from our records. I just haven't got around to it yet.'

'Why deleted?' Helen asked.

'Didn't you notice that they were all names of cartoon characters?' Audrey asked her. 'I've only been working here a couple of months, so I didn't know anything about it until Dr Taylor explained what had happened. Apparently a young man, who initially set up this new computer system, created a number of fake patient record files for testing purposes, to make sure it was all working properly. Dr Taylor says that these files were just cluttering up our system, so he downloaded all the information in them on to disc two days ago. Now I've just got to delete all the names.'

'Really?' Helen said thoughtfully. 'Do you know how long ago this new system was installed, Audrey?'

'Four years ago.'

'So these records are all four years old?' Helen asked.

'Yes. It was apparently a silly joke on the young man's part to give all the files names of cartoon characters. But at least it's made it easy for us to locate them and tidy up the system.'

'Quite so,' Helen agreed, gathering up the sheets she'd printed. 'Thanks for your help, Audrey. I think I'd better take Mr Paul back to his room now, so that you can get your staff back to work.'

It was a little after 4 p.m., and the weather was still glorious. Brilliant sunshine, but not uncomfortably hot, with a slight breeze moving the sweetly scented air.

'It's nice to be in the open air again after a stuffy hospital room,' Duncan commented as Helen pushed him across the courtyard in his wheelchair. 'Where are we going exactly?'

She stopped and looked down at him. 'It's your choice. I can take you on a tour of the grounds. There's a nice ornamental garden, with a couple of fountains, and even a small lake. Alternatively, I could show you my apartment.'

'Apartment,' he repeated with a smile. 'Is there any room in particular you think I should see?'

'The bedroom is very nicely decorated, and there's a very comfortable four-poster bed,' she replied. 'It's up to you.'

'There isn't really a choice, is there?' He looked upwards, narrowing his eyes at the glare of the sun. 'The weather isn't really right for a tour of the grounds. You never know, it might rain,' he added, surveying the cloudless blue sky. 'I think it best we go to your apartment, don't you?'

'Yes,' she agreed, pushing him forwards again. 'Luckily my place is on the ground floor.'

'I can climb stairs, I can do anything now,' Duncan said, lifting his foot, waving his ankle around as if it were fully healed. Duncan had been fitted with a lightweight cast – the very latest technology from the States, brought over by the company backing his movie. It meant he could get back to work earlier than expected.

185

Wardrobe was already altering his costumes so that the cast would be hidden during filming.

'Just don't get carried away, or do anything stupid when you get back on set,' Helen warned, pushing the wheelchair through the entrance doors of the apartment block. 'No silly stunts, no outrageous risks, Duncan, or your ankle won't heal properly. If you don't heed my warning, any damage you do could well turn out to be permanent.'

'Then no more big-budget action movies for me. I'm not that stupid, Helen.'

'I sense that you feel you have to live up to this macho image of yours. Sometimes you try to be what you are not,' Helen suggested.

'In that case perhaps you should come with me. Be my personal physician, always on call, day or night,' he teased, but in a way that she sensed was serious.

Helen was tempted to take up the offer. She really did need to get away from this place. She had become very attached to Duncan, and would love to spend more time with him. Once Duncan departed, and his steadying influence wasn't around, she feared that she might get sucked into the sexual morass if she wasn't careful.

'I'll get Paolo to send me a copy of the shooting schedule. That way I'll know exactly where you are at any given time. I can turn up at any moment to make sure you are behaving yourself.'

'You mean to check up on me and make sure I'm not banging away at some cute little bit-part player in my dressing room,' he commented with a wry chuckle.

'That part of your life is none of my business, Duncan. I was referring to your physical wellbeing, nothing more.' She stopped outside her front door, unlocked it and pushed Duncan inside.

Helen had only just pushed his chair into the sitting room, when he climbed out of it and walked over to the window, managing to move quite well on two feet, the restrictions imposed by his ankle cast barely visible. 'You mean you wouldn't be even the slightest bit jealous if

186

you found me bare-assed naked with some glamorous eighteen year old?'

'Why should I be?' she lied.

The thoughts didn't appeal at all to Helen, but she didn't own Duncan. She had managed to convince herself that this was purely a brief liaison with no expectations on either side. Anyway, what right had she to feel jealous after her recent erotic interludes with Ben and Justin?

'This place isn't bad for a staff apartment.' Duncan stepped towards her, barely limping at all.

'Would you like a drink or something?' she asked as he stared thoughtfully at her.

'No thanks. Where's the bedroom?'

'Through there,' she pointed, then gave a squeal of surprise as he lifted her into his arms.

Chapter Nine

'No,' Helen protested as Duncan started to carry her towards the bedroom. 'Be careful – your ankle.'

'Forget it,' he replied. 'I never break a promise. I'd taken a rain-check on this if you remember.' He set her down beside the four-poster bed. 'Now what?' He grinned wickedly, displaying no discomfort after his exertion.

'You could have damaged that ankle again, Duncan,' she remonstrated. 'I know you're very fit, but you're still not one hundred per cent after your accident.'

'I'm fine,' he insisted stubbornly. 'Now let's forget your medical concerns and concentrate on something far more important.' He removed Max's nipple clamps from his shirt pocket and very deliberately placed them on her bedside table.

'What would your adoring fans in records have thought if they'd known you had those in your pocket?' she teased, slipping off her white coat.

'They'd probably have been lining up to use them,' he said with a cheeky grin. 'You should take a look at my fan mail. Some of it is unbelievable – what they say – what they offer to do for me.'

'Like what, exactly?'

'I reckon you could hazard a damn good guess. We

could try some of their suggestions out. Start by taking off your dress,' he prompted, sitting down on her bed.

'This dress?' Helen slid down the zip, stepped out of it, and let it drop to the floor.

'You're definitely on the right track,' he confirmed, looking her up and down.

Helen had worn undies today: a provocative red lace bra and matching panties. The lace was so fine you could almost see through it, while her nipples peeped coyly out of the low cups. The panties were minute, a tiny triangle at the front, which didn't even cover her pubis, and a narrow band at the back which sat neatly between her buttock cheeks. As she moved, Helen could feel the thin string straining against her sensitive anal opening.

'Very cute,' Duncan commented, his breathing quickening, lust lighting his dark eyes.

'Now you must strip too,' she demanded, stepping out of her sandals and leaning forwards so that her scantily clad bosom was directly in front of his face.

'You smell great,' he said, inhaling her perfume. Duncan continued to stare hungrily at the lush curves of her breasts, as he unbuttoned his shirt and pulled it off.

'So do you,' she replied as her eyes fastened on the tempting bulge of his erection, encased in his snug-fitting jeans. Helen reached down to unbutton his flies and, as they opened, his silk-covered cock bulged provocatively through the slit.

Helen jerked the tight jeans down his legs, being careful not to hurt his damaged ankle as she pulled them off. Duncan was left wearing a pair of black silk boxers, with a designer logo splashed across one leg, which had probably cost far more than the dress he'd ruined last night.

'There's not much left to take off,' he said, eyeing her bra and panties.

'You first,' she insisted, pulling down the boxers, almost ripping them in her haste. She admired his hard, well-toned stomach, and his gorgeous cock, rearing out of its bed of jet-black curls. She found Duncan in all his naked glory far more stimulating than any other man – even Justin, with his bizarre body piercing and erotic leather harness.

'Now lie back and relax,' she softly commanded.

Helen had planned this romantic interlude and prepared for it carefully before seeing Duncan today, hoping he would agree to come to her apartment. As he lay back on the bed, he was unaware of that, not knowing what erotic delights she had in store for him. Helen wanted it to be an experience Duncan wouldn't easily forget.

'This is far more comfortable than the bed in my suite,' he said, settling himself on the soft mattress, eyeing her cautiously, suspecting she had something special in mind.

'Then let me make you even more comfortable,' Helen said, picking up one of the silk scarves she'd left ready, and looping it around his wrist, tying the end to the bedpost so that his arm was stretched tautly upwards. Duncan watched her intently, never saying a word, making no attempt to resist or protest as she moved round the bed and confined his right arm in a similar fashion. The air was electric with anticipation as she joined him on the bed.

'Should I be scared?' he teased. 'Are you in one of your dominating moods again?' he asked with a wry grin.

'Wait and see,' she said with a smile. 'Do you know, Duncan, men's armpits are so sexy.' She kissed the cup of flesh covered with its sprinkling of dark hair, inhaling the musky masculine smell. 'Deliciously inviting,' she purred, rising to her knees and adjusting her bra. She eased her bosom from the cups, but left the garment in place – supported like this her breasts looked even larger and fuller.

Duncan grinned seductively as she pressed her titties close to his face until her nipples were only a tantalising inch or so from his lips. She felt his warm breath on the

190

sensitive peaks as he jerked his head forwards aiming to pull one of the tempting teats into his mouth.

Just in time to prevent him reaching her, Helen pulled back. 'Spoilsport,' growled Duncan in frustration.

'You'll have all you want, eventually,' she promised him, reaching across his prone body to pick up the nipple clamps.

Helen pointedly played with her breasts, pulling and rubbing her nipples until they grew and hardened. Duncan watched and waited, clearly expecting her to attach the clamps to her own teats, an idea far from her thoughts. She leaned forwards again, allowing him to capture one pert little peak between his lips. Duncan enclosed it completely with the wet warmth of his mouth, stabbing at the teat with his tongue. Helen responded by gently rubbing his small flat nipples, pulling one away from his chest to swiftly imprison it in the neat little clamp.

Duncan gave a soft moan of surprise, but continued to pull more of her breast into his mouth, sucking on it like a hungry child. Helen felt the invisible cord between her breasts and belly tighten, her pussy growing warm and pleasantly moist, while she tried to concentrate her attentions on attaching the other clamp.

When she had managed to confine both Duncan's nipples she pulled away from him. Duncan's mouth tried desperately to follow her breasts, but he was brought short by his silken bonds. The sudden, sharp movement made the silver filigree flowers brush teasingly against his muscular chest. 'Very pretty,' he said as he glanced wryly down at the decorations. 'But not really my style.'

'You'll get used to them,' she promised. 'The longer you wear them the more intense the sensations become.'

'Is that so?' Duncan relaxed back against the pillows as she ran her hands teasingly over his body. Gradually she slid them downwards, trailing her fingers around the root of his rigid penis. His balls tightened automatically, and his cock twitched excitedly as Helen circled the base of the shaft.

Helen leaned forwards and blew softly on the stiff organ, watching a slight tremor pass across his stomach as she caressed the shaft with the warmth of her breath, making the tiny dewdrop on the domed head tremble.

'Do you want me to put your cock into my mouth?' she teased, sensing how desperate he was to feel her lips close around the pulsing head.

'Please,' Duncan groaned, out of his mind but reluctant to beg.

His cock twitched again, ready and eager. Helen lapped the tiny dewdrop from the tip of the glans then drew the head fully into her mouth. Duncan strained against his bonds, jerking his hips, desperately trying to push more of the shaft between her lips. She sucked on his flesh, slowly and sensuously, until he moaned with pleasure, then drew back, forcing him to lift his hips and follow her. Duncan was left lying there, his body twisted and balanced on his right hip, his buttocks raised from the mattress.

Helen savoured the musky saltiness of his flesh and the throbbing hardness of his cock as she felt the tip of it catch the back of her throat. She sucked harder, drawing his pleasure upwards, while she reached out and hit him hard across the buttocks with the flat of her hand, feeling Duncan tense in surprise.

'Hell, that stung,' he grunted.

Helen hit him again, and the large cracking sound of the slap was an amazingly satisfying sound. Two more strokes, then she let his cock slip smoothly from her mouth as she pushed him back down on to the bed, hearing his loud grunt of frustration.

'Some people enjoy being spanked,' she said with a smile, as she picked up a small wood-backed hairbrush.

'With that?' He gave a soft chuckle. 'It's too small to even hurt.'

'You'd be surprised.' Her words were followed by a faint gasp of surprise, as she hit him gently across his

inner thigh with the brush side of the implement. 'More?'
she asked teasingly, as she tapped the soft bristles over
his pubic area.

'What have I done to deserve this?' he asked, as she
applied the bristles in a hard regular motion around the
base of his dick. 'I never said I was into S and M,' he
added, half-jokingly.

'This isn't a punishment,' she said softly, running the
bristles up and down the side of his shaft, sharply
teasing the tender flesh. 'It's designed to give you
pleasure.'

'You're inventive, I'll give you that,' he grunted, tens-
ing as she lightly ran the bristles across the sensitive tip
of his cock head.

'Do you want me to stop?'

'Yes,' he growled. 'No,' he added, his body trembling
at the continuing onslaught, clearly turned on by the
tickling, scraping sensations of bliss. 'Just let me fuck
you, Helen.'

'All in good time,' she promised. 'Let's play a little
more first.'

'You're doing the playing, not me,' he said with a
harsh laugh, then winced as she continued the erotic
assault on his sexual organs, running the brush head up
his penis again, then over the soft sac of his balls. 'And
you're a prick teaser, Helen.'

'Very funny,' she conceded, smiling wryly. 'Now in
order to continue our game you have to be properly
confined.'

'Is that so?' he said, as she reached down and wrapped
a silk scarf around his damaged ankle, being extra careful not to hurt him as she tied the scarf to one end post
of the bed. Helen confined his other ankle, tying it to the
opposite bedpost, so that his legs were held wide apart.
Duncan looked so deliciously vulnerable Helen could
hardly wait to begin. 'So what do these games consist
of?' he asked.

'Patience is everything.' Helen kneeled astride his hips
and removed her bra, trailing it over his chest before

tossing it aside. Her panties were next, and she undid the bows at the sides, stretching the lace taut so that it slipped between her pussy lips. Duncan's eyes fastened on her sex as she stimulated herself with the strip of red lace, wetting it with her juices, before casually discarding it.

She leaned forwards to pull gently at the nipple clamps until he gave a soft groan. 'Do they feel tighter now?'

'Infinitely,' he said, through gritted teeth.

Helen lowered her body until she was poised tantalisingly close, only inches above his quivering cock-head. Duncan strained at his bonds, desperate to thrust his way inside her, and the tip of his glans brushed the entrance to her sex. Helen moved teasingly lower allowing his cock to slide partially into the smooth wet interior of her sex. He moaned with delight as he experienced the soft embrace of her flesh. 'Deeper,' he pleaded.

'Not yet,' Helen said, lifting herself away from him, ignoring his gasp of frustration then crouching between his open thighs. She had been tempted to let him fuck her there and then, but before she was filled with his hot hardness, she wanted to drive him insane with need. She intended to take his pleasure to a higher plane before she allowed him to reach total fulfilment.

She reached for the slim gold-plated vibrator she'd left tucked beneath the corner of the bedcover. It was small, designed for a ladies handbag, and quite perfect for what she had in mind. She laid it between his thighs and Duncan lifted his head, attempting to see what she was doing as she picked up the tube of lubricant. She felt him wince slightly, knowing the jelly felt cold to the touch as she smoothed it over the base of his penis and the sensitive skin of his perineum. She slid her fingers downwards, slipping them teasingly between the cheeks of his firm buttocks. Judging by the way Duncan instinctively flinched, Helen assumed that he'd never allowed this part of his body to be penetrated before. His flesh here was innocent of the joy such pleasures could bring.

194

Delicately she slid the tip of one finger into his arse-hole, spreading the icy lubricant around the tight opening until it gradually started to relax and the tenseness melted away from Duncan's limbs. Then she turned on the vibrator.

'What are you going to do with that?' he asked anxiously, his muscles tightening in nervous anticipation.

'Nothing you won't like,' Helen promised as she applied the tip of the vibrator to his penis, running it up and down the swollen shaft.

She slid it lower, letting it rest on the sensitive strip of skin between the base of his penis and his anus, concentrating on the acutely sensitive area until his body trembled with delight. When Duncan appeared to be ready and sufficiently relaxed, she pressed the tip of the instrument to the opening of his anus.

'No,' Duncan exclaimed nervously, as the vibrator buzzed relentlessly against the tight ring of muscle.

'Yes,' she insisted. 'Trust me,' she added, easing the rounded tip inside the tense rim. It tightened reflexively, but Helen persisted, holding it there until the constant vibrations forced the taut muscles to gradually relax. 'You'll be amazed at what a turn on it can be for a man,' she insisted, as she managed to breach the opening.

She pressed harder, forcing his virginal flesh to unlock and expand. Once past the initial barrier it became easier to thrust it deeper and deeper. As she penetrated a part of his body that had never been invaded before, Duncan gave an unwilling groan. Yet, judging by the way his belly and limbs trembled, he was enjoying this singular pleasure far more than he cared to admit.

She moved the vibrator, gently sliding it in and out of Duncan's anus until he was driven wild with excitement, his limbs moving restlessly as he reached the exquisite plateau where pleasure and pain intertwined. Helen lodged it neatly inside him, turned on by the sight of his bulging arsehole, distended by the buzzing gold dildo. Now she could hold back no longer. Her pussy was so hot, so wet, that it had to be filled by his hard male flesh.

Swiftly she straddled his hips, took hold of his cock, and guided it between the lips of her sex. She savoured the pleasure as it slid smoothly into her, while she heard Duncan give a loud gasp of relief. Shafting herself the last short distance, she ground her open pussy against his pelvis.

Helen felt her stomach tighten, and her sex contract around his smooth hardness. The twisted expression on Duncan's face told her that that he was periliously close to climax. She started to move, pulling up, thrusting downwards, the feelings of pleasure so irresistibly compelling that they forced her to move faster and faster. She fucked him in a smooth, unrelenting rhythm as Duncan strained beneath her, confined and helpless, his hands balled up in tight fists. She was certain that she could even detect the buzzing sensation in his arsehole, the vibrations travelling through his veins and nerve-endings until they passed into her.

The bliss gained strength, moving like liquid fire through her body and into Duncan consuming everything in its path. As the orgasmic waves swept over her they culminated in a sweetly perfect moment of pleasure, so profoundly intense that she didn't even hear herself cry out.

Helen and Duncan spent the rest of the afternoon and evening in her apartment. He would have stayed the night but she had promised Colin she would have Duncan back in his room by 11 p.m. at the latest – after all he was still a patient at the hospital.

'You'll have to get into the wheelchair soon,' Helen told Duncan. 'As soon as we enter the hospital building. It's official policy.'

'Why?' he asked. Duncan was pushing the chair himself, walking with a barely perceptible limp as they moved across the courtyard towards the main building.

'It's because of the hospital's insurance policy,' she said.

'I suppose I could do with the rest –' Duncan grinned cheekily '– after what you put me through this evening.'

'You enjoyed every minute.' Helen stopped and stared at him. 'Didn't you?'

'Surprisingly, I did.' He gave a soft chuckle. 'In the past I've always had a thing about anyone touching my arse. Never liked the idea of it before.'

'A trace of homophobia, perhaps?'

'Maybe,' he agreed. 'Frankly I never realised what a turn-on it could be.'

Duncan glanced across the courtyard as they heard the sound of a car engine approaching. Headlights came into view, as it turned the corner, moved slowly forwards and parked close to the rear entrance of the building. The security lights flickered on immediately, and they saw it was a large black limousine with dark tinted windows.

'Do you think your mystery patient might be leaving?' Duncan asked. At present they were out of the sight of the driver, hidden by a people carrier left in the courtyard.

'Not yet, surely. It's way too soon after major surgery.' The thought struck her that if someone could afford to pay for all the secrecy, they could also easily arrange private nurses and physicians in order to leave the hospital extra quickly. But if this was the patient leaving then she might never learn who he was.

She saw the door of the limousine open and the driver, wearing a smart pale-grey chauffeur's uniform, stepped out. He pulled open one of the rear doors with a flourish and the first passenger exited the vehicle. The man was dressed in flowing white Arab robes, with a chequered head-dress wrapped around his lower face, and sunglasses covering his eyes, even though it was night. A second passenger joined him, and he was obviously the more important of the two. He also wore Arab robes but these were fuller and trimmed with gold, while his face was similarly concealed by dark glasses and a head-dress.

'This gets more interesting by the moment,' Duncan whispered as they watched the two new arrivals enter the hospital. 'Let's follow them and see if the go to the annex,' he added, as the chauffeur followed the two men, struggling with a pair of heavy suitcases.

'We'll be rather obvious won't we?' Helen pointed out. 'Me pushing you in a wheelchair.'

She wanted to follow them too, but she couldn't desert Duncan. He was still a patient and her responsibility.

'Leave the bloody wheelchair,' Duncan hissed, then started to creep forwards stealthily, as if he was in one of his action movies. He could move even quicker than Helen had expected and before she could stop him he was halfway to the entrance door.

'Damn,' she muttered. Not wanting to leave the wheelchair in the middle of the courtyard, she went to follow Duncan, trying to be as quiet as possible as she pulled the wheelchair with her. She struggled through the double doors, scraping her shins, and banging the wheelchair loudly against one of the doors in her haste.

She spotted Duncan immediately, walking back up the corridor towards her, limping a shade more obviously than he had a moment ago. 'They went up in the lift, just around the corner ahead,' he said. 'I still find the layout of this place confusing. Does that lift lead to the annex?'

'Yes,' she confirmed, thinking it fruitless to point out that he shouldn't be doing any of this with his ankle still strapped up.

'We could follow them,' he suggested.

'I think that a high profile patient creeping around the place like an SAS commando in the middle of the night might be rather obvious. It may happen in movies but not in real life.'

He grinned, looking rather like an overgrown schoolboy, but still immensely appealing. 'I've always hoped that one day fiction might become fact. Where do we go from here then, boss?'

'We go to reception. They hold a list there of all

patients due to be admitted. If those guys weren't on it then we can presume they are part of Ben and Ralph's little game,' she said, wondering if Ralph had actually gone back to New York. She could perhaps try contacting him tomorrow, if she could think up a reasonable excuse for doing so. But if Ralph did turn out to be in New York, who would be operating on this new arrival? Like *Alice in Wonderland* this was getting curiouser and curiouser. 'Now get into the wheelchair, Duncan.'

Duncan seemed to be enjoying this immensely as he sat down obediently. 'It's great, isn't it?'

'I'm a doctor not a detective,' she muttered as she pushed him forwards.

They passed the lift leading to the maternity and the annex, just in time to see the down arrow light up, and hear the soft hum as it started its descent. Not wanting to be seen, Helen pushed Duncan faster, almost running in her haste. She glanced back, just before they negotiated a sharp corner, and got a quick glance of the chauffeur exiting the lift alone. With luck he didn't see them as she skidded round the bend in such haste that Duncan was forced to hang on to the arms of the chair to stop himself falling out.

By the time they reached reception, Helen's heart rate had slowed a little and she had her agitated breathing under control. The lobby was only dimly lit, the front doors were locked, and only a security man was on duty.

'Evening, Dr Dawson,' said the security man, glancing with interest at Duncan, obviously recognising him but not wanting to say so. 'You and your patient are up late.'

'Evening constitutional,' Duncan explained. 'I was getting tired of looking at four walls.'

'Mr Paul wanted to check up on a friend of his, George,' Helen smoothly lied. 'He heard his friend was due to be admitted today and we wanted to know which room he'd been taken to.'

'I wasn't aware that anyone was coming in today,' George said, sifting through the papers in front of him.

'I'll check the list – I may be wrong. What was the gentleman's name?'

'Cartman, Mr Cartman,' Duncan improvised.

George looked down at the list in front of him. 'No sir, nothing like that here. In fact no-one has been admitted or was due to be admitted today.'

'What about tomorrow?' Helen suggested.

'Or tomorrow for that matter,' George replied. 'It's very quiet at present.'

'Yes, I suppose it is,' Helen agreed. 'Thanks for your help, George,' she added, pushing Duncan towards the lifts. Once they were inside the lift and on their way up to the first floor, she glanced down at Duncan. 'Penny for them,' she said, as Duncan appeared deep in thought.

'I was thinking that we have to find some proof,' he replied. 'If, as we suspect, people are coming here to have their faces altered for some dodgy reason, then this should be brought to the attention of the authorities.'

'Having your looks changed drastically isn't necessarily illegal,' she pointed out. 'Not unless they're terrorists or something, looking for a total change of identity.'

'Then I suppose helping them would be classed as aiding and abetting,' Duncan concluded. 'But we couldn't go to the authorities with just suspicions.'

'If there's no proof, then I doubt they'd even bother to investigate.' She pushed his chair out of the lift and slowly along the near-deserted hospital corridors.

'So we need concrete evidence, like medical records, and their actual identities, just to build up a convincing case.'

'Ben downloaded all those suspect records on to a disc. He wouldn't have done that unless he intended to keep that information somewhere,' Helen said.

'And he must keep records of current patients, but where?' 'Maybe in his apartment, or an office somewhere – does he have an office in the hospital?'

'There's one, but it's shared by all the registrars,' Helen replied. 'However, he did once mention that he does a

200

lot of his work in Justin's office, because the lab is so quiet in the evenings.'

'Then we should try and break into it,' Duncan suggested, with rather undue enthusiasm.

'What's all this we?' she asked. 'I think it actually translates as "I", Duncan. You're due to leave pretty soon, and frankly I wouldn't have the faintest idea how to go about breaking into a locked office.'

'If I wasn't slap bang in the middle of filming, I'd stay longer and help you out.'

'But you can't,' she said, then fell silent as they approached the nurses' station on the East Wing, where a few night staff were on duty.

Neither of them said another word until they reached the privacy of Duncan's suite. 'You're right.' Duncan yawned as he climbed out of his chair. 'I'm not one hundred per cent at present. Usually I'd still be brimming with energy at this time of night, but I'm worn out.' He pulled her close. 'And another thing, my butt's sore!'

She gave a soft laugh. 'It is a rather enjoyable soreness, isn't it?'

'As a matter of fact, it is,' he agreed with a teasing grin.

'It's late. I'll help you into bed and leave,' Helen said, suddenly conscious of a slight headache in her right temple.

'Stay with me,' he said, kissing her forehead and cheeks.

'I can't, not in your room all night, it wouldn't be right,' she said awkwardly.

Such behaviour would compromise her position even more than she had done so already. Even taking him to her apartment had compounded her sins, especially while he was still an in-patient of the hospital.

'We'll discuss things tomorrow then,' Duncan replied, disappointedly. 'I'll help you figure out your next move. If needs be I could think of employing a private detective to help you. We might even be able to find a way of

201

getting him in here, either as a patient or member of staff.'

'I think that should be considered only as a last resort,' she said cautiously, fearing that someone like that might uncover some of the seedier sexual goings on in this hospital. Apart from what she knew about Justin, Ben and Sandra, she'd heard lots of rumours circulating. She was inclined to believe many of them, but any such sensitive information would reflect badly on the hospital governing board. She still cared for Max's wellbeing even though she no longer wanted to be involved with him.

'If you –' Duncan paused, as they heard a faint knock on the door. 'Come in,' he called out.

Colin entered dressed in jeans and a casual shirt, obviously ready to go off duty after his shift. 'I was hoping to catch you, Dr Dawson. There are a few phone calls you need to make tomorrow morning,' he said, well aware that he could speak freely in front of Duncan.

'About what?' Helen asked. 'And please don't forget that I asked you to call me Helen.'

'Yes, sorry. I've discovered some things about Dr Taylor which may be important,' Colin explained. 'Over the last few months he has taken on a number of extra duties. He's now the consultant physician for a couple of old people's homes in the vicinity, and a local home for maladjusted children. From what I can garner he's put a number of these patients on *Ampesoman*. I'm sure if you spoke to the people in charge of these places you could get far more information.'

'Could you find out more?' Duncan asked Helen.

'Probably,' she agreed thoughtfully. 'I'd have to come up with a convincing line as to why I was checking up on Ben though.'

'God knows how many people he's got on this drug,' Duncan added. 'He could be raking in a fortune.'

'I'm more than certain that he's not passing the payments on to the unsuspecting patients,' Colin added, frowning.

'I'll do what I can to find out more tomorrow,' Helen told them. 'You can give me a list of the addresses and phone numbers, Colin. If needs be I'll visit the places and try to get some concrete evidence.'

Up to now Helen had been inclined to blame Justin for all that was going on around here. She quite liked Ben, and had always considered him basically OK, but just weak and easily led. She had been totally wrong in her assumptions, and she began to see just how much she had misjudged this man.

'Another thing,' Colin continued. 'I managed to grab a quick word with Fran. She couldn't tell me much because her boyfriend keeps her pretty much in the dark. She did say that for some time now, Jack has been doing theatre work at odd times, late at night. Jack was deeply in debt when they first met, two years ago. Now he's free and clear, buying them a house, has a substantial amount in the bank and has just splashed out on a brand new sports car.'

Helen hid a yawn as she walked through the East Wing. She had spent a very restless night, her sleep filled with strangely erotic dreams in which Duncan, Ben and Justin figured, but she couldn't remember one single detail of what had happened between them.

She wasn't expecting to see Ben – according to the staff rota he wasn't on duty until after lunch – but she saw him striding towards her, coming from the direction of the annex. Obviously he had been visiting the new arrival, although the annex was officially still off limits to all staff.

'Helen,' he acknowledged. She didn't know if she was imagining it, but she thought that he was looking at her a trace oddly.

'Ben,' she smiled with extra warmth, hoping that appearing to be extra friendly might lull him into a false sense of security, although she despised him now more than she cared to admit. 'I was hoping to see you yesterday. I thought perhaps we might talk,' she said, lowering her eyelashes flirtatiously, noticing at the same time that he had a sample bag in his hand containing vials of freshly drawn blood.

'What exactly did you want to talk about?' he asked charily.

'Well –' Helen juggled the files she was holding, managing to drop a number of them and spreading papers across the floor. 'Oh, damn!'

Unenthusiastically, Ben bent to help her pick them up. 'There's no need to carry all this stuff around with you,' he said, laying the sample bag on the floor as he piled the papers together in a heap. Helen could see at least three vials of blood and a bloodworks request form in the bag. Samples from more than one patient were never sealed in the same bag. She couldn't see the name on the form as it was hidden by one of the blood samples.

'Thanks, Ben,' she said as he continued to gather up her papers.

'You surprised me,' he said softly, looking deep into her eyes. 'The other night, when we were all together. I didn't know that you were quite so liberated. Exotic sexual practices really turn you on, don't they?'

'It wasn't like me at all,' she admitted, feeling the colour rush to her cheeks. 'I don't know what came over me.'

'I do,' he replied huskily. Helen rose swiftly to her feet, as Ben straightened and placed her papers on the counter of the nurses' station. She vaguely heard the phone ringing as he put a hand on her arm and added, 'You were amazing, Helen. I thin – '

His words were cut off by the nurse calling his name. 'Dr Taylor!'

'Yes?' Ben sounded a little irritated.

'Could you go to X-ray straightaway, they need you.'

Helen heard Ben swear under his breath. 'Yes, nurse,' he agreed, smiling charmingly at the young woman. 'Tell them I'm on my way.' He stepped forwards and thrust the bag of samples into nurse Barker's hand. 'Dr Masterson is waiting for these. Take them straight down to the lab. Don't let them out of your sight, and don't give them to anyone but him. They're very urgent.'

By the time Helen had dumped the rest of her files on the counter, Ben was disappearing in the direction of X-ray and nurse Barker was walking briskly towards the nearest lift.

Helen hurried after her. 'I was hoping for a quick word, nurse Barker,' she called out.

Nurse Barker paused and turned to look enquiringly at Helen. 'Is something wrong, doctor?'

'On the contrary.' Helen smiled. 'It concerns the matter we spoke of the other day. Mr Paul will be only too happy to give you his autograph. He said to pop into his room, and don't forget to tell him what message you want him to write. I dare say he will give you some autographed photos for your friends as well.'

'Thank you.' Nurse Barker's face lit up. 'I'm so grate-ful, Dr Dawson,' she said with enthusiasm. 'Now if you'll excuse me, I have to get down to the lab.'

'I'd like to get a look at the samples first if you don't mind.'

'You heard what Dr Taylor said.' Nurse Barker clung determinedly on to the bag. 'That I shouldn't let them out of my sight.'

'They won't be out of your sight,' Helen said sooth-ingly. 'I know the samples are urgent. All I want to do is see if Dr Taylor included a request for an ESR,' Helen explained. 'It would be a pity to have to subject the patient to another blood test when the request can easily be added to this form.'

'I suppose so,' nurse Barker agreed reluctantly, as she handed Helen the bag.

'By the way,' Helen said as she opened the bag and examine the contents, thinking that a further sweetener wouldn't go amiss. 'Mr Paul suggested that you might like to visit the set of his latest movie. He'll be filming on location close by, quite soon. I'm sure it will even be OK if you want to take a friend.'

All nurse Barker's concerns about the samples disappeared in a flash as she stared in disbelief at Helen. 'You're really sure about this?'

'Quite sure,' confirmed Helen. Ben had written out a request for a Full Blood Count, including ESR, biochemical analysis and group and cross-match for imminent surgery. The name on the form was amusingly familiar – Mr Homer Simpson.

'This is unbelievable,' nurse Barker said, hardly able to contain her excitement, as Helen handed her back the small bag.

'Mr Paul's secretary will be contacting you with the details,' Helen said, certain Duncan could arrange what she had so rashly promised. 'Oh, and by the way, do me a favour, Nurse Barker. Don't mention to anyone that I looked at the samples. I wouldn't like Dr Taylor to think I was checking up on him – it could prove embarrassing.'

When Helen entered Duncan's room, to her surprise she found it in utter chaos. Duncan, dressed in a pale suit, was speaking agitatedly on the phone, while another guy was gathering up papers. A young, smartly dressed, rather plain looking young woman was sorting other files, putting some of them into a Gucci briefcase.

'Helen, there you are!' Duncan slammed down the phone, and walked over to her, running a hand through his hair. 'This is my secretary, Susanna,' he said, introducing the young woman.

'Hello.' She flashed a polite smile at Susanna, who appeared a trace concerned. 'Something wrong?' Helen asked Duncan.

'Isn't there always?' He sounded frustrated as he put an arm around Helen and led her into the bedroom. 'Sorry if I sound uptight, but this extra pressure – being producer as well as the star. There's so much to organise, and with my leg still strapped up –'

'Slow down,' she said soothingly. 'Just tell me everything, Duncan.'

'The backers have got into a panic. They think the delay, because of my ankle, will put us way over budget.

It's far too complicated to explain. What it means how-ever, is that I have to fly to Paris for a meeting and try to calm them down.'

'But I thought the insurers wanted you to remain in hospital a few days more?'

'Crazy isn't it?' he said. 'I'm being yanked in both directions at once, and they can't bloody well agree on anything.' He smiled at her. 'That's the movie business, Helen.' Duncan paused and pulled her close, kissing her with such passion that her knees grew weak. Then he cupped her face in his hands. 'You know I don't want to leave. I should stay and help you discover what's really going on around here.'

'It doesn't matter,' she told him. 'You go to Paris. The success of your movie is at stake.'

'It'll teach me not to be so keen in getting involved in production as well,' he said with a wry grin. 'I meant what I said last night. I could easily hire a decent private detective, employ them to help you.'

'No – not yet. Let's wait and see what Colin and I can find out for ourselves. I do have him, Duncan, and he is a reassuring presence.'

'I've asked him to keep a close eye on you and make sure you're OK.' Duncan pressed a card into her hand. 'Here's my secretary's number, she can get hold of anything you might need. And my private mobile num-ber. Only a very few close friends have that.'

'I'll be fine,' she insisted.

'I'll contact you as soon as I get back from Paris.' He paused and glanced towards the door at the sound of someone noisily clearing their throat. 'What's wrong?' he asked Susanna, who was standing awkwardly in the doorway.

'The car's here, Duncan. The driver has your passport and flight ticket,' she said, holding out his briefcase.

'Thanks.' Duncan looked back at Helen. 'Walk down with me?'

'Of course,' she agreed. 'But walk? Hospital policy

insists on wheelchairs for all patients checking out after surgery.'

'I obviously have some clout then, don't I?' He took the briefcase from Susanna.

'I worry about you, Duncan. You take too many chances with your health.' Helen grumbled as they walked out of his suite. He slid an arm about her waist, holding her close, and she gave up any attempt at lecturing him as they made their way downstairs to the lobby.

There was no chance of being alone to say their final farewells; at this time in the morning the lobby was crowded with patients arriving for treatment or due to attend various clinics. Helen saw a large black Mercedes parked outside, and Duncan's chauffeur waiting patiently just inside the entrance doors.

'We should say goodbye.' She turned to look deep into his gorgeous brown eyes. 'I'll miss you, Duncan.'

'Wait just a second.' He walked over to the chauffeur, and handed the man his briefcase. 'Give me a few minutes,' he said to the man, then moved back to Helen, all the while looking thoughtfully around the lobby. 'I want to kiss you,' Duncan whispered in her ear. 'In fact I need to fuck you – right here, right now,' he added softly, so that only she could hear.

His unexpected words made Helen glow as she experienced a sudden surge of lust. 'How can we?' she asked, as his warm breath brushed sensuously against her earlobe.

She couldn't contain her gasp of surprise as he grabbed hold of her hand and pulled her towards the unisex toilet, heedless of who might be watching them.

'Sssh,' he whispered, pulling her inside, and locking the door.

Duncan pushed Helen against the wall and jerked up her lacy top. His hands roughly caressed her breasts, arousing and exciting her as he ground his belly against hers. She felt the growing hardness of his cock and a wild hunger flooded her body. Her pussy ached, yearning for the feel of his lips, the delicious sensation of his tongue probing into her. Above all else, she had to have his cock pounding inside her, feel its power, its strength. She wished they could join together and remain that way forever.

Urgently Helen's hands moved to his flies, sliding down the zip, unbuttoning the waistband. They dropped around his ankles as he pulled up her skirt, bunching it around her slim waist, and pushed aside her panties, to burrow his fingers into her moist depths.

'God, how I want you,' he groaned, biting her breasts, while his fingers thrust harder into her.

'Now,' she begged, arching her hips, wriggling agitatedly until he jerked down her panties. His hands cupped her buttocks, his passion almost animal-like in its instinct, as he lifted her and thrust at the same time.

Helen sighed with relief as he impaled her on his prick, the sensation so utterly delicious as he buried the entire length inside her. She twined her legs around his hips as he pressed her back against the wall. Duncan began to pound into her, his desire vigorous and urgent, using quick deep strokes, his pubic bone smacking hard against hers.

Duncan's ramming shaft made her body quiver with pleasure as she felt the intense sensations spiral out of control. She could feel her orgasm moving closer, while each pounding thrust jammed her harder against the wall. Helen gave a muffled moan as her climax came in a sudden blinding rush. Duncan joined her, uttering a deep groan of surrender as the pleasure consumed his senses.

He leaned against Helen, his breath coming in laboured gasps, until he recovered enough to straighten and lower her gently to the ground. Helen's whole body trembled as she struggled into her panties and did her best to readjust her crumpled clothing.

'I can't seem to keep my hands off you,' Duncan said shakily, now fully dressed again, in his amazingly uncrushed suit. He was calmer now, but the passion still lingered in his dark eyes.

'Nor me you,' she admitted with a warm smile. 'Shouldn't you be going, you've got a plane to catch.'

'Yeah,' he agreed with a reluctance that heartened her immensely. 'I'd much rather stay here with you.'

'I'm flattered.' She tenderly smoothed his ruffled hair. 'You won't be in Paris long, will you?'

'Hopefully not,' he replied. 'Soon I'll be back in England and on location less than twenty miles away. You promise you'll come and visit me on set?'

'If only to make sure you're taking proper care of your health,' she replied, thinking that she would have to contact Susanna to arrange nurse Barker's visit. 'That's of course if I'm not busy playing detective around here.'

'Whatever you do, be careful. We don't exactly know what we're dealing with yet. You getting hurt isn't on the agenda.'

'Don't be silly, how would I get hurt?' she replied dismissively, appearing more confident than she felt.

'I'm still going to worry about you.' Duncan pulled her to him and kissed her with a tenderness that left her shaken to the core. It was a kiss of love not lust.

'I'll be fine,' she insisted, trembling with the intensity of her emotion.

'And I'd better go. If I don't turn up in Paris on time, all hell will break loose.' Duncan opened the door, letting Helen leave first, but following her immediately, heedless of what the occupants of the lobby might think. Helen didn't care about anyone else's opinion, and would have carried it off quite calmly if Sandra hadn't been standing there, pointedly waiting for them.

'Mr Paul,' she said, hurrying forwards, smiling charmingly at Duncan, but totally ignoring Helen. 'I had to come and bid farewell to such a high-profile patient.'

'So thoughtful.' Duncan replied politely. 'I'm flattered, matron.' He turned to look at Helen. 'I have to leave right now, I won't make the flight otherwise.'

'Then we mustn't keep you,' Sandra interjected before Helen could reply.

'Look after yourself.' Duncan smiled tenderly at Helen, totally ignoring Sandra. 'I'll phone you as soon as I get back – goodbye, matron,' he added as an afterthought, then flashed Helen another loving smile before he walked towards the door and climbed into his Mercedes.

Chapter Ten

*H*elen stood there watching until Duncan's car disappeared from sight, trying to contain her own unhappiness. She would miss him far more than she cared to admit.

'Helen.' Sandra's tone was sharp.

'Yes?' Helen turned to Sandra, her thoughts still focused on Duncan.

'You can't stand here in the lobby all day like some mooning fan,' Sandra said curtly. 'Pull yourself together and come with me. I need to speak with you in private.'

Helen couldn't refuse, even though she wanted to be alone with her thoughts for a few minutes. She followed Sandra along the corridor, and into matron's inner sanctum. 'Well, what was it you wanted?' she asked, thinking Sandra intended to discuss hospital business.

Sandra's face twisted into an expression of disgust. 'You're supposed to be a doctor, not Duncan Paul's whore!'

'I beg your pardon?' Helen could hardly believe what she was hearing.

'You stink of sex,' Sandra said bitchily. 'Are you so desperate to fuck that guy that you're prepared to do it practically in front of the entire hospital?'

'It wasn't like that –' Helen stammered, then gave a

bitter laugh. 'You're jealous!' she said, realising that there was a very simple explanation for Sandra's sudden hostility. 'You fancy Duncan, and you are jealous – because he wanted me, not you.'

'He may have wanted you for a quick shag because he was frustrated and there was no one else around at the time,' Sandra sneered. 'You obviously threw yourself at the man. But in real life, in his life, surrounded by beautiful actresses, he wouldn't give you a second look. I'm not jealous, just utterly disgusted with your behaviour.'

'And you think that *you* have the right to judge me?' Helen snapped back. 'You are unbelievable. You're the promiscuous one, not me. I saw you, Sandra, tied naked to your bed, turned on by being whipped. You were all too eager to let anyone and everyone slather all over your body and push their cocks into every willing orifice.'

Helen's venomous reply surprised even herself. She didn't usually rise to the bait that easily. Yet the erotic vision her words conjured up clouded her thinking for a moment, exciting her beyond explanation, as the simmering heat in her pussy grew stronger. Not that long ago she'd had her face buried in this woman's sex. Life got weirder by the moment.

'I don't recall you objecting at the time. When you were invited to join in you responded with alacrity!' Sandra reminded her. 'Justin and Ben can both attest to that. 'However, what we choose to do in our private lives is nobody's business but ours. Just as long as it doesn't affect any of our professional responsibilities. That wasn't the case with you, Helen. I should remind you that you are on duty this morning, and patient care does not extend to shagging them in the lobby before they leave.'

'Is that so?' Helen retorted. 'That's not what I've heard.'

Colin had acquainted her with even more of the rumours circulating in the East Wing. It was said that the majority of the nursing staff in the West Wing were all too eager to provide services to their patients way above the call of duty.

Helen had to admit that she was a little perturbed by Sandra's words. Helen knew full well that she had let her desire for Duncan get out of hand. Having sexual relations with a patient in these circumstances might be more a moral than factual crime, but her behaviour had been foolhardy all the same.

'Rumours always circulate in places like this,' Sandra said curtly. 'You don't have to believe them. They are mostly started by a few disgruntled staff in the East Wing. It's just sour grapes that's all. The staff in the West Wing have been here longer and are consequently better paid that those in the rest of the hospital. However, your relationship with Duncan Paul was no ill-informed rumour, and it wasn't even conducted with discretion. It was made obvious to all and sundry.'

'Perhaps I did let matters get a little out of hand,' Helen admitted. 'But Duncan has left, so it won't happen again.'

'No, it won't,' Sandra agreed, her anger appearing to cool a shade. 'We still need to have a serious talk about certain matters. First, I have something to show you. You had better sit down.'

'I can't stay long,' Helen pointed out as she sat down reluctantly on the floral couch. 'I have patients to attend to,' she added, confused by the fact that Sandra had turned on the TV.

'They can wait, this can't.' Sandra picked up the video remote. 'I'll show you my favourite part first.' She relaxed back on the sofa. 'I'll be interested to hear if it's your favourite too.'

For a brief second, when the picture first appeared on the screen, Helen thought she was watching a movie. Her face turned scarlet in embarrassed disbelief as she recognised the two naked people. 'How did you get this?' she gasped in horror, seeing herself inserting a gold vibrator into Duncan's arse.

Helen was filled with such fury, such disgust, that her

214

mind went blank for a moment. Yet for all her anguish, the sight of her and Duncan together was highly arousing. Watching herself make love was an amazingly hedonistic experience.

'Judging by your expression, you're enjoying this part best as well.' Sandra stared intently at the screen, watching Helen energetically shaft herself on Duncan's cock. 'What does it feel like having sex with such a famous actor?'

'Unbelievable,' Helen hissed furiously. 'How the hell did you get hold of this? Are there hidden cameras in my apartment?'

'I could fast forward it if you like.' Sandra smiled. 'I love the bit where Duncan goes down on you. Who's better at licking you, him or me?'

'You are foul,' Helen snapped. 'Just tell me how the hell you got this.'

'Your apartment used to be occupied by Justin,' Sandra said with a goading smile. 'Justin installed the camera – he's always liked watching himself on the job. He used to bring the tapes with him, and we'd watch them while having sex ourselves. They are a great turn on, believe me. We often used to place bets on how long it would take him to seduce a new member of staff. He's amazingly successful, you know.'

'What is the point of this?' Helen glanced back at the TV, growing wetter as she watched Duncan kissing and caressing every part of her naked body. 'Is your intention to humiliate and embarrass me? Well, it won't work.'

'Oh, but it will,' Sandra said confidently. 'You played right into our hands, acting so indiscreetly in taking Duncan Paul to your apartment.'

'It might have been foolish,' Helen conceded. 'But it's not a cardinal sin.'

'In the eyes of the British Medical Association it is.' Sandra clearly thought she was on a roll as she stared at Helen, appearing so confident, so sure of herself.

'I beg your pardon?'

'I presume you know that a doctor can be struck off

for having sexual relations with a patient,' Sandra stated, as if Helen was some kind of idiot. 'You did know that, didn't you?'

'Of course I knew,' Helen snapped. 'But officially Duncan was never my patient,' she added, as a frisson of fear passed through her. 'Ben Taylor was the admitting physician. He assisted during the surgery. I took no part at all in Duncan's treatment. The only thing I did was check up on his post-op condition when requested to by Ben.'

'You're clutching at straws,' Sandra replied, sounding chillingly sure of herself. 'I suggest you examine Mr Paul's hospital records. I'm certain you will find that your assumptions are incorrect.' Sandra smiled triumphantly. 'Your name is on every piece of paper in that file. Officially you were his attending physician.'

'So you alter medical records when it suits you.' Helen managed to hide her concerns amazingly well. 'Strangely, that doesn't surprise me.'

'Not only was Duncan your patient, I have very visible proof that you were having sex with him. You'll find not one person in this hospital who will be prepared to back up your side of the story. If I choose to do so, I can destroy your medical career in a moment.' Sandra snapped her fingers loudly. 'It will take no longer than that.'

'What do you intend to do with this information, then?' Helen challenged, fearing the worst.

'Why nothing, darling.' Sandra put on a good display of charming innocence as she looked with thoughtful consideration at Helen. 'You're a friend, a very intimate friend. Why should I want to hurt you? This tape will remain part of Justin's secret library and will never be shown to anyone outside our little circle, unless –' she paused to give extra emphasis to her next words '– unless you plan to continue your curious little forays into matters that are not your concern. I understand Justin spoke to you about this the other night. The problem is that you are looking for things that just aren't there.'

'Really?' Helen raised her eyebrows. 'I think there are some pretty weird things going on around here, Sandra. Such as non-urgent surgery being carried out in the middle of the night.'

'You're clearly troubled about the two patients we have lodged in the new annex,' Sandra said coolly. 'There's nothing to be suspicious about. They are both very high-powered individuals who want to keep their treatment totally private. We offer a service second to none at the Princess Beatrice, and when we are asked to be discreet, we arrange to be just that.'

'But why are they in the annex when it isn't completed? And why the stories about problems with the structural integrity of one of the rooms?' Helen challenged, certain that Sandra still wasn't being truthful with her.

'Why do you have to complicate everything? Duncan Paul is the one who deals in fantasy, not you. Doctors rely on cold, hard facts,' Sandra replied calmly. 'Rumours had reached us about a member of the tabloid press infiltrating the hospital. So we decided to place these patients in rooms in the annex which were already finished, and make it out of bounds to everyone but a few select members of staff that we knew we could trust – those staff members who wouldn't see something suspicious or underhand in our motives. You were new here, Helen. We didn't know how safe it would be to confide in you, so we chose to keep you in the dark.'

'I'm sorry if my suspicions were wrong,' Helen said, thinking it wiser at present to appear to accept Sandra's explanation of events – at least until she decided what to do about the videotape. She saw no point in examining Duncan's medical records; they would be exactly as Sandra said, falsified just as she'd promised.

'In future I would suggest that you keep your mind wholly on your work,' Sandra said, smiling at Helen. 'If you do that everything will be fine,' she continued, putting her hand on Helen's thigh and squeezing it in a very familiar fashion.

Colin jogged through the hospital grounds, trying to control the anger that simmered deep inside him. It was a long time since he'd felt like this; he had managed to smother most of his aggressive tendencies since he'd left the army. Yet now they were surfacing again, whether he wanted them to or not.

Ben Taylor's behaviour was the main cause of his anger. Created out of concern for Zara, it had taken root and flourished as he discovered more of Ben's perfidy. Helen Dawson had contacted one of the old people's institutions, and the children's home, pretending to be a physician involved in monitoring the *Ampesoman* trials. In order to protect herself, she'd given a false name, so that even if Ben did get to hear of her visit, he wouldn't know it was Helen.

Helen had discovered that a number of patients had been put on the drug – so far twenty-one in all – and she still had the second old people's home to check up on. Some of the patients on *Ampesoman* had already begun to suffer a variety of unpleasant side effects, but Ben had insisted that they must all continue and take the entire course of tablets. This was because he wouldn't get the $10,000 pay-out if the patient's six-week trial wasn't satisfactorily completed. He seemed to display no concern for the wellbeing of his patients. His only interest was the money he hoped to make.

Zara had taken no persuading to stop taking the drug but she had yet to acquaint Ben of that fact. Helen, meanwhile, had promised her friend Peter Caxton at the FDA in Washington that she would try to find proof that Ben was falsifying his records, and intended to appropriate all the cash due to be paid to those on the drug trial. Somehow they had to get hold of concrete evidence, both on Ben and the patients lodged in the annex. To those ends, Colin had casually befriended one of the girls who worked in the bacteriology department. She had told Colin that Justin kept his office locked, and even the lab staff weren't allowed in there. Both Justin and Ben had keys to the office which they kept on them at all times. All Colin had to do was figure out how to get hold of one of the keys and surreptitiously break into Justin's office to find some corroborating evidence. There was no way he would let Helen try to do anything like that. He was convinced that he could adequately protect himself if things got nasty – but she couldn't.

Colin ran the last few yards, then slowed to a brisk walk as he entered the building, making his way to the gym. He intended to have only a short exercise session before going to see Zara. She was due to check out tomorrow and fly off to the Bahamas. Then he wouldn't see her for two weeks. He hated to say goodbye to her, but he had to stay here, work out his notice, and also help Helen.

Usually, at this time of day, a little after 6 p.m., the gym was empty. Most staff favoured the early morning sessions. The locker room was unisex, with separate cubicles for the more modest, so most people just changed together and left their stuff on the benches. It was never locked away because nothing was ever stolen at the Princess Beatrice.

Colin towelled the sweat from his face and slipped off his singlet. After spending time with Zara, he planned to hang around near theatre round about midnight, as it was more or less definite that the new arrival from the annex would be undergoing surgery tonight. Fran had left him a message on his answerphone: Jack was due to work this evening and intended to get to the operating theatre just after 11p.m., when most of the night staff would have carried out their evening routine and be settling down for a quiet few hours of relaxation.

Wondering if anyone was in the gym, Colin peered through the glass panel in the gym door. He was surprised to see both Ben and Sandra working out on the machines. Both were wearing only brief shorts and singlets, and it was obvious that Ben had no pockets to keep his keys in. If the keys were in Ben's bag, here in the locker room, Colin thought he might have just enough time to steal them, break into Justin's office, then replace the keys before Ben finished his workout. Pathology closed at 5 p.m., so he was more or less safe from discovery.

Glancing round the locker room, Colin spotted two bags close together, one pink, one navy. Dropping his sweat-stained top on the bench, he began to rifle through the dark-blue canvas bag. The first thing he found of any interest was Ben's wallet, with a number of credit cards and nearly five hundred pounds in cash; a lot of money especially for a none-too-well-paid doctor. Rifling deeper, Colin still couldn't find any keys, but he did pull out a loose-leafed, leather-covered book about the size of a personal organiser. There were lists of names and dates, even brief medical notes on some of the patients, probably all pertaining to his *Ampesoman* trials. However, there were thirty to forty names on the list, far more than Helen had found so far. Also there was a word, written in capital letters in a red felt-tipped pen on the back page of the book: PANDORA. Colin had no idea what that meant.

If Colin's instincts hadn't been honed by the years he'd spent in the army, he would never have heard the faint sound of someone approaching. He dropped Ben's stuff back in the bag and turned around to see Justin stroll casually into the locker room.

'Hi, Colin,' Justin said, not appearing at all suspicious of Colin as he stepped nonchalantly away from Ben's bag. 'Planning a workout?' Justin asked

'I was,' Colin replied. 'But my run took longer than I initially intended. I haven't much time to spare so I think I might just take a shower.'

'Nothing like strenuous exercise to work out one's demons,' Justin joked.

'I don't have any demons,' Colin replied, stepping away from Justin.

'Don't forget this.' Justin picked up a navy towel edged in scarlet. 'It's yours isn't it?'

'No, it's not,' Colin replied hurriedly. 'I came over here to examine it, because I thought it was the towel I left here by mistake a couple of days ago.'

'Any stuff left around at the end of the day gets gathered up by the cleaners, and lodged with matron's secretary,' Justin pointed out .'Didn't you know that?'

Colin shrugged his shoulders. 'Guess I forgot.'

'Guess you did.' Justin eyed him thoughtfully. 'By the way, could you do me a favour?'

'Favour?'

'Yeah. With all your service training, you must be able to give me a few pointers on body building. I'm having a little trouble with my bench presses.'

'Sure,' Colin confirmed, hiding his reluctance to have anything to do with Justin. 'When?'

'Now, if you wouldn't mind.' Justin looked at him expectantly. 'It'll only take a moment.'

'It'll be my pleasure,' Colin said with a fake smile, then followed Justin into the gym.

Ben and Sandra, both sweating and breathing heavily, turned to look at Colin. He had never seen Sandra out of uniform before, and he couldn't believe the skimpiness of her shorts and top. The brief white singlet clung damply to the curves of her large breasts, and her nipples stood out like organ stops. Her shorts were so tight that they rode up at the crotch, the fabric slipping tautly between her pussy lips, drawing Colin's eyes like a magnet. Sandra seemed equally fascinated by him as she stared at his muscular chest.

'Colin's going to give me a few pointers,' Justin announced.

'Is he?' Sandra stepped forward and squeezed Colin's muscular upper arms. 'Very impressive.' She glanced downwards, as if also trying to gauge the size of his sexual organs.

Justin moved over to the first weights bench, and

221

placed a number of weights at either end of the thick steel bar. 'One hundred kilos OK?'

'I can manage that,' Colin agreed, feeling a little self-conscious as he lay down on the bench, tucking his knees down over the end, while all three of them stared at him expectantly. 'I usually work with a little less weight and do more reps.'

Ben moved to the head of the bench, ready to help Colin if the need arose, watching him intently as he positioned his hands on the bar.

'That's the right position, is it?' Justin asked.

'About perfect, I'd say.' Sandra moved closer to Colin. 'Now lift, and lower slowly, keeping your breathing just right.' Colin demonstrated, his muscles bulging under the weight, as he eased it down across his chest then lifted. 'Don't forget to exhale as you lift it up from your chest.'

Colin did four more reps, then went to replace the bar, thinking he must do this more often, as his arms were feeling a trace weary. He'd not been exercising much recently; first there had been the course on aromatherapy, then Zara.

'Don't stop yet,' Justin pleaded. 'A few more, just so that I can really get the hang of the technique.'

Colin didn't like to refuse – he was a well-built guy and didn't want to appear weak in front of Ben and Justin. He did three more reps, now able to feel the faint burn as the lactic acid built up in his muscles.

Just as he lowered the bar to his chest for the last time, Justin stepped astride his prone body, and placed his hands between Colin's on the steel bar, pushing down with his entire weight. If Colin had been fresher, he could have easily pushed Justin off and lifted the bar back on to its rack. But Justin had timed his move well, and Colin was just a shade too tired to gather enough momentum to lift the bar away from his chest. All he could do was tense his muscles and keep a tight hold on the bar to prevent the entire thing slipping forwards and crushing his throat.

'Ease off, Justin, the joke's over,' Colin gasped, staring up at him.

'It's not over by a long chalk,' Justin sneered. 'I want to know why you were rummaging around in Ben's bag. I didn't figure you as a thief, Colin.'

'My bag?' Ben exclaimed in angry surprise.

'Thief,' Colin muttered, finding it hard to speak as he struggled with the weight, trying to prevent it crushing him, his muscles screaming under the pressure. 'I'm no thief.'

'Then what were you doing in Ben's bag?' Justin challenged. 'Tell me, and this can be over.'

'I'm no thief,' Colin insisted, unable to tell Justin the truth without compromising himself and Helen.

'Tell me,' Justin pressed. 'Or I'll have to force it out of you.'

'By killing me?' Colin's muscles were threatening to give way, but he dare not let go if he wanted to survive.

'We don't want to harm you,' Sandra assured him.

'We just want the truth.' Justin eased his weight from the bar, still applying just enough extra pressure to stop Colin from lifting it. 'Think how unhappy Miss Dawn would be if there was an unfortunate accident.'

'No, Justin,' Sandra said sharply. 'This has gone far enough.'

He flashed her a sullen, angry look. 'I can make him tell me, eventually.'

'Ease off me, and I'll tell you,' Colin begged, desperately trying to retain control of his aching muscles. He could feel them trembling now under the pressure, and feared they could give way at any moment.

'For God's sake, help him, Ben.' Sandra sounded genuinely concerned. Colin summoned all his strength and, without waiting for Justin's approval, Ben somehow managed to help him lift the hundred kilos and place the barbell back on its stand.

Colin lay there, panting with exertion, his arms feeling weak and shaking slightly, while Ben rolled the stand back, away from Colin's head. Justin didn't move, he just sat heavily on Colin's chest, making sure his weakened captive wouldn't be able to sit up. Colin was past caring; he was giving his body time to recover its strength, while he desperately tried to think of an innocent reason why he would be rifling through the contents of Ben's bag. Unfortunately he could think of nothing convincing, other than the truth, and that wasn't a viable option.

'If you're not a thief, what are you, Colin?' Justin taunted. 'How about a spy?'

'Spy?' Colin repeated. 'Spying on what in a bloody hospital? I'm just a staff nurse, Justin.'

'Who rifles through other people's belongings,' Ben accused.

'And chooses to mix with the wrong kind of people. You seem very pally with Dr Dawson. Why, may I ask?' Sandra quizzed.

'Because I like her,' Colin retorted. 'My friends are, after all, my business.'

'Not in this hospital.' Sandra stepped closer, running appreciative hands over Colin's bare chest. 'You've found yourself a rich older woman. You'll be leaving soon to live off her millions. Wouldn't it be safer to keep your nose clean until then?'

'You wouldn't want anything to jeopardise your future,' Justin added, as Colin felt something touch his legs. He realised, way too late, that Ben was fixing a thick leather weight lifting belt around his calves, strapping his lower limbs to the legs of the bench.

'Hey,' Colin growled. 'What's going on?'

'Didn't you hear what Justin said?' Sandra trailed her fingers over his nipples. 'You don't want to compromise your position with Zara, do you?'

'Of course I don't,' he gasped. Sandra was pulling on his nipples, teasing them into pert peaks, and Colin began to feel very nervous – everything was getting way out of control. 'I've no intention of doing that.'

'I think you might have already compromised your position,' Justin said softly, easing himself back so that

224

he was sitting astride Colin's stomach. 'Getting dismissed for attempted theft might make Miss Dawn think twice.'

'Do you think it would scare her to know that her gigolo was also a thief?' Sandra leaned closer, her breast pressing against Colin's side, while she trailed her fingers down his arm. He didn't realise what she was up to as she circled his wrist, not until the warmth of her finger was replaced by the cold hardness of metal. Hearing a slight click, Colin tried to move and discovered that she had handcuffed his wrist to the underside of the bench. He struck out with his one free arm, but Justin and Ben acted swiftly. Catching hold of his forearm they manhandled it down, just managing to confine his wrist in a similar fashion.

'This is insane,' Colin gasped, watching in disbelief as Sandra slipped off her clothing. She was amply built and as she moved, her breasts jiggled enticingly.

'Insane?' Justin grinned wickedly. 'There are many ways to compromise people, Colin. If one doesn't work, we try another.'

Sandra rubbed her full breast against Colin's chest, and he tried to fight his arousal, all too aware that this exercise was designed to compromise rather than cause physical harm. But his body didn't appear to want to do what his mind told it. He tensed, struggling to keep tight control over the sudden overpowering sensation of lust, but almost of its own accord his cock begin to harden.

'Zara might not be willing to believe you are a thief, but I bet she won't be too happy to learn that when you're not with her, you spend your time engaged in hedonistic pursuits with other members of staff,' Sandra purred.

'Perhaps photographic evidence,' Ben suggested.

Colin stared at Sandra's breasts, never having seen such huge nipples on a woman. As she rubbed them teasingly across his small paps, he experienced an even stronger surge in his libido, knowing that the very positive evidence of his arousal now distended his tight jersey shorts.

'Let me see his cock.' Sandra tried to peer past Justin. 'Is it hard yet?' she asked, grinning wickedly at her erstwhile boyfriend.

She gave a delighted laugh as Justin stepped aside and jerked down the captive's shorts to allow Colin's rampant cock to rear away from his flat stomach. 'Deliciously hard,' Justin replied.

'You'll enjoy yourself, Sandra,' Ben said, eyeing Colin's cock. 'He's pretty well endowed.'

'You'd be amazed, Colin. Lots of muscular guys have tiny dicks,' Sandra confided, seeming pleased with herself as she settled down by his side again. 'It's the steroids they use.' She tweaked his nipple, then pinched it until it turned red. 'Does Zara like to feel your big cock thrusting inside her, or does she like you going down on her best?'

Not waiting for an answer, Sandra lapped at his nipples sucking on one, gnawing at it with her teeth. Colin felt the blood rush to his groin, as sexual need overwhelmed his senses. There was something perversely arousing about being tied down and forced to endure this, however much he disliked and despised his tormentors. Then he felt hands stroking his private parts, hands that could only belong to Justin or Ben. They cupped his balls, caressing them gently before teasing fingers slid up and down the shaft of his penis. He felt his balls tighten, and his cock stiffen even more. He was being touched by a man, yet those gentle fingers knew how to titillate beyond endurance. Colin had never had a homosexual experience, but he had always wondered what it would be like.

He closed his eyes for a second, thinking that, male or female, it made no difference – the tantalising touch felt delicious all the same. There was no point in trying to resist, or fight the onslaught on his senses. He was bound and totally helpless. Colin relaxed, allowing the caress-

226

ing movements to further seduce his senses, as his cock stiffened even more.

Sandra stroked his chest, sucking greedily on his nipples, while he felt other lips touch his sex; a soft, wet mouth, kissing, licking, inciting his passions, sending them spiralling out of control. A moist tongue circled his penis, lapping at his balls, then his cock-head was pulled between willing lips. They sucked so hard on the shaft that his insides cramped. The pleasure was utterly exquisite and he wanted it to continue forever. So many hands, so many mouths, all pleasuring him at the same time.

Colin's cock was buried deep in the warm, moist cavern of Ben or Justin's mouth, while Sandra kissed him, stabbing her tongue against his. Colin allowed himself to drown in the sea of hedonistic pleasure, surrendering himself completely as somewhere in the distance he heard a man moan, never realising it was him.

Justin, Ben and Sandra toyed with his senses, taking him higher and higher and Colin's desire rose swiftly, quick and sudden lust ripping through him as his balls tensed ready for climax. Then nimble fingers squeezed his cock head, and he felt his passion start to deflate, stifling his rush of pleasure, preventing him from coming.

Colin groaned in frustration, but was compensated by the sight of Sandra's shaved quim as she straddled his chest. She moved her body forwards, gradually lowering her open sex on to his face, almost smothering him with her soft, ample flesh. She smelt stronger and muskier than Zara but good all the same.

He pressed his lips to the scarlet slit, pulling the fragrance of her pussy deep into his lungs. Sliding his tongue between her labia, he ran the tip of it along her moist slit, pausing to circle her generously sized clit. Colin pulled it into his mouth, sucking on it hard, only vaguely conscious of Sandra's moan of pleasure.

He needed to tear his arms from his bonds and thrust his fingers deep into her, to finger-fuck her beyond endurance. Instead, he stabbed his tongue into her moist fleshy depths, caressing her soft internal walls until her belly trembled with bliss.

Sandra was close to coming when she pulled away from Colin, sliding down his prone form to straddle his hips. Colin wanted her desperately, yet he still despised the physical hunger that consumed his senses as she sheathed herself on his sex. Colin felt her soft, wet flesh embrace his cock, tightening around it until strong sensations of lust flooded his body, blocking out all negative thoughts.

He strained upwards with his hips, thrusting deeper, but his movements were held in check by his bonds. Sandra responded, pushing her hips downwards so that her pelvis was jammed hard against his pubic bone. As Sandra continued to ride his body, thrusting wildly up and down, Colin lost himself in the lewd pleasures of the senses.

Suddenly Justin stepped astride his upper chest and Colin found himself facing an engorged prick, which waved tantalisingly in front of his face. Colin was surprised to discover he was far from repulsed, and instinctively he reached forwards and pulled it between his lips, turned on by the feel of the silver balls that pierced its head.

Lust overtook his entire being, and the lewd carnality of the experience was so powerful that it blocked out everything but the search for ever increasing pleasure. Sandra continued to bounce up and down on his throbbing dick as Colin pulled Justin's penis deeper into his mouth, sucking on it tenderly, while Ben moved behind his head, leaning forwards to push his organ into Justin's willing mouth.

All four of them were melded together in a tableaux of intimacy so exquisitely hedonistic that the logical part of Colin's brain couldn't even begin to believe this was happening. Justin's cock slid deeper, forcing Colin's throat muscles to contract around the head. Colin sucked hard with his lips, filled with the sudden need to draw

Justin's spunk into his mouth at the very moment he achieved his own release. Tension built swiftly, then a sudden surging pressure swept through Colin's groin, shooting out of his cock, as Justin's creamy offering spurted down his throat.

No matter how hard she tried to convince herself that everything would be fine, Helen couldn't bring herself to look forward to the party she was due to attend tonight. She felt obliged to go as Sandra's invitation had been tantamount to a command.

Trapped in a corner by circumstance, Helen had little control over her own life at present. She felt like a puppet on a string being controlled by Sandra, Justin and Ben. It was either that or chance jeopardising her career.

Helen was going to the annual party, organised for the staff of the West Wing, and to be honest she wasn't even certain why Sandra wanted her to be there. Helen had deliberately kept her distance from Sandra and her cronies since the threatening incident in matron's office. She was scared of being pulled into the sexual morass they inhabited, their only needs appearing to be a constant search for physical gratification. Helen was made even more fearful because she found something highly seductive about this strange way of life.

The party was being held in the newly renovated ballroom, and the invitation stated erotic fancy dress. As Helen didn't have anything to fit that category, Zara had arranged to lend her a costume from one of her movies – a sci-fi extravaganza called *Starfest*.

It was a little over five days since Duncan had flown to Paris. He was back in England now, the problems all sorted out, and had already resumed filming. Helen had spoken to him on the phone a number of times and hoped to visit him soon, but she hadn't told him about the videotape, or Sandra's threats. Even if he knew, Duncan could do nothing to help Helen. Not only was the videotape capable of destroying her career, it could also harm Duncan. If the press got hold of it they would both most likely be compromised beyond endurance, and Duncan's international fame would make the situation even worse.

Helen hadn't even spoken of Sandra's threats to Colin. He had been acting a little oddly himself lately. Perhaps he was missing Zara, or was just troubled about all they had discovered. Whatever was wrong, he definitely wasn't showing much enthusiasm for their investigations at present. But as things stood, maybe she should consider his lack of zeal a blessing in disguise.

However, Colin had found out that the Arab gentleman had been operated on, and once again the surgery had been extensive facial reconstruction. Colin hadn't been able to discover the surgeon's identity, so at first they'd both presumed it to be Ralph. But Helen had phoned him in New York less than twenty-four hours later, and he mentioned a gala he'd attended at Carnegie Hall the night the operation had been carried out. Further investigation had confirmed his presence at the event, so Ralph was ruled out. Neither Helen nor Colin had any idea who the other surgeon might be.

Still trying to muster some enthusiasm for the evening ahead, Helen put on her outfit, which was skimpy in the extreme. The side lacing proved difficult to manage and she struggled with it for a short time. The garment, if one could call it that, was fashioned out of a fabric which looked but didn't feel like shiny black PVC. The front panel was so narrow and brief she had been forced to shave off the majority of her pubic hair. Level with her breasts it extended outwards into a 'T' shape which served just to cover her nipples. The equally narrow strip at the back was held to the front by elaborate lacing at the sides. To all intents and purposes she was nude, with just her nipples and the crack of her sex and buttocks covered. Yet the outfit looked good, amazingly sexy.

A silver studded belt was slung low around her hips. Attached to that, just at the sides were narrow, floor length panels of the black, shiny fabric, which revealed the length of her shapely thighs and her high-heeled, tight-fitting boots. Helen wore far more make-up than usual, especially around her eyes, and when she looked in the mirror she barely recognised herself. She had to admit she had never felt more sexually alluring than she did in this scanty outfit.

Thinking of Duncan for a moment, she looked up at the grille set high in the wall opposite her bed. She'd found Justin's hidden video camera soon after she had spoken with Sandra, and put it straight in the refuse bin to be carted away by the dustmen the very next day. Then she had conducted a search of her apartment, ensuring there were no other nasty little hidden surprises. She was still thinking of this when she heard a faint rap on her door.

'Colin!' she exclaimed, surprised not only by his unexpected arrival, but also by his outfit. 'Come inside,' she said as they were being careful not to be seen too often together.

'You look amazing,' he gasped, looking her up and down, clearly turned on by her scanty costume. 'No man could resist you.'

'I hope that's an exaggeration,' she said with an awkward smile. 'I don't want to spend the entire evening fending them all off.'

She looked at Colin, only dressed in tightly-cut, brown leather trousers and long boots, never having realised what an attractive man he was until now. He was well built and muscular, with slim hips and a firm flat belly. His outfit was in some ways similar to hers, laced at the sides like her dress, with only his groin and the inner parts of his legs covered.

'Same movie,' he told her, adjusting the metal studded leather bands around his wrists, which matched the leather collar decorating his neck. In his hand Colin held a brown leather head-dress which would mask most of his features and make him unrecognisable to the other guests. 'I asked Zara to organise it for me, after you told me that Sandra wanted you to attend the party tonight.'

231

'Were you invited as well?' she asked, feeling a little self-conscious about the way his eyes kept straying back to her scantily covered body.

'No. I'm gatecrashing,' he told her. 'With most of the guests masked, they'll probably never realise that I've not been officially invited. Dressed like that, Helen, you'd make a monk feel horny. I can't let you go in there alone; I intend to come too, and make sure you'll be OK.'

'I'll be fine,' she insisted. 'After all this is just a staff party.' She looked down at her outfit. 'I admit this is pretty outrageous, but I'm a big girl, I can look after myself.'

'Don't forget it's being organised by Justin and Sandra,' Colin said very seriously. 'From what I hear last year's party got pretty wild and totally out of hand – it turned into a full-blown orgy. That's worrying enough, but I also don't trust Sandra and her cronies. They must have some nefarious reason for wanting you to be there, Helen.' He frowned. 'They know damn well you're on to them, and you can't ignore that fact.'

Of course Colin didn't know about the videotape – she had told nobody about that – and she was certain that Sandra and Justin felt quite safe in the knowledge that they could ruin her in a moment if they chose to. 'They also know that we don't have one shred of definite proof. The only person we could harm with any certainty is Ben, and he isn't aware of that yet.'

'I'm still not happy to let you go alone,' he insisted. 'Duncan called me, not long after you told him Sandra had invited you. He asked me to watch your back.'

'Did he?' she said with a thoughtful frown.

Gauging her thought correctly, Colin added, 'It's not as if he's checking up on you or anything – he'd never do that. He just doesn't trust Sandra, Justin or Ben.'

'Who does?' she said, lightly. 'Just don't get caught gatecrashing, and keep a low profile once you're in.'

'My own mother wouldn't recognise me in this get-up, and when I put on the head-dress –' he grinned. '– I'm a different person altogether.'

232

'I don't think my mother would recognise me either,' Helen admitted with a rueful smile.

'By the way,' Colin continued. 'Did you make up your mind whether to contact Professor Fenton?'

'I did. I left a message on his mobile yesterday evening,' she confirmed. 'All I said was that I was concerned about Ben Taylor's behaviour, with regard to a drug trial he was carrying out without official authority from the hospital board. Peter Caxton is going to contact the manufacturers of *Ampesoman*, and suggest they check up on the methods Ben is using. I wanted Max to be prepared, just in case things get ugly, although nothing can be totally proven until the trial is completed and Ben withholds the money from the patients concerned.'

'So in other words, we're off the hook?'

'Peter still wants any documentary proof we can provide, just to back up the FDA's investigations. He's concerned that Ben might decide to give the patients fake identities so that they'll be more difficult to trace.'

'Frankly, I think we'd better let the experts deal with this now,' Colin said cautiously. 'Justin and Ben are not nice guys. If they discover you were involved in putting the finger on Ben –'

'I know,' she interrupted. 'I'll worry about that, if and when it happens, not before.'

Colin did not appear altogether happy with her reply. 'Maybe, now that Professor Fenton knows, he'll get back here and make sure you are OK. If I was him, I'd be back in a flash.'

'Then I'll have to tell him that we are finished, which won't be easy. Max can be very possessive at times.'

'I'd prefer him to Ben or Justin any day,' Colin pointed out.

'I suppose you are right,' Helen agreed, glancing at the clock. 'It's getting late, I should be leaving.'

Colin slipped on his head-dress, and Helen examined him with thoughtful consideration. 'Nobody will know who you are,' she agreed. 'It masks your features completely. All I have to do if I get worried is keep my eyes peeled for the masked stranger,' she added teasingly.

'And he'll fly to your rescue,' Colin responded jokingly, as he moved towards her front door.

After Colin had departed, Helen walked into her bedroom to turn off the TV. She had left it on mute, and as she picked up the remote she glanced at the screen. She froze in surprise as she recognised the hook-nosed man whose picture had just flashed into view. He probably looked very different now that Ralph had performed such radical surgery on him, she thought, as she turned up the sound. His name was Carlos Alcazar, and he was a South American drug baron who had built up a massive distribution system in the United States. He was being hunted by the FBI, and was wanted for murder and various other unpleasant crimes. It was thought he had fled to Europe and all ports and airports were being watched.

Helen had tried to persuade herself to believe Sandra's explanation, but deep down she had always known it wasn't true. Now she had discovered the true identity of Mr X, and it appeared that Ben and his accomplices had been involved in committing a criminal act by aiding and abetting a wanted man.

Chapter Eleven

*H*elen's thoughts were still full of her staggering discovery as she made her way to the party. If Ben, Ralph and the others were branded criminals her career might be safe after all. Once they were arrested, all she had to do was locate the videotape of her and Duncan, and destroy it immediately.

The newly renovated ballroom looked wonderful, and Helen felt as if she had stepped back into a place where past, present and future intertwined. The room was illuminated by flickering candles and magnificent glass chandeliers, while swathes of black silk covered the windows, blocking out any remnants of evening light. Helen, like all those present, was masked, making it difficult to figure out anyone's true identity. The costumes were a strange mixture from Baroque to the foreseeable future, all highly erotic, some more blatantly sexual than others.

Two young women walked past Helen, touching each other intimately and totally oblivious to the presence of the other guests. They both wore facsimiles of a nurse's uniform, but their breasts were uncovered, and their skirts so short that it was easy to see they wore nothing underneath.

Helen saw both ends of the spectrum here, from highly

elaborate bejewelled garments to brief costumes consisting of chains and leather straps which lifted and exposed genitalia in a variety of different ways. The air was heavy with the odour of incense, and a heady atmosphere of promiscuity permeated the entire ballroom, oozing over the partygoers, filling their minds with wild lustful thoughts, and the need to fulfil every bizarre fantasy their minds could dream up. Helen found this strange aura highly addictive and she was obliged to constantly remind herself that she must not allow her senses to be seduced by its mesmerising spell.

Out of all the people present, there was only one Helen recognised immediately – Sandra. She walked towards Helen, modestly draped in a red silk cape, a matching red mask covering her eyes. A faint breeze brushed the silk, making it shimmer as she moved. Helen paused, waiting for her to approach.

'Very unusual,' Sandra conceded, looking Helen up and down, aware that the eyes of every man and most of the women in the room were lustfully fastened on the beautiful doctor. Helen's outfit was stunning and she looked spectacularly sexy.

'Thank you,' Helen replied, as Sandra tossed back her cape to reveal an outfit much like the one Justin and Ben had dressed Helen in that fateful evening in Sandra's bedroom. Sandra's breasts were much fuller than Helen's, and were forced into the tight garment, so that they bulged through the leather straps. Her nipples swelled obscenely through the confining metal rings, making them appear even larger. Her shaved pussy was covered by a thin strip of leather, also held on by straps, which cut into Sandra's wide fleshy hips.

Helen was filled with a complex variety of emotions as she stared at Sandra; a weird mixture of anger, abhorrence and lust. She was tempted to grab hold of those exposed titties and twist them hard until Sandra screamed with painful bliss. Keeping a strong control over herself, she did nothing but glance down at the naked man who crouched on his hands and knees at Sandra's side.

He wore a dog collar around his neck, and Sandra held the leash attached to it in her hand. The man's rather unimpressive genitals hung down between his scrawny legs, and he looked a little too well-fed and portly to be a proper slave. Helen couldn't see his face, as his entire head was covered by a tight-fitting leather mask, with holes near his nose for him to breathe, and a zip fastener covering his mouth. It was presently closed, but Helen presumed it would be opened when his mistress wanted pleasuring.

'Where exactly did you get that outfit?' Sandra asked.

'It's from one of Zara's movies,' Helen replied, trying to prevent herself from staring with compelling fascination at the man crouched by Sandra's side.

He moved, shuffling about, probably because the wooden floor was uncomfortably hard on his unprotected knees. 'Behave yourself,' Sandra snapped, hitting him with the end of the leash. 'Or you'll be punished.' She hit him again, and this time the leash left a small red mark which merged tastefully with the others that already marred his back and buttocks.

'This is certainly a party with a difference,' Helen conceded, as a man strode determinedly towards them. Judging by his build, and the way he walked, it was Ben, encased from head to foot in black rubber. There were press-studded panels at pertinent spots in the garment, which could be ripped away to expose nipples, buttocks, and sexual organs if the need arose.

'Enjoying yourself, ladies?' he asked. Only Ben's lips were visible, and they twisted in amusement as he noticed the aggressive stances of both women, even though they were smiling politely at each other.

'Immensely,' Helen replied sarcastically. Ben lifted the front of his mask to expose a face already pink and shiny with sweat. Helen thought the rubber garment must be incredibly hot on a warm summer evening such as this. 'Who wouldn't enjoy themselves at such a party?' she added in the same tone, although she did find the event amazingly fascinating. She had never seen so many uninhibited, and sexually adventurous people in one place, and now she was here she intended to stay and witness the orgy she knew would eventually occur. 'Now if you'll both excuse me . . .'

Helen strolled over to the refreshment table and helped herself to a tall glass of chilled white wine. She surveyed the ballroom thoughtfully as she sipped her drink, hoping to catch sight of Colin, but there was no sign of him yet.

Helen didn't notice the short, skinny man sidling towards her, who wore a bizarre mixture of straps and chains which did nothing but emphasise his lack of a decent physique. He didn't look even remotely sexy, just a little ridiculous. 'Hello, my beauty,' he said.

Helen didn't bother to reply, she just looked derisively down at his paltry sized cock and walked away from him. She intended to move anyway, because she had seen a number of guests gravitating towards the far end of the ballroom and she wondered where they were going. She found that they were aiming for a number of smaller rooms leading off the main concourse, all of which had been decorated with different themes.

One was a bedroom, and there were already four naked people writhing on the bed, all clearly enjoying themselves, while others watched. The second contained a number of pieces of medical equipment which could be put to good use in a variety of ways. The centrepiece was one of the new birthing chairs they had recently imported from the States. A plump young woman reclined naked in the chair, legs spread wide, while other guests took turns in stimulating her. Helen didn't find that sufficiently arousing to encourage her to stay.

The third room was even more dimly lit, and set up as a medieval torture chamber, with some surprisingly bizarre looking instruments, including a rack. A tall, slimly built, masked man was bent across a padded post, hands and feet chained, buttocks raised in the air, while a pretty dark-haired nurse, dressed as a dominatrix, beat him with a small leather-stranded whip.

Curiously, Helen wondered who the man was as he gave a moan of pleasure, which made the simmering heat in her quim increase.

'Does watching this turn you on as much as it does me?' Justin whispered in her ear as he slid his arm around her waist and pressed his belly hard against her buttocks.

'It's interesting to me, that's all,' she replied coolly, making no effort to pull away from Justin as she watched the young woman drop her whip and walk round to face her victim.

The woman picked up a leather harness, which was attached to a massive black rubber dildo, far larger than Helen imagined a real penis could ever be. Just looking at the massive instrument made moisture in her pussy increase, until her flesh stuck slickly to the narrow strip of fabric between her legs.

'Do you want a taste of this?' the dominatrix taunted her chained victim, lifting his head so that he could see the dildo more clearly.

The man gave only a soft groan in reply, as he trembled, whether from fear or lust Helen didn't know.

'He enjoys it,' Justin whispered in her ear. 'He loves being misused by either sex, but he prefers men arse-fucking him to women,' he added, obviously knowing the victim's tastes all too well.

Justin stepped away from Helen, and she saw that he hadn't chosen to wear such an outrageous outfit as most of the other guests. All he had on were his skin-tight leather trousers, and long leather boots, but just the sight of his nipple chains were erotic enough in themselves. Helen watched Justin grab the dildo from the young woman, and dangle it in front of the victim's face.

'Please, Justin,' he whined. 'I want you inside me, not that thing!'

'We don't always get what we want,' Justin replied with a cruel, salacious grin as he strapped on the dildo.

It looked even more outrageously fascinating on a man, and Justin reminded Helen of a high priest of some ancient sect, about to perform some bizarre ritual on his willing captive. She shivered with excitement, hearing the clicking sound his boots made on the polished wood floor as he moved slowly round his victim.

Picking up a silver container, Justin dribbled a sweet-scented oil over the prisoner's reddened buttocks, letting it drip between the cheeks and pool around his anus. He rubbed it into the trembling flesh, easing his thumb inside the tender ring of the man's anal opening until he gave a faint moan of surrender.

Helen held her breath, shuddering with excitement as Justin eased the tip of the dildo into his helpless victim. Very carefully, Justin gradually forced the fake organ deeper, ignoring the man's soft groans. They eventually culminated in a gasp of bliss as the last few inches were buried between his buttocks.

'Oh, yes,' Helen heard the man whisper, in a voice so tight and strained that her pussy contracted at the thought of the blissful sensation of fullness that he must be experiencing at this very moment.

Helen clenched her hands, pressing her hot thighs together, her quim afire and chafing hungrily against the slick PVC that covered it. She watched Justin move his hips, thrusting in and out of the prisoner's anus, all the while hearing the man's grunts of painful pleasure.

'Harder, Justin,' the man groaned, and something about the inflection of his voice made Helen stiffen. She'd not noticed it until now, but there was a familiarity about it she found troubling.

Without thinking of the consequences, she stepped forwards, lifted up the victim's head and pulled off his mask, disconcerted to discover she was right: the man was Ralph Kalowski.

'You continually manage to surprise me,' she said to Justin, who had stopped mid-thrust to stare at her in amazement.

'And you me, Helen,' he grunted, then again began to strain manfully against Ralph's buttocks.

Justin twined his arms around the prone body, grabbed hold of Ralph's rigid cock, and started to wank it in time with his powerful thrusts, while Helen just stood there staring at them both, trying to make sense of what she had discovered. She couldn't despise Ralph for his behaviour; in truth she pitied him. Ralph was inherently a moral man, and he wouldn't have got mixed up in all the underhand occurrences at this hospital, just for money. Justin was clearly in control of their relationship, and Ralph the willing but totally misguided victim.

Both men were now utterly caught up in the pleasures of the moment, and after Helen's momentous discovery, she didn't find the spectre quite so arousing as she had before. She turned and slipped silently from the room, still filled with a strong sexual need for fulfilment. Yet she couldn't chance letting it be sated here, because she feared losing control of herself and being caught up in this wild sea of orgasmic delights.

Perhaps it would be safer to leave right now, she decided. Helen was about to make her way to the exit when, just to her left, she noticed Ben being led into a small, silk-draped cocoon by a tall man dressed from head to foot in black silk. Helen had no idea who Ben's companion was, and curiosity prompted her to follow them. Reaching their refuge, she cautiously pulled back a loose piece of curtain and peered through the narrow slit. She saw the two men standing in the middle of the small tented chamber, their black-covered forms looking eerily menacing in the flickering candlelight.

Helen had expected Ben and his companion to be engaged in a prequel to intimacy, or already involved in a sexual act, but to her surprise they appeared to be having a violent argument. Ben gesticulated angrily, and she strained to hear what was being said, but the music being played in the ballroom was very loud – there was a speaker not far behind her and the heavy beat drowned out every word they spoke.

For a moment the beat softened as it reached a less intrusive passage of the music. 'You greedy idiot, you'll jeopardise all I've worked for,' she thought she heard the tall man yell.

'I didn't do it out of greed,' Ben shouted in reply. 'I need the money. How can you blame me – this is all your fault. If you hadn't arranged for . . .' The rest of the sentence was drowned out by a final crescendo from the overloud music track, frustrating Helen as she was certain that she'd been about to hear something of paramount importance.

Ben ripped off his mask, his teeth drawn back in a rictus of fury, his face red and shiny in the flickering light. He shouted as he raised his fists, looking as though he was about to punch the tall man. With an almost causal display of restrained violence, the man shoved Ben backwards, sending him staggering back against the hard wall hidden behind the silk curtain. The tall stranger turned on his heels and strode away before Ben had time to recover himself, passing only inches away from where Helen stood, frozen in surprise. She was unable to even hazard a guess as to who the stranger was; she couldn't distinguish any recognisable feature beneath his black satin mask.

Seconds later Ben had recovered himself, and left the tiny chamber. He stomped past Helen, looking extremely hot and agitated as he pulled open the neckline of his sweat-stained rubber garment. Helen cautiously stepped back, hopefully out of his sight, but Ben was too furious and too preoccupied to notice her or the fact that a silver chain had slid from his neck and fallen to the ground.

As Ben disappeared among the partygoers, Helen bent to pick up the broken silver chain; still attached to it was a small Yale key. She felt exhilarated and excited, certain that this was what she had been looking for – the key to Justin's office. Helen had no pockets, so she tucked the key safely into the top of her boot, and moved determinedly towards the exit. She decided that while everyone was still here, enjoying themselves, she would break into Justin's office and find the proof she and Colin had been looking for.

There were a number of people standing around the main door of the ballroom, and at first she couldn't figure out why they had congregated in that spot, not until she got close enough to see that a small semi-circle of people were gathered around Sandra and her slave. Now bereft of her cloak, Sandra stood there staring angrily down at the naked man crouched at her feet. Helen heard the slave's harsh agitated breathing beneath his tight-fitting leather mask. The zip fastener covering his mouth was still closed, so he couldn't beg for mercy, even if he wanted to.

At a nod from Sandra, a stocky man, who Helen recognised as a medical technician, hauled the slave to his feet, jerked his arms upwards and confined the slave's wrists in leather handcuffs that dangled from a high wooden frame.

There was a mutual sigh of appreciation from the crowd as they stared at the slave hanging there, quivering with anticipation, all too eager for the punishment he was about to endure. Sandra stepped forward, slashing the thin, leather-covered switch she carried through the air. It made a menacing sound which caused the slave to tremble even more.

Sandra slapped him hard across the buttocks, then across the curve of his hip, and he tensed excitedly, welcoming his chastisement with a moan of capitulation that pierced Helen's belly like a sword, making her feel hotter and hornier than ever. All around her people waited with bated breath for the next painful stroke, eager to enjoy every moment of the slave's erotic punishment.

Helen despised them all, yet in doing so she also despised herself, and she shivered with excitement as she saw Sandra hit her slave again. The thin cane stroked his flesh, bringing with it a subtle mixture of pain and pleasure that was even more arousing to him than it was to the watching crowd. By now the slave's breath was

243

coming in short gasps, as his struggles to survive his retribution were hampered by the all-enveloping mask.

'I wouldn't want you to suffocate before I've finished,' Sandra said, unfastening the mask and ripping it off to reveal Christopher's hot sweaty features to the watching crowd.

Helen was vaguely aware that she recognised the slave as someone well-known but, like the rest of the audience, she didn't care who he was. Her only interest was in what was to happen next, her senses aroused and intoxicated.

Sandra applied the switch, punishing Christopher with exact precision – an accomplishment she had honed and perfected over the last two years. Because Sandra also enjoyed being on the receiving end, she knew just how much discomfort to inflict to create the ultimate pleasure. Helen watched Sandra display her skills, feeling her body grow warmer, her sex even hotter, her skin glowing with the sheen of lust. Two further blows, this time aimed directly across the base of Christopher's red stubby cock, made it twitch and stand proudly out from his groin. His penis looked tight and turgid, ready to explode at any moment, as the switch kissed it yet again.

Helen was so caught up in the fervour of the ogling crowd, she wasn't even conscious of a man moving closer to her. Not until she felt his warm breath on the back of her neck, and smelt the spicy odour emanating from his flesh. He twined his arm around her body and jerked her back against his muscular chest. She could feel the hardness of his erection digging into her buttocks, yet she never even glanced down, or tore her gaze from the man being beaten by Sandra.

She felt fingers slide under the brief slither of fabric covering her breasts and rub her nipple. It felt so good she relaxed back against her seducer, sighing with relief as he pushed his hand between her thighs, pressing the heel of his palm against her aching pussy, forcing the sticky strip of PVC that covered it between her swollen sex lips.

Sandra didn't appear to be hitting her victim so hard now, only cruelly caressing his penis with the tip of the switch. Helen moved restlessly against her seducer, wanting the sensations he was arousing within her to become stronger. She was filled with delighted relief when he eased his fingers under the PVC gusset and dipped them into her quim. His sweetly teasing fingers felt good as they gradually explored the narrow valley of her sex, her hungry flesh welcoming his tantalising touch.

'Do you give yourself to any person who wants you?' he whispered in her ear in a low grating voice.

'No,' she gasped, pressing her buttocks back against the hard line of his erection. 'Deeper,' she begged. 'Push your fingers deeper.'

All around them others were doing the same. Helen could hear their moans of pleasure, the soft, wet sounds of sex, and her seducer's heavy breathing, while centre-stage Christopher, still being punished by Sandra, gave a loud grunt of bliss.

The gusset of Helen's garment was so snug fitting that it prevented her seducer from thrusting his fingers fully into her hungry vagina. In frustration he tore at the tight laces, managing to loosen the garment enough to allow him access to the very depth of her being. His fingers plunged deep into her cunt, just as Sandra hit Christopher one last time. His cock reared angrily upwards, and spunk spurted from the tip in an almost never-ending stream.

'You say you don't give yourself to everyone, but that's not what I hear,' her seducer said in an all too familiar voice, while his fingers rubbed Helen's clit, leading her closer and closer to her climax.

'Max!' she gasped in disbelief, as her orgasm came in a sudden rush, her flesh contracting in wild waves around his fingers.

'I hear you've been extraordinarily busy while I've been away,' he growled, his voice tight with fury.

Helen was still trembling in the aftermath of her

climax as Max spun her round to face him and ripped off her mask. His pale-blue eyes were cold and merciless as he stared at her through the slits of his black silk mask. Max looked even taller, even more threatening now than he did when he'd been arguing with Ben.

'I never thought . . .' She stared up at him, overcome by amazement at his unexpected appearance at this event.

'It appears you didn't, my sweet,' he grated, unfastening her belt, letting her decorative skirt drop to the floor. 'I received your agitated phone message and flew halfway around the world without a second thought – like a knight to the rescue of his damsel in distress.'

'I wasn't in distress,' she insisted, as Max's hands pulled at the laces which held her brief garment together. 'I just wanted to warn you –'

'– Warn me that you've spent your time in an endless round of shagging!'

Helen knew that Ben must have accused her of betraying Max, probably in an effort to deflate his anger over the drugs racket and turn his fury towards her instead. 'That's not true!' she insisted.

'Every bloody person in the hospital knows you were at it with Duncan, and goodness knows how many other men,' Max added, pulling so roughly at the laces of her dress that they cut into her flesh. 'I've spent the last few years listening to my entire family withering on about how handsome and successful Duncan is, now you do this to me.'

'So?' she countered furiously, trying unsuccessfully to stop Max from undressing her completely as she hung determinedly on to the front of her brief garment. 'We can talk about this more calmly later. Don't you have more important considerations? After what I told you about Ben –'

'– Bugger Ben,' Max hissed, angrier that she had ever seen him. 'You're mine, Helen. You seem to have forgotten that.'

'I belong to no one but myself,' she responded, as he

managed to divest her of every inch of her clothing, ripping the tattered remains out of her hands. Helen was left standing naked, apart from her high-heeled boots, in the ballroom. All eyes were salaciously focused on her, and she couldn't even run or hide because Max was holding on to her purposefully, forcing her to endure this horrible humiliation. 'No,' she begged, feeling embarrassed and fearful, but her mortification was mixed with a much darker emotion she couldn't define.

When Helen realised what Max intended to do next, she tried determinedly to get away from him. Struggling with all her might, as he dragged her towards the leather handcuffs that dangled menacingly down from the tall wooden rack.

She might have managed to get away from Max, if someone hadn't helped him by grabbing her from behind. She couldn't see her other assailant as two pairs of strong male arms held her, forcing her wrists upwards and confining them in the handcuffs. Helen was left hanging there, her feet barely reaching the ground, naked and totally helpless, all too conscious of the crowd moving closer, their eyes hungrily trained on her nude body.

Max slowly circled her hanging form, giving a harsh laugh as she tried desperately to lash out at him with her booted foot, missing his crotch by only inches. Helen's cheeks turned scarlet as she realised the sudden movement had exposed her to everyone's gaze. As Max stepped closer, running his hands sensuously over her bosom, she clenched her teeth and didn't move a muscle, consumed by shame as he rubbed her breasts harder, pinching and squeezing her nipples. He rolled them roughly between his fingers and thumbs, and Helen tried to fight the sudden surge of desire that consumed her senses.

'I intend to teach you a lesson, Helen. In future you fuck no one without my express permission,' he said cruelly, while twisting one of her nipples until she whimpered with painful bliss.

247

'Damn you,' she hissed. 'I do what I like. You don't own me, and you never will!'

'You're mistaken, Helen. I do own you and I always will.'

Max ran his hands down over her trembling stomach towards her sex and Helen squeezed her thighs tightly together. She stared with anguished concentration at his chilling blue eyes, only partially visible through the slits of his mask, knowing that he would give her no mercy. Max was strong and determined, he easily forced his hand between her legs, and into the moist slit of her sex. Despite her fury, the sensation of his fingers stroking her made her feel horny and highly excited. Her thigh muscles automatically relaxed, as she welcomed the delicious pleasure of his fingers sliding smoothly inside her.

Max slapped her hard across her buttocks and she winced, turned on by the stinging discomfort. He slapped her again with the flat of his hand, while roughly thrusting his fingers deeper into her. Helen tried to fight the steadily rising sensations, but Max knew her body well, and the movements of his thrusting fingers made her shudder with bliss. The eyes of the watching crowd seemed to devour her, feeding on both her pleasure and her pain, causing Helen to experience an unexpectedly exhilarating sensation which suddenly burst free from a deep, dark part of her psyche. Inexplicably she was turned on by the thought of so many people watching intently as Max finger-fucked her, every one of them eager to witness and share her climax.

Each of Helen's individual nerve endings became electrifyingly attuned to the cloud of carnal lust that hung over the people in front of her, seeping sensuously through their bodies into hers. She shuddered, the spiralling sensations rising, but Max knew how close she was to her climax and he jerked his hand away from her sex.

Swiftly, he pulled opened his flies, and his cock sprang from the black silk opening, looking impressively huge.

Helen couldn't tear her gaze from it and she shivered with wanting, desperate to feel it pounding inside of her. Grabbing hold of her calves, Max lifted her legs, pulling them apart so that the pink slit of her pussy gaped crudely open, and Helen heard a low sigh of anticipation from the watching crowd.

Helen's arm muscles protested under the strain of her own body weight, as Max held her thighs open and entered her with one smooth stroke. As he buried his cock the last few inches, Helen twined her legs around his waist, loving the feel of his silk-covered groin pressing against her open quim. The continued strain on her arms held her breasts in taut perfection, and Max fastened his lips around one swelling peak as he began to thrust into Helen. He fucked her in a smooth, unrelenting rhythm that sent the crowd wild with delight. Some joined in her pleasure, openly touching their own or another's genitals. Helen could almost taste the purity of their lust, the strange aura that permeated the warm night air.

Max's powering thrusts, and her rising pleasure, combined with the strange excitement of being watched by so many, meant that she started to peak all too swiftly. Max gnawed at her breast, thrusting into her so violently that it made her entire body shudder from the pounding pressure.

Max gave a loud grunt as he came, then pulled away from Helen, letting her feet drop to the ground. She was still trembling from the onslaught as he eased his penis back into his trousers and turned away from her, not saying a word.

Max strode off, never looking back, leaving Helen still bound and helpless, totally at the mercy of the crowd. She gave a whimper of trepidation as a number of them stepped towards her. Helen felt confused and frightened, longing to be touched, yet fearing what they might do to her. Her mind half-numb with anguish, she felt a plethora of hands and lips touch her in her most secret places. A wriggling finger buried into her anus, while lips sucked teasingly at her open quim, and she felt herself being drawn deeper and deeper into a morass of carnal delight.

Then someone tall and commanding stepped forwards, pushing her erotic tormentors roughly aside, employing so much force that a couple of them fell at her feet. A gentle hand supported her, while another released her wrists. She fell against her deliverer as he half-carried her through the door of the ballroom and into an ante-room heaped with bags and coats.

'Are you OK?' Colin asked, as he sat her down on the nearest couch. 'Sorry I couldn't get to you earlier, Helen.'

'I'm fine,' she said, still shaking slightly, feeling aroused yet appalled by what had just happened.

'Here.' Colin handed her a velvet caftan that someone had obviously used as an evening coat. 'Put this on,' he added, easing her trembling arms into the sleeves and wrapping it tightly around her naked body. 'Now you've got to get out of this place,' he continued, worriedly.

'We'll leave right now,' she said, fastening the row of buttons down the front of the caftan. 'You'll come too, won't you?' Helen was so furious with Max, so amazed by his cruel behaviour, that she didn't care what happened to him any more. She now had every intention of ensuring that Sandra, Ben, Justin and Ralph were brought to justice and paid for their crimes. If Max's reputation was destroyed in the resulting scandal she didn't care one jot.

'I can't,' Colin replied very seriously. 'I think I'm on to something, I have to stay.'

'I'm on to something too,' she said, still feeling very overwhelmed by all that had happened. 'Look,' she added, fishing the key she'd found out of her boot. 'I saw Ben drop this, and I'm certain it's the key to Justin's office. Let's try it now.'

'We will, together,' Colin agreed, with a thoughtful frown. 'You go back to your place, Helen. Wait for me there and I'll join you in a half hour or so. We'll break into Justin's office together.'

'Why not now?' she asked, filled with a zealous longing to get her own back on all of them.

'You can't go running about the hospital half-naked,' he pointed out. 'Change into jeans or something first. I've just managed to get one of the theatre nurses who assisted at those secret ops to open up to me. She's pretty pissed and doesn't seem to care what she tells me. It seems stupid not to learn all I can. Waiting a short while won't hurt, will it?'

'I suppose not,' she agreed reluctantly.

Helen almost did go back to her flat, but when she reached the passage that led to the courtyard, she had second thoughts. At present she was sure that Ben and Justin were fully occupied in some erotic pursuit or other, but the later she left it the more chance there was that one of them might leave, and her perfect opportunity could be lost.

She didn't come across a single soul as she made her way to the Pathology department. Fortunately moonlight streamed through the windows, and the labs weren't as dark as they might be. She navigated the rooms without the help of a torch or any lighting, and reached Justin's locked office without being seen. To her relief it was the right key – she opened the door and she slipped silently inside. The office had no external windows, so she chanced putting on a small desk light, hoping she wouldn't be discovered by one of the infrequent nightly security patrols.

The office was very tidy, which made it easier for Helen to search it systematically. She looked for any written records that Ben and Justin might have kept which could be used as evidence against them. She found nothing, only normal hospital paperwork, a few personal bills and files, plus in one cupboard a vast array of different sex toys, some of which looked incredibly bizarre. The only computer discs she found were still in a cellophane sealed box, and had obviously not been used.

Helen's last chance was the computers; there were two of them in this small room. As she turned them on, she discovered that one was linked to the hospital mainframe, and wouldn't tell her anything more than she had found in the Records Department. The other was a high-powered personal computer, which seemed far more promising. Helen opened up the system and searched through the files, soon discovering that most of them were protected by passwords: one for Ben, and one for Justin. She logged in under Ben's name and tried every conceivable sexual word she could think of, but none proved correct. Desperately she tried to think, remembering what Colin had told her about Ben's Filofax, and the word PANDORA sprang to mind.

Hoping that she was about to open Pandora's box, she typed in the name. It worked, and she began to search through the protected files. Ben hadn't bothered to conceal them with fake names, and she went straight to the one marked 'Ampesoman.doc'. There she found everything: a list of patients, medical tests pertaining to the trials and even a rough calculation of the eventual profit Ben hoped to make.

Swiftly she opened the fresh packet of discs, slipped one into the computer slot and downloaded all the information on to disc. Then she searched through the other files, eventually finding what she was looking for in one named 'FK.Interface.doc'. The downloaded files from Records were there, along with other equally important information.

Beneath the fake name of each patient, their true identities were also logged. Helen recognised the name of a Balkan who was wanted by the United Nations for war crimes; a former dictator who was supposed to have stolen millions from his poverty-stricken country; and a man who had managed to destroy a well-known bank while salting away large amounts of money for himself at the same time. All these people had disappeared and were still being sought by the relevant authorities.

Helen turned to Mr X's file, and there was the name

Carlos Alcazar. Every suspicion she'd had was confirmed, and she knew that she had to pass all this information on to the police, after she and Colin had read through it at their leisure. That would take quite a while, she thought, as she clicked the mouse, hoping there would be enough room on the disc to also save all this information.

The computer made a faint buzzing noise as it downloaded the files on to disc. Eventually, after what seemed like an age, the download was complete and with a sigh of relief she pulled out the disc.

She then froze as she thought she heard a sound from somewhere in the distant recesses of the lab. Helen listened intently, hearing the faint hum of machines, the strange creaks buildings always made at night, but no matter how hard she tried she could hear nothing else. Obviously her imagination was playing tricks on her senses, she thought, her ears still trained for any suspicious sounds as she turned off the computer screen.

Tucking the disc in the pocket of her caftan, she turned off the light and crept to the door of the office, opened it and peered nervously into the dark recesses of the rest of the laboratory. It seemed safe enough, so she crept cautiously forwards, conscious only of the loud noise of her own breathing. A sudden faint creaking sound made her tense apprehensively as she glanced around trying to detect even the slightest sign of movement.

Then her heart leaped in her chest as she was unexpectedly grabbed from behind. Helen was too surprised to even struggle as she was roughly manhandled back into Justin's office. She heard the door slam as the centre light clicked on, blinding her for a moment with its brightness.

Helen found herself facing a very angry-looking Ben, accompanied by Justin who was holding tightly on to her arms.

'I said it must be that bitch who found my key,' Ben said angrily.

'You shouldn't have lost it, you idiot,' Justin responded, running his hands over Helen's body. 'You were just bloody lucky that Kirsty thought she saw Helen pick it up,' he added, grinning when he found the disc in Helen's pocket. 'What have we here now?' he asked, holding it aloft.

Helen said nothing, just stared anxiously at Ben as he grabbed the disc from Justin. 'You think she downloaded our files?' Ben asked.

'How could she?' Justin replied sarcastically, pulling Helen towards the computer, holding on to her with one hand, while turning on the screen with the other. At once he discovered that Helen had made a great mistake in failing to both exit the file and log off. The proof of her perfidy was right in front of his eyes. 'If she didn't know either of our passwords, then would you like to tell me how she managed this?' Justin asked Ben, as he pointed to the name Carlos Alcazar.

'I don't know,' Ben muttered, stepping forwards to examine the screen himself. 'It should be impossible. She's no hacker; she couldn't have done this.'

'She must have got the bloody password from somewhere,' Justin snapped. 'Perhaps from someone stupid enough to write it down?'

Ben blanched. 'There's no way she could have seen it,' he stuttered awkwardly.

Justin's fury was cold and merciless as he glared derisively at Ben. 'I told you yesterday to download everything on to disc and put it somewhere safe, then wipe the records from the hard drive. Why didn't you do it?'

'I just didn't get around to it.' Ben looked uneasy, as if he was scared of what Justin might do to him.

'You're a fucking idiot!' Justin growled, unconsciously relaxing his hold on Helen as he glared accusingly at Ben.

Helen took the opportunity to tear herself from Justin's grasp and dart towards the door. She pulled it open, intending to run for her life.

'Oh, no you don't,' Justin roared, lunging towards her.

He grabbed a chunk of her hair and her arm, and yanked her back into the room.

'Ouch!' Helen exclaimed as he swung her round to face him. 'That hurt.'

'That's nothing in contrast to what I feel like doing to you,' he growled, pulling her closer and pressing his thumb against the pulse that beat agitatedly at the base of her neck. 'Ben, find something to tie her wrists together. I don't want her trying to get away again.'

'What are you going to do with me?' she asked, trying to hide her fear as he pressed his hand harder against her throat, as if he wanted to squeeze the life from her body. The way Justin was looking at her made Helen more scared than she'd ever been in her life.

'Make damn sure you keep your mouth shut, of course,' he said with an evil grin, as Ben rummaged through the cupboard containing all the sex toys they'd collected.

'Will these do?' Ben stepped forwards, holding a pair of handcuffs with fur-padded wrist restraints.

'Fine,' Justin said, holding tightly on to Helen while Ben pulled her hands behind her back and confined her wrists.

'Now what?' Ben asked.

'You do what I told you to do,' Justin replied curtly. 'Download everything, then wipe the hard disc. I'll take Helen back to my place. We can decide what we do with her later,' he continued with a cruel smile that made Helen's blood run cold. She had thought she might be taking a chance coming here, but it had never crossed her mind she might be putting her life in jeopardy.

Suddenly she heard a noise from the adjoining lab. Helen turned her head just as the tall, commanding figure of Max appeared in the doorway. Her past anger was forgotten in an instant, and she'd never been more pleased to see anyone in her entire life.

'Helen!' Max sounded as surprised to see her as she him.

Twisting away from Justin, Helen ran towards Max.

'We've got to get out of here,' she said agitatedly, as Max put his arms around her and held her close. 'We're in danger,' she urged, unsure what Ben and Justin might do next. Max was a strong guy, but it was still two against one.

'It's all right,' Max said comfortingly, as he held her trembling form close.

'No,' she insisted. 'Please get me out of here, Max. It's not safe.'

Max stared questioningly at Justin and Ben. 'What exactly is going on?' he asked coldly.

'She found out,' Justin replied, with an awkward shrug of his shoulders. 'She managed to get into the computer files and download them,' he added, as he waved the disc at Max. 'I presume she intended to go to the authorities with this.'

Helen tensed in surprise and she took a couple of steps back to stare in pained disbelief at Max. 'You knew what was going on around here?' she asked, not wanting to believe this heinous discovery.

'I had hoped that when Justin tried to warn you off it would be enough to put a stop to your amateur investigations. Obviously it wasn't,' Max said, smiling regretfully. 'I underestimated you, Helen. Totally underestimated you, as it happens.'

'It never crossed my mind that you were involved . . .' Helen stuttered, glancing nervously round at Justin and Ben. They were standing there looking at Max, as if waiting for him to tell them what to do next. 'Why?' she asked, turning back to look at Max. 'You're successful, famous – a brilliant surgeon.'

'I had my reasons,' Max replied, stepping further into the room, while Helen backed away from him, 'which mainly consisted of a number of rather pressing financial problems I never told you about.' He smiled wryly. 'Over the last couple of years I've managed to sort most of them out, thanks to my people at the Princess Beatrice.'

Helen shook her head. 'My God! You're running the whole thing, aren't you?'

'It's a pity you had to find out,' Max said with regret. 'For a time I believed we had a future together. I never wanted you to know any of this, Helen. In retrospect I realise I should never have arranged a temporary job for you here. Sometimes we don't truly know people until it's too late, do we, Helen?'

'It appears not, Max,' she confirmed. 'I was as wrong about you, as you were about me. But I just don't understand how you could do it – these people you've operated on, they're criminals.'

'A lawyer doesn't judge whether his client is guilty or innocent, so why should a doctor?' he said. 'And it's amazing how many people are prepared to pay exorbitant sums to have their faces changed and start all over again with a clean slate.' Max gave a harsh laugh. 'If needs be we can all do that as well.'

'And what happens to me?' Helen asked, wondering if he still held even a shred of affection for her. 'Would you believe me if I said I wouldn't talk, Max?'

'Poor Helen.' He cupped her face in his hands, kissing her tenderly on the lips. 'Sadly, my sweet, I can't bring myself to believe any soulful promises you might come up with. But don't worry about the future.' Max eased his hand inside the front of her top to fondle her breasts. 'I've no intention of letting any harm come to you. I think we'll take a holiday somewhere quiet. I've a friend who owns a delightful estate in the depths of Columbia. It's beautiful and very isolated. I'm sure once we've spent some time together you'll look at this matter very differently.'

'Ben, get to work,' Justin said quietly to his companion. 'Download everything.' He looked back at Max. 'Shall I contact the pilot, tell him to have the helicopter ready to leave in – '

Justin didn't have time to complete his sentence as two men barged into the room. Colin lunged towards Ben while Duncan moved anxiously towards Helen.

Justin, with a growl of fury, launched himself at Duncan, aiming a hard kick at his damaged ankle. As Duncan turned, with amazing speed, nimbly avoiding his attacker, Max grabbed hold of Helen and held her in front of him.

Duncan was a good few inches taller than Justin and far stronger. Because of his movie career he was well versed in a number of martial arts, and his ankle barely hampered his movements as he parried a blow from Justin. Yet Duncan employed none of these skills as he grabbed Justin, jerked him forwards and head-butted him hard in a move worthy of the toughest street-fighter.

Helen heard the sickening crack, and saw Justin crumple bonelessly to the ground as Max started to drag her towards the door. She struggled to get away from him, while Ben arched his back, his mouth open in a silent scream, as Colin lifted him and flung him against the desk. Ben fell, like a crumpled rag doll, landing on the floor in a tangle of arms and legs.

'Let her go, Max,' Duncan said, his face tight with fury as he moved towards his cousin.

'No,' Max hissed, never taking his eyes from Duncan, holding Helen tightly across the throat as he dragged her out of the room.

Helen saw Duncan's concern for her etched on his face as he continued to move slowly and cautiously towards them. 'Don't hurt her,' he warned. 'I'll kill you if you do.'

'Fuck you,' Max muttered, pulling Helen back another few yards into the dark laboratory. 'Have her then!' Max shoved Helen forwards.

Helen stumbled, about to fall, but Duncan caught her and held her close. 'It's OK,' he said, making no attempt to follow his cousin as Max turned and ran.

'I'll get him,' Colin said breathlessly, brushing past them and pounding after Max.

Duncan half carried Helen back into Justin's office and leaned her against the wall, as if fearing she might fall if not supported.

'The keys to these handcuffs,' she said, realising she was trembling uncontrollably. 'I think Ben might have them.'

Duncan poked Ben's prone body with his foot. Gauging him still safely unconscious he bent to search him. 'There's no key here,' he said. 'And short of stripping him . . .' he added, eyeing the all-enveloping rubber garment Ben still wore.

'In the cupboard behind Justin,' Helen said, seeing Duncan tense and turn swiftly as Justin made a faint whimpering noise. 'The key may be in there.'

Justin's body was limp as Duncan rolled him away from the cupboard, pulling it open to rummage among the various sex toys. 'This'll be useful.' He pulled out a thick roll of silver duct tape, then a small bunch of keys. 'I'll try the keys in a minute after I've attended to these two guys,' he added, pulling Justin's hands behind his back and fastening his wrists together with the tape. He stepped over to Ben and confined his wrists in a similar fashion. Then, when Ben made a faint groaning sound, he pulled off two extra strips and fastened the tape across both their mouths. 'Don't want them interrupting us, do we?' he continued, straightening and moving over to Helen.

While he had been tying up Ben and Justin, Helen had been scanning the room for any sign of the disc. She had spotted it eventually lying half under an overturned chair. However, she knew it wasn't as important now because all the information was still on Justin's computer. With luck the authorities might be able to find even more information than she had already among the many files.

'Do you think Colin caught Max?' she asked Duncan, as he unfastened her wrists and gently rubbed her arms to help relieve any stiffness.

'If he didn't, the authorities will,' he said, confidently. 'I heard enough before we burst in here to know that Max was in this as deep as all the others,' Duncan continued, looking at her thoughtfully. 'I think we should be more worried about you.'

'I'm fine,' she insisted, a single tear sliding from her eye and running down her cheek.

'You're far from fine,' he said, lovingly brushing away the tear. 'And you've not got an easy night ahead of you. I should phone the police.'

'Yes, you should,' she agreed, sliding her arms around his waist and holding him tightly, never wanting to let him go.

The sun was rising, bathing the hospital building in a rosy glow, as Helen and Duncan walked across the courtyard towards her apartment. It had been one of the longest nights of Helen's life and her head still buzzed with the many questions she'd answered.

She'd watched Justin, Ben and Sandra being carted away, along with Justin's computer. A police search of the annex had revealed one heavily bandaged man they suspected was a terrorist wanted by both Interpol and the CIA. There was no sign of Carlos Alcazar – he had already left the hospital.

Max was also in custody, although he hadn't been easy for Colin to catch and he'd put up a good fight. Colin cheerfully sported a black eye and a number of other cuts and bruises, but apart from that he was intact.

'What now?' Helen asked, as Duncan led her into her apartment. 'You still haven't told me how you managed to turn up here at the right moment.'

'It's a long story,' Duncan said, smiling. 'Way too long to tell now. We've only got a little over five hours before we're due to report to the police station and give our statements in full.'

'Then we should get some sleep,' she said, as he pulled her close.

'Sleep wasn't exactly what I had in mind,' Duncan replied, as he began to unfasten the line of buttons down the front of her caftan.

Visit the Black Lace website at
www.blacklace-books.co.uk

**FIND OUT THE LATEST INFORMATION AND TAKE
ADVANTAGE OF OUR FANTASTIC FREE BOOK OFFER!
ALSO VISIT THE SITE FOR . . .**

- All Black Lace titles currently available
  and how to order online
- Great new offers
- Writers' guidelines
- Author interviews
- An erotica newsletter
- Features
- Cool links

**BLACK LACE — THE LEADING IMPRINT
OF WOMEN'S SEXY FICTION**

**TAKING YOUR EROTIC READING
PLEASURE TO NEW HORIZONS**

LOOK OUT FOR THE ALL-NEW BLACK LACE BOOKS – AVAILABLE NOW!

All books priced £6.99 in the UK. Please note publication dates apply to the UK only. For other territories, please contact your retailer.

THE HAND OF AMUN
Juliet Hastings
ISBN O 352 33144 5

Marked from birth with the symbol of Amun, the young Naunakhte must enter a life of dark eroticism as a servant at his temple. She becomes the favourite of the high priestess but, when she's accused of an act of sacrilege, she is forced to flee to the city of Waset. There she meets Khonsu, a prince of the Egyptian underworld whose prowess as a lover is legendary. But fate draws her back to the temple, and she is forced to choose between two lovers – one mortal and the other a god. **Highly arousing and imaginative story of life and lust in Ancient Egypt.**

Coming in June

MIXED SIGNALS
Anna Clare
ISBN 0 352 33889 X

Adele Western knows what it's like to be an outsider. As a teenager she was teased mercilessly by the sixth-form girls for the size of her lips. Now twenty-six, we follow the ups and downs of her life and loves. There's the cultured restaurateur Paul, whose relationship with his working-class boyfriend raises eyebrows, not least because he is still having sex with his ex-wife. There's former chart-topper Suki, whose career has nosedived and who is venturing on a lesbian affair. Underlying everyone's story is a tale of ambiguous sexuality, and Adele is caught up in some very saucy antics. **The sexy *tours de force* of wild, colourful characters makes this a hugely enjoyable novel of modern sexual dilemmas.**

WHITE ROSE ENSNARED
Juliet Hastings
ISBN 0 352 33052 X

England. 1456. The young and beautiful Rosamund finds herself at the mercy of Sir Ralph Aycliffe when her husband is killed in battle. Aycliffe will stop at nothing to humiliate Rosamund and seize her property. Only the young squire Geoffrey Lymington will risk everything to save the honour of the woman he has loved for just one night. Against the Wars of the Roses, the battle for Rosamund unfolds. Who will prevail in the struggle for her body? **Vicious knaves and noble gentlemen joust in this tale of courtly but not so chivalrous love.**

Black Lace Booklist

Information is correct at time of printing. To avoid disappointment check availability before ordering. Go to www.blacklace-books.co.uk. All books are priced £6.99 unless another price is given.

BLACK LACE BOOKS WITH AN HISTORICAL SETTING

BLACK LACE ANTHOLOGIES

BLACK LACE NON-FICTION

To find out the latest information about Black Lace titles, check out the website: www.blacklace-books.co.uk or send for a booklist with complete synopses by writing to:

Black Lace Booklist, Virgin Books Ltd
Thames Wharf Studios
Rainville Road
London W6 9HA

Please include an SAE of decent size. Please note only British stamps are valid.

Our privacy policy
We will not disclose information you supply us to any other parties. We will not disclose any information which identifies you personally to any person without your express consent.

From time to time we may send out information about Black Lace books and special offers. Please tick here if you do not wish to receive Black Lace information. ❏

Please send me the books I have ticked above.

Name ....

Address ....

....

....

....

Post Code ....

Send to: Virgin Books Cash Sales, Thames Wharf Studios, Rainville Road, London W6 9HA.

US customers: for prices and details of how to order books for delivery by mail, call 1-800-343-4499.

Please enclose a cheque or postal order, made payable to Virgin Books Ltd, to the value of the books you have ordered plus postage and packing costs as follows:

UK and BFPO – £1.00 for the first book, 50p for each subsequent book.

Overseas (including Republic of Ireland) – £2.00 for the first book, £1.00 for each subsequent book.

If you would prefer to pay by VISA, ACCESS/MASTERCARD, DINERS CLUB, AMEX or SWITCH, please write your card number and expiry date here:

....

Signature ....

Please allow up to 28 days for delivery.